Norah

THE MCKADES OF TEXAS, BOOK 2

KIMBERLY LEWIS

This book is a work of fiction. Names, characters, places,
and incidents are products of the author's imagination or
are used fictitiously. Any resemblance to actual events or
locales or persons, living or dead, is entirely coincidental.

Norah (The McKades of Texas, Book 2): Kimberly Lewis
ISBN-10: 0-9852752-5-1
ISBN-13: 978-0-9852752-5-9
Printed in the United States of America

Cover Design by: Kimberly Lewis
Cover images purchased RF from Dreamstime.com

First Edits by: Jennifer Pitoniak
Second Edits by: Samantha Wheaton, Red Line Editing

For my mother.
Words cannot describe how grateful I am for you.
Thank you for everything! I love you!

ACKNOWLEDGMENTS

It has been such a long road to finally getting this book completed, and I feel that I have so many people to thank for helping make this happen. Once again, I'd like to thank my dear friends Ashley, Renee, Megan and my wonderful mother for reading the book and giving me their honest opinions. Your helpful advice and input helped get me through the writing process. I'd also like to thank my husband for putting up with my grumpy attitude when things in the book weren't going my way and for encouraging me to just keep writing because "I can do this." And I really want to thank all of my readers for sticking with me this entire time while you patiently waited for this book to be completed. It's been a long time coming and I'm very happy that you all understand that sometimes life happens and certain things get set to the side. Y'all are the best!

CHAPTER ONE

Beep beep beep. "Move!" Chase O'Donnell swore under his breath at the cow standing in the middle of the road. "Come on, you stupid thing. Move!"

He honked the horn again. Nothing. The cow stood there like she had no better place to be. Chase couldn't believe this was happening now.

He shifted his vehicle into park and stepped out onto the gravel road, slamming the door behind him in an attempt to spook her. She still didn't move. Sighing heavily, Chase slowly walked towards the large animal and waved his arms.

"Go on. Shoo!" He kicked at the gravel, sending the tiny rocks skittering along the top of the road.

With a lazy turn of her head, the cow looked at Chase.

"Don't give me that look," Chase said. "Get. Out. Of. The. Road." He spoke each word through gritted teeth.

Still nothing.

Muttering to himself, Chase stomped back to his vehicle and reached in through the open window and pressed firmly to the horn.

Again.

And again.

And again.

The cow gave Chase one final look and "mooed" before moving along.

"'Bout damn time." He shook his head and let out an exasperated sigh. "Absolutely ridiculous," Chase muttered as he got back in his SUV. Nothing said "Welcome to the country" better than a random cow in the road. The gravel road slowly faded into dirt as he drove away. He cursed as he swerved to miss one pothole only to hit another.

If there was one thing he disliked about the country it was dirt roads filled with potholes. And the smell. And the never ending dust that now covered his freshly waxed Chevy Tahoe.

Sure, visiting the country as a child was fun and exciting. There was always a new adventure to be had and coming home dirty and filthy at the end of the day made up most of his childhood memories. But that was a very long time ago and Chase wasn't a child anymore.

Gently shaking his head, Chase let out a long sigh and stared out the windshield at the never-ending pastures of cattle. This scenery was a far cry from the city life he was accustomed to: coffee shops on every corner, ATM machines, and cell phone reception. He'd been on the road for about four and a half hours now, and he was already missing all of those modern luxuries—especially the cell phone reception.

No sooner had the thought popped in his mind when his phone beeped signaling a voicemail. He pulled his SUV to the side of the road and punched the numbers on his touch screen to access the message.

"Hello, Mr. O'Donnell, this is Shelly from Bryant and Holmes Real Estate. I apologize for the short notice, but I have to cancel our appointment for this evening. However, I will be available first thing tomorrow morning. If you'd like to meet then please let me know. Thank you and I apologize for any inconvenience this may cause you."

Chase pressed the end button on the touch screen and tossed his phone to the passenger seat. He scrubbed both of his hands over his face then through his hair before shifting the SUV into drive and pulling back out onto the road; a cloud of dust filled the air behind him as he sped off.

Inconvenience.

This whole ordeal was a big freakin' inconvenience. The news of his Great-Uncle Eli's passing had surprised and saddened him. But when Chase had received the news that he had inherited his great-uncle's ranch he was shocked—shocked beyond belief because Chase hadn't seen or spoken to the man in over ten years.

As he drove, he thought back on the conversation he'd had with his mother after the visit with the lawyer.

"I don't get it," Chase had said to his mother as he rested his elbows on the table and stared at the legal document naming him the new owner of the Caldwell Ranch. "Why me?"

Susan O'Donnell shook her head and shrugged, taking the document from Chase to read over it silently. "I'm not sure, son," she told him softly. "He was always fond of you. I think he saw you as the son he never had."

Chase had let that information sink in for a moment and then let out a long sigh. "What am I going to do with a ranch?" He leaned back in the kitchen chair and ran a hand through his hair. "I appreciate the gesture, but I really don't want it."

"You could always sell it." Susan slid the piece of paper across the table back to Chase. "People are always looking for property, and a well established ranch like your great-uncle's would most likely sell very easily."

Those last few words rang in Chase's mind as he pulled off the road and onto the bumpy dirt driveway that led to the house. The once bright and sunny yellow home was now faded and in severe need of a new coat of paint. He looked to the left and noticed the barn roof was missing a piece of tin and he didn't even want to think about what the inside of the building looked like.

How the hell was he supposed to sell it when it looked like it had been vacant for years?

Parking his SUV in the driveway, Chase stepped out of the vehicle and shut the door behind him. He stood there for a long moment, with his hands in the front pockets of his jeans, and stared at his surroundings.

Not exactly the postcard image now, is it?

The grass, mostly brown, crunched beneath his boots as he walked across the yard. Chase took in the appearance of the place and wondered why his great-uncle had let it fall apart like this. The front porch, once a welcoming part of the home, was now missing railing and a few of the floorboards were cracked. Taking in a deep breath, he placed a cautious foot onto the first step. He tested it out before placing all of his weight on it and, when he was satisfied it would hold, he slowly made his way up to the porch. An old rocker lay flipped over and he carefully walked over to it and sat it upright. Stepping over a missing plank, Chase crossed the porch to the front door and turned the handle. It opened with an audible creak, and he stood in the open doorway for a moment in silence.

The room looked exactly the same as Chase remembered—older, but exactly the same—from the wood paneled walls down to the golden tan carpet. The green plaid sofa and matching loveseat still sat in the same exact spot they had sixteen years ago, and his great-uncle's giant brown recliner did as well. He stepped into the house and began to walk around the small space, noticing a thin layer of dust covering the wood furniture. The inside of the home was surprisingly well kept, minus the dust, and looked drastically different from the outside.

As his journey through the house led him to the eat-in kitchen Chase came to an old china cabinet, the same one his Great-Aunt Mary had kept her best dishes in, and stopped. Not only did the cabinet still hold all of the delicate, floral patterned dishes, it now held old photographs as well. His eyes scanned back and forth over the photos that ranged from black and white to color and stopped on one particular picture.

Opening the glass door, Chase reached inside and took hold of the old photograph. He stared down at the image and smiled as he took a seat at the table. A younger version of him smiled back from atop a painted pony with his Great-Uncle Eli standing next to him holding the pony's reins. He had a lot of fond memories here in this house and on the ranch, like waking up at dawn and helping his great-uncle with the chores, learning how to ride a horse, fishing and swimming in the creek, and his great-aunt letting him help cook and bake—which was only a one time affair after Chase bypassed the list of ingredients and threw in a bunch of random things.

He had loved this place, and his great-aunt and great-uncle very much, and he had looked forward to visiting them every summer vacation. A wave of guilt swam over him in that moment and Chase placed the picture back it in its rightful spot and closed the cabinet door. He felt like an ass. His great-uncle had obviously still cared and thought about him over the years, and how did Chase repay his memory? By not even bothering to keep in touch, and by whining like a little brat about how big of an inconvenience this inheritance has been. Hell, forget feeling like an ass, he *was* an ass.

CHAPTER TWO

"Son of a—!" Norah McKade quickly balanced the tray of beers she was carrying and set it down on the table next to her, breathing a sigh of relief that none of the glasses had toppled over. Ignoring the sharp, stinging sensation on the left side of her rear, she turned around slowly to face her admirer.

"Is there something I can help you with?" she asked the man, her voice thick with annoyance as she placed a hand on her hip and stared down at him. This was one of the only downsides of working in this small town bar: the grabby customers. Of course, this wasn't an every night occurrence. Normally the crowd that filled the old building known as the Rusty Spur was nothing but local ranchers and townsfolk—people Norah dealt with on a regular basis in and out of the bar. These were people she treated with respect and kindness and who returned the same courtesy. But every once in a while there'd be a night where some jerk would show up with his buddies and get a little too touchy-feely. Apparently it was going to be one of those nights.

The man was slouched casually in his chair, with one arm draped over the edge of the table and the other resting on his jean clad thigh as he gave her a thorough once over. His roaming eyes sent a chill of disgust down her spine and made her skin crawl.

Scumbag.

"Oh, I could think of a lot of things you could help me with, blondie." The cowboy gave her a devilish smile and reached for his mug of beer while the other men joining him at the table laughed and watched the awkward interaction.

Norah rolled her eyes. She knew this man's type— attractive, cocky and thought he was God's gift to women—and she just wasn't in the mood to put up with anyone's crap tonight. Plus, she'd be damned if she was going to just let him get away scot-free for that downright rude ass slap. A devious little thought popped in her mind and she pasted on her best seductive smile as she stood in front of him, leaned down to his level and rested her hand on the back of his chair.

"What exactly did you have in mind, cowboy?"

He leaned back, brought the front two legs of the chair slightly off the ground and balanced on the back two. His smile grew wicked as his eyes moved from her lips to the neckline of her low-cut, fitted black shirt, and stayed locked there.

"Well, blondie, I'm more of a show than tell kind of guy. Why don't we go out to my truck so you can see what I mean?" He slowly moved his gaze back to her face and sent her a wink. "What do ya say?"

Oh, she was saying a lot of things in her mind right about now and even inventing some new words in the process. But instead of ripping him a new one, she bit her tongue. Moving her hand from the back of the chair, Norah let her fingers glide over the man's shoulder to his chest where she began to toy with the pearl snap buttons on his shirt.

"Mmm," Norah replied in a throaty, sultry moan. "That sounds like a nice plan, but first…"

She brought the toe of her boot up and nudged one of the front chair legs, sending the chair and the man flying backwards to the floor. A loud thud followed by some groaning and sputtering filled the area as the man wiped his beer away from his face and attempted to get up.

"You should learn some respect and how to keep your hands to yourself," Norah chided as she looked down at the man. "Maybe then you wouldn't end up looking like a fool." She gave him one last look and a smart-ass smile before righting herself and going back to the table where she had set her tray of beers. Amongst the laughter and whistles that filled the tables around her, Norah grabbed her tray and successfully delivered the drinks before making her way back towards the bar.

"Well, that looked fun," Andi told her with a smile as she reached in the cooler, popped the tops off of two beers, and then handed them over to the waiting customers.

Norah returned her sister-in-law's smile and laughed. "I just love seeing their shocked faces. But I've gotta tell ya, that guy got me good. My butt still stings."

"What's wrong with your butt?" Luke asked, claiming an empty barstool in front of Norah.

"Some out-of-town cowboy was trying to say 'Hi,'" Norah explained to her older brother. She watched as he turned around in the barstool and scanned the crowd, apparently looking for the loser who had nerve enough to touch his baby sister.

"Which one is he?" Luke leaned back and asked Norah. "I swear I'll—"

"Relax, Luke," Andi said, moving to stand next to Norah. "Don't get your Wranglers all up in a bunch. Your sister handled it, and Trace just took care of walking the guy and his buddies out."

"What'd you do?" Luke asked, directing his question to Norah.

"Well, he almost knocked me on my behind so I returned the favor," Norah explained. When she saw that her simple explanation didn't seem to be enough for Luke she elaborated. "I kicked his chair over, sent him flying to the floor, and he spilt his beer all over himself."

A wide smile spread across Luke's face and he shook his head. "Subtle much, sis?"

"Oh like you've got room to talk," Norah told Luke. "What were you going to do? Get Zane and give that man a good ol' butt whoopin' for messing with your little sister?"

"Speaking of my husband," Andi interrupted, tucking a stray strand of her dark brown hair behind her ear. "Where is he?"

"He's over there talking to Henry White." Luke jerked his thumb towards the door where Zane was indeed engaged in a conversation with the older rancher.

Norah watched as Andi stared adoringly across the room at Zane and decided to take the opportunity to tease her favorite, and only, sister-in-law.

"That must suck," Norah said with a grin as she took care of filling a pitcher of beer and instantly gained Andi's attention.

"What sucks?" Andi asked, tearing her gaze away from Zane to give Norah a perplexed look.

"Hitting that year mark of marriage and not being a newlywed anymore," Norah teased. "Now you're just an old married couple."

"Oh really?" Andi retorted, leaning against the counter and sending a smirk at Norah. "I'll have you know that your brother and I are far from being an old married couple."

That comment brought a snort from Luke and both women turned to look at him, unaware that he'd been listening in on their conversation.

"And just what was that for, Luke McKade?" Andi

asked as she placed a hand on her hip.

"Nothing," he said with a laugh, shaking his head and looking down as he crossed his arms onto the lacquered wood bar top.

"No, no, it's something," Norah said. "Come on, spill."

"Can I get a beer?" Luke asked, looking to Norah and seemingly trying to avoid explaining himself.

"You'll get your beer when you tell us what's so funny," Andi told him.

Bringing his hand to his face, Luke rubbed his smooth, clean-shaven jaw and grinned. "I just have this image of Grandpa Zane and Grandma Andi sitting on the porch in their rockers, talking about the weather while he whittles a piece of wood and she knits."

Norah and Luke laughed while Andi shot them both a dirty look.

"Ha, ha, very funny, Luke," Andi said sarcastically.

"What'd I miss?" Zane asked as he approached the bar, greeting his younger brother and sister before turning his attention to his wife. "Hey, baby." He leaned over the counter and pulled Andi in for one long, lingering kiss.

"All right, all right," Norah said, waving a bar towel at Zane and Andi to break them up.

Andi turned briefly away from Zane to stick her tongue out at Norah, and then turned back to her husband. "Your brother and sister here were making fun of us. They called us an old married couple."

"Is that so?" Zane said with sly smile as he sat down on his barstool and held his wife's gaze. "They're just jealous, sweetie. And I think you know well enough that we aren't an old married couple," he told Andi with a wink.

Norah glanced over at Andi just in time to see her

cheeks turn slightly pink. She absolutely adored the love that her brother and sister-in-law had for one another, and she also knew darn well that they were the farthest thing from being an old married couple. But she had to admit that it was fun teasing them about it.

As Norah took care of loading her tray with another customer order, she overheard Zane ask Andi for a beer followed by an impatient sounding huff from Luke.

"Good luck with that," Luke mumbled. "I've been waiting fifteen minutes for a cold one."

"Oh, you're so whiney," Norah said to Luke as she finished placing the mugs on the tray to accompany the pitcher of beer. "Why don't you go hunt down some lonely girl and cheer her up? Isn't that why you come here anyway?"

Luke smiled at his sister and adjusted his cowboy hat as he accepted the long neck bottle Andi handed over to him. "Yes, ma'am, that's exactly why I come here. And I've been waiting on you two women to quit gabbin' long enough so I could get my beer and get going," he said to Norah. "Now if you'll excuse me…" He nodded towards the corner of the bar where a sad looking brunette sat all alone staring down at her untouched mixed drink. He scooted off of his barstool and made his way through the crowd towards the young woman.

Shaking her head, Norah laughed, rolled her eyes and then turned her attention to Zane and Andi. "I swear, one of these days he's going to fall and fall hard."

"Pfft!" Zane said. "Luke falls in love every night."

"She's right, babe," Andi said to Zane. "One of these days it's going to hit him and these little one-nighters aren't going be his thing anymore."

"I'll believe it when I see it," Zane muttered, then took a long sip of his beer.

Pulling the tray from the counter, Norah lifted it and balanced it with the palm of her hand. "I'll be back in a few, Andi. I've got to deliver these drinks to that table over by the jukebox."

"No problem," Andi told her. "I've got things covered here."

Norah rounded the corner and maneuvered her way through the crowd. The speakers from the jukebox blared an upbeat country tune that had dozens of line dancers scooting around on the old wooden floor. She could actually feel the vibration through her feet from their non-stop boot stomps as she dropped off the beer and mugs to her waiting customers.

She was on her way back towards the bar with her empty tray in hand when a man pushed his chair back from his table and stood abruptly, knocking into Norah in the process. Stumbling backwards, she thought she'd found her footing but her boot slipped in something—no doubt some of the beer left over from that jerk earlier—and the next thing she knew her feet were flying out from underneath her. She flung her arms back and felt her tray smack against something before she dropped it and braced herself for the fall on the hardwood floor.

"Shit!" she heard a deep voice say from behind her and then a pair of masculine arms circled her waist.

The tray hit the floor with a light thud and Norah grasped onto the arms around her as she attempted to find her balance. When she was standing upright, the arms around her loosened and she heard the man ask, "You okay?"

"Yeah," she said as she turned around slowly to see who her savior was. Her breath caught in her throat as she stared at the man before her.

Oh. My. God.

Attractive didn't even begin to describe what this man was. Hell, you might as well throw the term good-looking away too. This man could easily grace the cover of those magazines that listed the year's sexiest men. His thick, dark, almost black hair was combed away from his face and—*oh my*—what a face it was. He had a strong, defined jaw with just the tiniest bit of a five o'clock shadow, full, kissable lips, a straight nose and killer green eyes that were framed with dark lashes. It was those eyes staring back at her that brought her out of her trance and she blinked a few times to clear her head.

"Thank you," she managed to say, but she found herself staring again. And that's when she noticed the tiny trickle of blood seep down from the man's eyebrow. "Oh my gosh, you're bleeding!"

CHAPTER THREE

"I'm out." Chase threw his cards down on the table in front of him and picked up his beer, downing the last of it with one swig. Tonight was just not his night. Actually, if he were going to be honest with himself, this whole day just sucked in general. And losing hand after hand of poker wasn't making him feel any better.

"Thanks for letting me join in on your game," Chase said as he slowly pushed his chair away from the table and stood.

"You out for the night, son?" one of the older players asked as he scooped up the cards and began to shuffle the deck.

"Yes, sir, I am," Chase replied. "You gentlemen have pretty much cleaned me out. I think I may have just enough money left in my pocket to pay my bar tab." He laughed after that last statement, and the men joined in with him.

"Son," the older man said. "You come on back tomorrow night and see if you can win some of your money back."

Chase smiled and nodded. "Will do, sir."

He excused himself from the table and began to make his way towards the bar. The place was crowded—too crowded for his sour mood. Why did he think going out to a bar, a honky-tonk at that, would make him feel better?

His thought was cut short when a hard object collided with his head just above his eye.

"Shit!"

Chase winced but then looked and saw one of the

waitresses, the blonde one he had noticed as soon as he entered the bar, falling back into him. Caught off guard for only a moment, he threw his arms out and grabbed the woman around the waist just in time. He held onto her and pressed her back against his abs as she found her balance.

"You okay?" Chase asked as he slowly loosened his grip.

"Yeah," the blonde replied, letting out a sigh of relief as she turned around slowly to face him.

Damn.

She had to have the biggest and bluest eyes he had ever seen. He knew he was staring, but he honestly didn't care. He took his time taking in the rest of her features and settled his gaze on her soft, luscious, pink lips. The blonde's expression went from soft to shocked, and Chase saw her mouth moving but hadn't heard a word she'd said. Afraid he'd offended her, Chase removed his hands from her waist and took a tiny step back.

"Huh?" Chase said, tearing his gaze away from her mouth.

"I said you're bleeding," the woman informed him as she rested her hand on his arm and stepped closer.

Chase took a breath as she leaned in to get a better look at the cut on his eyebrow and—*good Lord*—she smelled amazing. Delicate. Flowery. Completely intoxicating. He realized he was staring again and snapped himself out of it as he brought his hand up to his eye and touched the cut with his finger.

"Oh, wow, I guess I am," he said looking at the streak of blood on his fingertip.

"Come on," the blonde told him. "We've got a first aid kit in the back."

"Nah, I'm okay," Chase told her. "It's fine, really."

The woman shook her head. Clearly she wasn't going

to take no for an answer. "I'm cleaning you up, so put your pride away and follow me."

Trying his best to hide his amused smile, Chase allowed the woman to take him by the hand and lead him to the backroom; they received many curious stares from the crowd along the way.

"Have a seat," the blonde told him and practically pushed him down into the kitchen style chair. "I'll be right back." She flipped the switch on the wall, and the light from the ceiling fixture illuminated the room.

And that's when Chase got a *real* good look at her— well, a real good look at her from behind that is. He let his gaze travel down the length of her body starting at her hair, which she wore back in a low ponytail that rested in waves between her shoulder blades. Following the curves of her body, Chase's gaze moved down her back and to her trim waist before settling on her perfectly round bottom.

He watched as she made her way over to the bookshelf on the far wall and reached for the first aid kit on the top shelf. Seemed kind of an inconvenient place to keep something as important as that, but right now Chase was thanking his lucky stars and praising whoever decided to stick it up there in the first place. Watching her stretch her body and stand on her tiptoes to reach the darn thing was the highlight of his day—well, aside from having her in his arms just a few short minutes ago. He felt a familiar stirring sensation begin to build and tried to clear his mind as his jeans quickly started to become uncomfortable.

"There," the blonde said, stepping away from the bookshelf and adjusting her shirt as it had ridden up her stomach in the process of getting the kit. "I think he tends to forget that I'm not as tall as he is." She walked towards him looking down at the first aid kit in her hands.

"He?" Chase asked. He wasn't sure why, but something that felt an awful lot like a jealous twinge jolted through him.

"Oh, sorry," she said. "I was just talking about Red. He's the owner of the bar and my boss. He tends to just put stuff wherever he sees fit. Stuff is always getting 'misplaced' as he likes to put it." She sat down in the chair across from him and placed the first aid kit on the table.

"Sounds like you're used to it though," Chase said as he watched her open the white box and pull out two square packets of what he assumed was an antiseptic wipe, another packet that read *Butterfly Bandage,* and a pair of latex gloves.

A soft laugh escaped her lips as she proceeded to pull the gloves on one at a time. "Yeah, I guess I am." She took one of the square packets and ripped it open, pulling out the moist, towelette and unfolding it. "This may sting," she said, then looked up at him and locked her eyes with his.

Sitting there under the bright light of the ceiling fixture, all Chase could do was stare at her. Yes he thought she was attractive when he saw her in the dim light and the smoky air of the main bar, but now that he could clearly see all of her perfect features, he wasn't sure how to describe her. She was so darn beautiful, and the thing that made her even more so was the fact that she didn't even seem to notice how hot she really was. She didn't have that I'm-out-of-your-league attitude that most women with her appearance had.

Chase couldn't help himself. He just sat there and watched her. He took in everything about her: her big, blue eyes, her perfect nose, those luscious lips, and that sun-kissed skin that looked so soft and was practically begging for him to reach out and touch it.

"You're not gonna pass out, are you?"

Chase blinked a few times and gave the woman a questioning look. "Pass out? No. Why?"

She smiled in a cute way with her head just slightly tilted to the side, and his heart literally did a double skip.

What the hell? What am I, in junior high? Get a hold of yourself, O'Donnell.

"I mentioned that this might sting," she said and held the wipe for him to see, "and you got this blank stare on your face. I think you may have even stopped breathing."

Shit. "Umm, no, I'm all right." He gave her a playful smirk and added, "It's probably just a side effect from being hit upside the head."

"Very funny," she told him with a smile and scooted her chair closer to him. Taking his chin in her hand, the woman angled his face and began to dab at his cut with the antiseptic wipe. "I am really sorry about this."

She had positioned herself so that his thigh rested between hers—which he knew she'd done in an effort to get closer so she could clean his wound properly. But every once in a while her thigh would brush against his and he was back to square one trying his hardest to control his traitorous hormones.

"It's okay, really," he told her, hoping that if he engaged in a conversation with her that he'd be able to get a hold of himself. "It's not like you meant to beat me to a pulp with your tray."

She kept her focus on cleaning the cut above his eye, but she laughed and shook her head. "Oh, believe me. You wouldn't be sitting here if I had 'beat you to a pulp.'" Placing the used antiseptic wipe in the wastebasket next to the table, she reached for the other one and tore it from its packet.

"I guess that's your subtle way of telling me you're a

woman who knows how to handle her own business?" Chase asked as she dabbed the newer wipe along his cut.

"Years of working in a place like this you kind of have to," she told him and tossed the wipe in the wastebasket along with the other.

"That a job requirement?" Chase asked with a teasing grin. He watched her as she reached for the bandage and pulled the tape from the back of it.

The blonde shook her head slightly and let out a soft laugh.

"So what else do you do besides bartend and hit people in the head with trays?"

"You sure do ask a lot of questions," she told him with a smile as she secured the bandage over his cut.

"If I'm not mistaken, you're the one who's supposed to be asking me all the questions."

"Oh, is that so?" she said, removing the gloves and tossing them in the basket with the other trash.

"Yeah, you know, in case I have a concussion." He pointed to the cut above his eye. "Head injuries can be serious."

The blonde shook her head and closed the first aid kit. "Laying it on pretty thick, aren't you?" She rested her hand on his knee, patted it twice, and then pushed herself up from the chair. "I think you'll pull through."

Chase reached for her hand as she started to walk away and watched as the woman stopped and look at his hand before she looked to his face. "You're not just gonna leave me hanging like that, are you?"

She carefully peeled her hand away from his and held onto the first aid kit with both hands. "Look, I'm sure you're a real nice guy, but I'm just not into sharing my personal life with strangers. I'm really sorry about hitting you with my tray but—"

Chase stood and slowly pushed the chair under the table. "I completely understand," he told her, then held his hand out for her to shake. "I'm Chase O'Donnell."

The woman looked at his hand, then up to his face, and placed her own hand in his. "Norah McKade."

"Now we ain't strangers," he told her and cringed inwardly at his choice of words. Less than a day in hickville and he was already using the local lingo. But then Norah let out a soft laugh, and he smiled curiously. "What's so funny?"

"Nothing," she told him and shook her head. "You do realize you just quoted *Forrest Gump*, don't you?"

Chase chuckled, removed his hand from hers and used it to rub the back of his neck. "Shoot, I guess I did."

Still smiling, Norah nodded her head, walked over to the bookshelf, and placed the first aid kit on the shelf directly in front of her.

"Hey, Norah." She turned and Chase found himself face to face with her. His eyes trailed over her face as he searched for the words, any words, to say. But she was staring up at him with those big blue eyes that he found irresistible, and Chase's mind went blank.

"I've been back here far too long, and if I don't get back out there soon, someone is probably going to come looking for me," Norah told him, holding his gaze for a moment before smiling. "And with the way both of our luck is running tonight it'll be one or both of my older brothers."

So she has two older brothers? "Did you just share some personal information with me?" Chase asked with mock shock.

Norah laughed and gently pushed him towards the door. "Only for your own safety, O'Donnell," she said. "Trust me. I don't have enough bandages or the kind of medical training needed to patch you up if they find you in here alone with me."

So she has two very over-protective brothers? "Fair enough," Chase said but stopped in the doorway, blocking her path. "You think your brothers would mind if I bought you a drink? You know, as my way of thanking you for patching me up."

Norah looked up at him and held his gaze. "I don't drink on the job."

"How about when you're not on the job?" Chase asked.

"You sure are persistent," she said.

"What can I say?" Chase grinned and shrugged. "Is that a yes?"

"I'll think about it." Norah slid her body between his and the doorframe and gave him a genuine smile as she walked away.

CHAPTER FOUR

Her heart was hammering in her chest. Jesus. What was it about this guy that had her insides going crazy? One little interaction that lasted less than fifteen minutes had her feeling like a hormonal teenager. She hadn't had that kind of a reaction since she was thirteen-years-old and her crush at the time, J.T. Thompson, snuck her behind a tree during his family's barbeque and kissed her.

She wondered...if her body was reacting this way just from a little small talk and a few non-intimate touches, then how would it have reacted if he *had* kissed her? And—*great*—now she was imagining making out with a complete stranger.

Way to keep it classy, Norah.

"Where'd you run off to?" Andi asked when Norah came back behind the bar.

"I had to take care of something in the back," Norah told Andi.

"Something? Or *someone*?" Andi asked, amusement on her face as turned away from Norah to fill an order.

"Andi!" Norah said.

"What? All I saw was you holding some guy's hand and hauling him into the back room," Andi said. "It sure did seem like you were in an awful rush to get him alone."

"Okay, one, I was not in a rush to get him alone," Norah stated. "And, two, he was bleeding. All I was doing was patching him up."

"Why was he bleeding?" Andi asked with a raised an eyebrow.

"I hit him in the head with my tray," Norah casually

told Andi, then prepared two mixed drinks and handed them across the counter to the waiting customer.

"Good Lord, Norah," Andi said as she shook her head and helped the next customer. "You're two for two tonight."

Norah laughed. "It wasn't like that." She quickly explained the situation to her sister-in-law and ended the story with Chase asking to buy her a drink sometime.

"So what'd you tell him?" Andi asked.

Norah shrugged as she wiped up condensation rings from the bar top. "I just said that I'd think about it and left it at that." She turned to find Andi gawking at her with a confused look. "What?"

"You'll think about it?" Andi repeated, her voice thick with disbelief as she furrowed her eyebrows.

"Was I supposed to say something else?"

A sarcastic snort escaped from Andi. "Uh, how about 'Sure, I'd love to.' Or even a simple 'Yes' would've been a better answer than what you told him."

"Yeah, I could've," Norah said. "He did seem like a nice enough guy."

She glanced out the corner of her eye at Chase. He still leaned casually against the open doorway as his eyes scanned the crowd before they settled on Norah. Her heart flip-flopped and she quickly looked away.

"Not to mention he's smokin' hot," Andi added.

"Umm, you're married," Norah said, coming back to their conversation and letting out a soft laugh. "To my brother, at that."

"I'm married, not blind," Andi said. "But even though your man over there is very good-looking, he's got nothing on your brother."

"Okay, can we please stop comparing the two," Norah said. "I'm getting a little weirded out by the whole thing."

Andi laughed at that and agreed. "It's a shame you didn't take that guy up on his offer, though. You haven't been out on a date since the whole Wade debacle."

"Be that as it may," Norah said, bristling up at the mention of her ex. "What's done is done, and I can't take it back now."

A knowing smile spread across Andi's face as she looked past Norah. "I wouldn't be so sure about that."

Norah turned her head. Chase was slowly making his way towards the bar, weaving through the crowded room until he stood across from her.

"What can I get you?" Andi chimed in as she moved to stand next to Norah. "Beer? Whiskey? A tall glass of water?" She bumped Norah's hip with her own and let out a soft laugh.

"Oh my God. Stop," Norah muttered under her breath to Andi and rolled her eyes.

Chase leaned an elbow on the bar top and smiled. "I'm okay, but thank you."

"Suit yourself," Andi said, then excused herself to help a customer at the end of the bar.

"Your friend seems nice," Chase told Norah.

Norah nodded and smiled. "And crazy. Sorry about that."

"Don't apologize," Chase said. "I just wanted to thank you again before I headed out for the night."

She felt her face drop. Why did it matter so much that he was leaving? "Calling it quits, huh?" she said. Even though her chest felt heavy and hollow, she managed to keep her voice even and upbeat.

"Not a chance," Chase said.

And the look he gave her made every bone in her body turn to mush. That sly, crooked grin of his was a dangerous thing.

Chase's phone buzzed in his pocket as he stepped out of the bar. One look at the screen told him exactly who the caller was, and he smiled.

"Hey, sis."

"Hey," Sarah replied. "I'm not calling you too late, am I?"

"Nope," Chase said. "What's up?" The lights on his SUV blinked twice and the horn beeped as he pressed the button on his key ring to unlock it.

"I finally got the girls to bed a few minutes ago, and I wanted to check in with you to see how things are going."

Chase opened the vehicle door and then slid into the driver's seat. "Those nieces of mine giving you a run for your money?"

Sarah laughed genuinely but the exhaustion was clear in her voice. "You wouldn't believe what I've been through tonight." She took a deep breath and let it out in a huff. "So how'd it go with the realtor?"

"I actually didn't see the realtor today," Chase told her and then explained the voicemail from earlier.

"So…what? Are you staying there overnight? In Uncle Eli's house?"

"I'm sure as hell not driving back to Dallas tonight," he said. "And if you want to get technical about things, it's really *my* house."

Chase heard muffled voices from Sarah's end of the phone and then Sarah was back with a loud sigh.

"Chelsea's awake and wants a glass of water," Sarah told him. "I've got to let you go but call me tomorrow after the meeting and let me know how things went."

"Will do," he said. "Night, sis."

"Goodnight, Chase."

He sat in the parking lot for a long moment, watching the lone pole light flicker on the weather beaten building, and all his thoughts went to Norah. He just couldn't seem to get her out of his head.

You're only in town for another day, he told himself. *Long enough to get things started with the realtor and then you'll be handling everything from Dallas.*

Chase expelled a heavy sigh because he knew his conscious was right. This little trip to Buford was for business only. What was he thinking anyway?

You're thinking about how nice it was to hold a woman in your arms again.

It *had* been nice holding her in his arms. The recent memory of her sweet curves pressing against him had his mind and his heart racing.

And now he needed another drink to settle his nerves—needed a cold shower, too.

He needed to stop thinking about Norah McKade and just drive the hell back to the ranch, get some sleep, and get back to his day-to-day life. He could do that. Just put her out of his mind for good. Besides, it's not like he'd ever see her again anyway.

CHAPTER FIVE

Sunlight beamed through the sheer lace curtains and shined directly in Norah's eyes. She cracked open an eyelid, moaned, and pulled her covers over her head.

"Go away sun," she mumbled, the sound of her voice muffled from beneath the fluffy, white comforter.

She was suffering from some major lack of sleep thanks to one Chase O'Donnell. The image of him flitted in and out of her mind all night long, but Norah wasn't going to complain. She had rather enjoyed having Chase visit her in her dreams. Smiling to herself, Norah snuggled deeper into her bed. She closed her eyes tightly and attempted to fall back asleep just so she could experience Chase again...and again.

But then her cell phone rang, interrupting her thoughts of Chase, and Norah reached from beneath the covers to retrieve it.

"Hello?"

"Hey, Norah, where are you?" Zane asked.

"Good morning to you, too," she replied and pulled the covers away from her face so they only covered the lower half of her body.

"Seriously," Zane said, his voice taking on a no nonsense tone. "Are you still at your house?"

"Yeah," Norah told him. "Why? What's up?"

"Luke and I were out early mending some fence at the ranch, and he cut his arm on a rusty nail," Zane explained.

"Is he okay?" she asked, sitting up in bed and brushing her tangled hair away from her face.

"The cut is pretty deep, so I think he's going to need stitches," Zane said. "I'm taking him over to the emergency room now, but I need you to do me a favor."

"Sure. What do you need?"

"It's Luke's turn to go over to Eli Caldwell's place and take care of the livestock," Zane told her. "But seeing as he's on his way to the hospital..."

"You need me to go over there and take care of the livestock for him."

"That'd be great."

"All right, but he owes me," Norah said with a teasing tone. "And Zane?"

"Yeah?"

"You do remember that Luke has a fear of needles, don't you?"

Zane laughed and replied, "Oh yeah, I remember."

"Have those smelling salts ready," Norah said, laughing along with Zane. "Let me know how he makes out, okay?"

"Will do. Thanks, Norah."

"No problem."

As Norah neared the Caldwell Ranch's driveway, a flicker of light caught her eye. She zeroed in on the silver SUV parked to the side of the house and wondered who the hell had nerve enough to be trespassing on the private land—especially since the place had been vacant for the past two weeks.

Her curiosity peaked, but she knew better than to let it get the best of her. Pulling her truck to the side of the road, Norah grabbed her cell phone from the center console and punched the numbers. As she waited, she impatiently drummed her fingers on the steering wheel and watched the house for any signs of movement.

"Sheriff's Department, this is Deputy Woodson."

"Ernie, it's Norah McKade, listen I—"

"Now, Norah," Ernie drawled, "you know you're supposed to call me Deputy Woodson when I'm on the job."

Norah rolled her eyes. Even though she and Ernie Woodson had gone to school together since they were in kindergarten, had gotten into trouble numerous times throughout their high school days, and even graduated together, he still insisted she call him Deputy Woodson whenever he was in uniform.

"Sorry, Deputy," Norah replied, trying not to sound annoyed. "Listen, I'm over here at Eli Caldwell's place, and there's a vehicle parked next to the house that I've never seen before."

"Hmm," Ernie replied. "I don't recall hearing that anyone had bought it yet. And you're sure you ain't never seen that vehicle before?"

"Never," Norah told him.

"All right," Ernie said, grunting into the phone as she assumed he was standing up. "The Sheriff is out right now, so I'll be by there shortly. Don't go up to the house. Just stay right where you are."

"Okay," Norah said. "Thanks, Ern—I mean, Deputy Woodson."

Bang bang bang! "Sheriff's Department."

What the…?

Chase cracked open his eyes and sat up with a groan. He ached all over from awkwardly sleeping on the old sofa. It had been his only other option besides the one bed in the house, which had belonged to his great-uncle and great-aunt, and sleeping there had been out of the question—a decision he was now regretting.

In an attempt to ease some of his discomfort, Chase brought his hand up to his neck and firmly rubbed the back of it. He then remembered what had woken him up and looked to the front door.

Bang bang bang! "Sheriff's Department. Open up."

What the hell is the Sheriff's Department doing here?

Chase stood, picked his t-shirt up from the arm of the sofa, and slipped it over his head as he crossed the room. He opened the door and found a man, probably around his own age if not a few years younger, dressed in a tan law uniform complete with the hat, sunglasses, and badge.

"Yes, officer?" Chase asked, thoroughly confused as to why he was receiving this morning visit.

"Sir, I'm gonna have to ask you to step out of the house." The officer stepped back and gestured for Chase to follow.

He complied with the man's request, stepped out onto the wooden porch barefoot, and crossed his arms over his chest.

"What's this all about, officer?"

"What's your name, sir?"

"Chase O'Donnell."

"You have any I.D. on you, Chase O'Donnell?"

Oh, it was too early for this. "In my wallet," he told the officer, "but it's in the house. Can I ask what the reason is for this visit?"

"We got a call about some trespassing," the officer explained, tucking his thumbs into his belt. "See this here is private property."

Good Lord. "Yes, officer, I'm fully aware that this is

private property. But I—"

"Then you must also be fully aware that trespassing is considered a criminal offense and I can arrest you."

Okay, now he was pissed. "It's not trespassing when you legally own the place," Chase said, attempting to calm his voice. "Eli Caldwell, the previous owner, was my great-uncle. I just inherited the entire ranch two weeks ago when he passed away."

"I wasn't aware Eli had any living kin," the officer said, the skepticism clear in his voice. "You got any documentation proving your statement?"

CHAPTER SIX

Her curiosity was starting to get the best of her. What the hell was taking so long anyway? Norah leaned against the front of her truck, arms and ankles crossed, as she waited to find out what was going on.

Ernie had gone into the house and had yet to come back out. She looked at her watch.

Ten minutes.

She sighed. It sure felt a hell of a lot longer than ten minutes. She didn't understand why Ernie just hadn't arrested the guy. Isn't that what happened to trespassers? This was taking too long. Something wasn't right, and she knew it. Maybe Ernie had tried to arrest the man and things had gotten out of hand? Maybe Ernie was tied up and defenseless? Maybe he was knocked unconscious? Or hurt? Or maybe she needed to stop watching so many crime shows on TV. Her imagination was now getting the best of her and starting to run wild. Everything was fine.

She proved herself right when Ernie stepped out of the house seconds later, shook the man's hand, and walked over to his police cruiser. Uncrossing her ankles, Norah stood and waited for Ernie to meet her. He stopped his cruiser next to her truck and rolled the window down.

"Well?" Norah asked, uncrossing her arms long enough to tuck her hair behind her ear.

"Well, it turns out he's the new owner," Ernie told her.

Her eyes widened. "New owner? I didn't know anyone had bought it."

"He didn't buy it," Ernie explained. "He inherited it.

Apparently he's Eli's great-nephew."

"You don't say," Norah said.

"Yep," Ernie said. "I suggest you go introduce yourself to your new neighbor."

"Hmm." Chase said as he studied the old enamel coffee pot sitting on the stove. He'd found the coffee grounds, and now he just needed to figure out how to actually brew the darn stuff. Picking up the contraption, he opened the lid and looked inside.

"Now where are you supposed to put the coffee?" he asked himself out loud when he found no filter.

A knock at the door distracted him, and he placed the pot back on the stove, a little more forcefully than he'd intended, and knocked over the hen shaped saltshaker.

"I'm coming," Chase shouted from the kitchen as he fixed the saltshaker and headed towards the front door.

For being in the middle of nowhere he sure was getting an awful lot of visitors, way more than he had living in his apartment in the city, and it was starting to annoy the crap out of him. He wasn't much of a morning person to begin with, and with everything that had happened already that morning, plus the fact that he hadn't had his coffee yet, Chase was already past the boiling point. He swung open the front door with an exasperated "What?" and froze.

"Oh," Norah said, staring at him with a confused yet surprised expression. "It's you."

Holy shit. "Uh, yeah, it's me," he replied, pleased to see her yet wondering why she was standing on his front porch.

Norah let out a tiny laugh and shook her head. "I'm

sorry. I'm just…surprised to see you here."

Think of something clever to say, O'Donnell.

"So you aren't here to make a house call?"

And boy did *that* come out all wrong. He regretted his choice of words as soon as they came out of his mouth.

Way to make her sound like a prostitute.

"Excuse me?"

"Checking up on your patient," Chase quickly explained and pointed to the bandaged cut above his eye. "Like doctors do."

"Oh…umm," she said and let out another soft laugh. "No, I, uh, honestly didn't know you were here." She looked up and held his gaze for a moment before directing her eyes to his cut. "How *does* your head feel this morning?"

"Fine," he replied, smiling and leaning against the doorframe. "So if you're not here to check up on me, can I ask why you *are* here?"

"Oh, God, yes of course you can," Norah said. "I was just on my way over to take care of the livestock, and I saw this SUV parked up here that I've never seen before, which now I'm assuming is your SUV."

"You'd be correct," he said, still smiling as he watched her explain herself and enjoying how downright adorable she was when she was nervous.

"Anyway, I wasn't sure who was up here so I called the Sheriff's Department and—"

"So *you* called the cops on me?" His smile widened at her obvious discomfort.

Letting out an embarrassed sigh, Norah brought her hand to her face and covered her eyes. "Yes." She took her hand away and looked him in the eye. "God, I'm so sorry. That must've been some wake up call."

He laughed. "You could say that."

"Well, when Ernie, I mean Deputy Woodson, told me you that you were the new owner he suggested that I introduce myself."

"And why would he suggest that?"

"Because technically we're neighbors," she told him, then jerked her thumb to the left. "My family's ranch borders yours."

He followed her gesture and looked out upon the land, seeing nothing but miles and miles of tall grass against the morning sky. It was a rather beautiful sight, but not as beautiful as the sight before him. Chase hadn't been able to stop thinking about Norah since he left the bar the night before, so it was quite a shock for him to see her standing on his front porch at seven a.m.—almost as if his mind had conjured her here.

"Well," Chase said, then held his hand out. "It's very nice to meet you, neighbor."

She let out a soft laugh and shook his hand. "Very nice to meet you too."

God, she looked good. He'd bet everything he had that she woke up looking like that, and he'd give everything he had to get the chance to find out.

CHAPTER SEVEN

Chase O'Donnell was the new neighbor. She couldn't believe it. Never would she have guessed that he would be the one greeting her. Her heart had damn near jumped out of her chest when he swung that door open. For a moment she thought she'd been seeing things or that her brain had been so stuck on Chase's image that every man was starting to look like him. But it was him, and seeing him standing there in the doorway looking all sleep disheveled was making her all kinds of flustered.

"I, uh, was just going to make some coffee," Chase said. "But it, umm, looks like we're all out. If you want to come in I can make you…a glass of water."

He laughed and Norah joined him.

"I'll take a rain check," Norah said with a flirty smile. "I really should be tending to the livestock now. I mean, that *is* why I came over here in the first place."

Chase returned her smile. "Shut down again."

She bit the corner of her lip and shook her head as she started to walk away, but she stopped near the edge of the porch and turned back to Chase.

"Sorry about calling the cops on you." She took a step back onto one of the steps.

"And the early wake up call." She took another step.

"And hitting you in the head last night." She took another step but this time her foot slipped and she missed the last step, making her awkwardly catch her balance on the ground.

"I'm okay," she said, holding her hands up. "I'm just gonna…" And with that she scurried off towards the barn before Chase could see the mark of pure embarrassment on her face. When she knew she was out of his view she began to fan herself and took in deep breaths to rid her cheeks of the blush.

Good Lord. What was the matter with her? She'd never lost her cool around a guy before. Confidence was something she always exuded when dealing with the opposite sex. So what was it about this guy that threw all her senses off and literally had her falling for him?

Maybe it's those gorgeous green eyes and the way he looks at you. It's as if he knows what you look like na—

She stopped that thought dead in its tracks and quickly made her way towards the tack room of the barn. Grabbing three halters from their hooks, Norah looped them and a lead rope over her shoulder and made her way back out to the stalls. Tossing two of the halters on a hay bale, Norah crossed the walkway to one of the stalls that held a large bay gelding.

"Hey there, Doc," she said as she rubbed the palm of her hand up and down the white blaze that marked his face.

The horse nudged her hand but then backed away and let out a whinny as it looked in the direction of the door. She turned and found Chase walking across the dirt packed floor towards her and the horse.

"I hope I'm not intruding," he said. "But you really don't have to do this. I can take care of the animals."

"I see," Norah said with a teasing tone. "What you really mean is you don't feel right about letting a woman do all the work."

"No, that's not it at all," Chase said.

She raised an eyebrow and smirked.

"Okay, you're right." He laughed and walked over to the hay bale, picked up one of the halters and went to the next stall. "What kind of a man would I be if I just sat in the house and let you do all of this?"

"Well, thanks," Norah told him but stopped him before he placed the halter on the gray mare. "You can put the halter on her, but wait for me to let this guy out first."

"Okay," Chase said as he stroked the mare's neck and gave her a few gentle pats. "You know, I don't remember either of these horses."

Norah hooked the lead rope to the bay's halter. "Well, this fine lookin' fella is Doc," she said as she led the horse from the stall and out of the barn.

"Here," Chase said, catching up to her and gently taking the rope from her hand. "Let me."

She let go and followed in step from the other side of the horse. "I believe Doc's been here for about ten years now," she told him. "When's the last time you were here?" Stepping ahead of Chase and the horse, Norah opened the gate that led to the pasture.

"It's been about sixteen years."

She blew out a breath of air. "That's a long time."

"Yeah," Chase said, "but I remember that Uncle Eli had a lot more horses back then. The barn was also a lot bigger if I remember right." He removed the halter from the horse and looped it along with the lead rope over his shoulder.

Norah closed the gate behind them as they made their way back to the barn. "Yeah, there was a whole other side with six stalls, but the wood was all rotted and it collapsed a few years back. By that time your uncle had gotten out of the horse business and was only down to the three that are here now."

"I remember he had this brown and white pony that I used to ride when I was younger," Chase said, a smile drawing up the corners of his mouth. "He was an ornery son of a bitch; he hated my sister and even bit her once. But he and I got along great for some reason. I wonder what happened to him?"

"Buckshot?" Norah asked and knew she was correct the moment she saw Chase's eyes light up.

"Yeah, that was his name," he said. "Crazy little pony."

She wondered for a moment if she should suggest just finishing the chores by herself. Maybe then she'd be able to help Chase hold on to that memory he seemed to cherish so much. But this was his ranch now, and she couldn't very well hide things from him that he'd find out sooner or later.

"Come with me for a second," she told him as they entered the barn.

"Aren't we taking this one out?" Chase asked as they passed the gray mare.

"Yes, but I want to show you something first." Norah stopped at the last stall and gestured for Chase to step forward. "Take a look."

He gave her a bemused grin and stepped up to the stall. His mouth fell slack as he looked in and saw the painted pony from his childhood. "Holy shit. Is that…?"

"Yep," Norah said. "That's him."

Chase crossed his arms on the ledge of the stall and stared. "Wow. He looks so old."

"He is," Norah said.

"I know that but…" Chase reached his hand over the stall, clicked his tongue against the roof of his mouth, and called for the pony to come to him. The pony slightly moved his head towards Chase but didn't move. "He probably doesn't recognize me after all these years."

Norah let out a soft sigh. "He won't be able to recognize you, Chase. He's blind."

CHAPTER EIGHT

"Blind?" Chase asked. With a heavy heart, Chase stared across the stall at the once vibrant pony. It was as if all that remained of the animal he knew was a hollow shell. "So does he just stay in this stall all day long?" *That can't be any kind of a life for the poor thing.*

"Oh, no," Norah told him and nodded to the gray mare in the next stall. "Missy and he are companions. They get turned out to the small pasture together. She keeps him company and sticks close to him so he knows where he is and where he's going."

"Well, that's good to know," Chase said. Even though that bit of information eased his mind, he still felt horrible for the animal. "I'll get him," Chase said to Norah as he opened the latch on the stall door.

"Okay, just make sure you talk to him so he knows you're coming," Norah instructed. "So he won't be startled."

Chase entered the stall and saw the pony's ear twitch and turn in his direction. Walking slowly, he spoke calm and gentle words until he stood by the pony's side. He carefully brought his hand up and rested it against the pony's neck, stroking back and forth against its shaggy mane.

"It's good to see you again, old fella." Chase spoke in a barely audible voice as he carefully placed the halter over the pony's head. "Even if you can't see me."

"You good?" Norah asked as Chase led the pony out of the stall.

"Yeah," Chase replied.

She nodded and Chase followed behind her out of the barn. Once both of the animals were in the pasture, Chase propped a foot up on the bottom rail and rested his arms over the top rail as he watched the old brown and white pony saunter along next to the gray mare.

"This feels so weird," Chase said.

"What?" Norah asked, turning from the horses to Chase.

"Being here on the ranch again," Chase told her as he watched both animals stop to graze. "I haven't been here since I was fourteen, but it feels like I never left." He turned to look at her. "Everything's the same. A little run-down and older, but still."

Norah nodded. "Did you come here often?"

"For two weeks out of every summer since I was six," Chase answered, removing his foot from the bottom rail to lean casually against the fence.

A soft breeze blew through the air, slightly tousling Norah's hair. He fought the urge to gently brush the stray strands away from her face. Even though it may have felt right at that moment, he knew it was borderline crossing a boundary. They barely even knew each other.

"It feels weird to say this since I've lived next to your uncle my entire life," Norah told him, "but I just don't remember ever meeting you."

"It's not weird at all," Chase said. "We pretty much stayed on the ranch for the duration of our visit."

"We?" Norah asked.

"My sister and me."

"Oh right," Norah said with a knowing smile. "The one who got bit by the pony."

Chase let out a soft chuckle. "That's the one."

"She older or younger than you?" Norah pushed herself away from the fence and walked over to the water trough.

"Older," Chase answered as he walked past her to the hose on the side of the barn and began to pull it free from the reel. "She's married and has two daughters. Maddie's seven, and Chelsea just turned five."

"Uncle Chase," Norah teased.

Chase held up his hands. "That's me." He smiled as he handed her the hose. "What about you? Do you have any nieces or nephews?"

"Not yet," she told him with a smile. "My oldest brother just got married last year. My other brother isn't married, and I don't think he ever will be." She laughed at that.

"A bit of a ladies' man, is he?" Chase asked, then walked back to the barn and turned the water on.

"A bit," Norah agreed.

"And are these the same brothers that you were afraid would find us last night?" Chase asked with a sly smile as he moved towards her.

"I was only afraid for your sake," Norah told him, placing the hose in the trough before turning to look back at him. "It would have been a shame if they messed up that pretty little face of yours."

The warmth that flushed her cheeks at that moment and the sheer look of embarrassment on her face would have made any other woman appear awkward. But on her it was sexy, and it became even more so when she ran her fingers through her hair, giving her that bed head look that one of his exes used to spend an hour and a half in the bathroom trying to achieve.

"Anyway," Norah said, breaking eye contact and walking past him to the barn. "Your uncle has some chickens in that coop over there. They lay eggs regularly, so you'll need to make sure you check it every morning."

"Okay," Chase said, hiding an amused smile as he followed a few steps behind her.

"I'm sure it's been a while since you've collected eggs so I'll help you after we get the horse stalls all clean, but there's really nothing to it."

"All right," Chase said as he smacked his hands together. "Let's get to work." He started to walk past Norah but paused when she gave him a curious glance. "What's that look for?"

"Hmm?" Norah said as she pointed to his feet. "I didn't pay any attention until now, but…are you sure you want to muck horse stalls wearing *those* boots?"

"What's wrong with them?" What the hell else was he supposed to wear?

"They look brand new," Norah said.

He looked down and—*yeah, okay*—so they were brand spanking new. Wearing cowboy boots was about as country as Chase got these days. He even wore them to the office on occasion, which drove his father absolutely crazy.

"No, they're not new," Chase lied.

"All right," Norah said. "But don't come crying to me when you get manure on your pretty boots."

"So I never did ask," Chase said, basket of eggs in hand as he and Norah walked out of the chicken coop. "How did you end up taking care of my great-uncle's animals?"

"Oh, well it was my brother's turn to do it today," Norah told him. "But he had a minor accident this morning and needed me to fill in for him."

"No, no," Chase said with a soft chuckle. "I didn't mean today." Then with a more serious tone he added,

"Although I do hope your brother's okay now."

"I'm sure he's fine."

She tried to hide a smile, but Chase saw it and instantly became curious.

"Why's that funny?"

"No reason," she told him. "Getting back to your question...my brothers have actually been the ones taking care of the animals. I filled in occasionally, but I mainly helped look after your great-uncle by bringing him meals and keeping the house tidy. My mom helped out as well."

"How long have you all been taking care of things?" he asked as they walked towards the house.

She turned to him with a frown and shrugged her shoulders. "It was just after his first stroke so about six or seven months now."

"Ah," Chase said with a slight nod, silently berating himself that he'd forgotten all about his great-uncle's first stroke, and the fact that he'd been too involved in his own life that he didn't even bother to offer to help out. "Well, thank you for doing all that you've done. I'm sure it was hard taking care of things around your place plus his." He stopped as they neared where his SUV and her truck were parked. "If I can repay you and your family in any way—"

Norah held up her hand to stop him and smiled. "It was our pleasure," she said. "Eli was a great man and your Aunt Mary was a wonderful woman. If the roles had been reversed I know they would have done the same for us."

Chase returned her smile. "Well, thank you again."

"You're welcome."

"And thank you for sticking around and showing me how you all have been handling the chores," Chase told her. "It'll come in handy for when I hire some help."

A soft laugh escaped her lips as she looked at him with a perplexed expression. "It's only three horses, well, two and a half really, and some chickens," she said. "Nothing you can't handle on your own."

"It's not a matter of me not being able to handle it," Chase explained. "It's a matter of me not being here to handle it."

Her expression deepened. "Am I missing something here?"

"I'm, umm," Chase said, pausing for a moment as he stared into Norah's questioning eyes. "My plan, actually, is to sell the ranch."

"Oh." Norah's expression changed then to one of realization with a hint of shock. "I'm sorry," she said with a slight shake of her head. "I just assumed that, since you had inherited the place, you'd be staying here."

"And that was a fair assumption," Chase told her. "But this whole inheritance thing came as quite a shock to me, and I really wasn't prepared for it and all that it entails."

"I see," Norah said softly. "You know, if it makes things easy for you, my brothers and I can keep taking care of the place."

"I couldn't ask you to do that," Chase said.

"It's okay, really," Norah said. "We've been doing it for so long now that it's become part of our routine."

"Are you sure?"

She nodded. "I'm positive."

"Well, thank you," Chase told her. "I really don't expect you to do all this work for free, so if you let me know what I can pay you—"

Once again, Norah put up her hand to stop him from talking. "Like I said before," she said, "it's really not necessary."

He nodded as silence filled the space between them. After a few moments, Norah brushed her hair behind her ear and let out a soft sigh. "Well, I really hate to rush off, but I sort of need to be heading out now."

"Of course," Chase said. "Here, I'll walk you to your truck."

They walked the short distance and, when they had reached the driver's side, Chase opened the door for her.

"Thanks," she told him as she slid onto the seat.

"Don't forget these," Chase said and handed her the basket of eggs.

"Are you sure you don't want to keep them?" Norah asked.

"I'm sure," Chase said. "I don't need them. Plus I'm not about to cut off that family you've been giving them to."

"Thanks," Norah said and smiled, as she placed the basket in the floorboard on the passenger side. She turned back to him and he held her gaze. "So how long are you in town for?"

He hesitated for the briefest moment before answering her. "A few more hours. I have a meeting with my realtor and then I'll be handling the rest of the sale from back home."

"Well," Norah said with a heavy sigh, "I guess this is goodbye."

"I guess it is," Chase agreed.

"It was nice meeting you, Chase O'Donnell."

"You too, Norah McKade." He stepped away from the truck and closed the door for her. "Maybe I'll see you around, though. I'm sure I'll be back sometime during this whole process."

"Yeah." She laughed softly. "Maybe."

He nodded and grinned.

"Oh," Norah said. "Before I forget, the phone number to our ranch is on the notepad by the phone. If you need anything or, you just want to check in and see how things are going with the place, give us a call."

His grin widened. "I'll do that."

CHAPTER NINE

The smell of bacon, sausage, and fresh biscuits greeted
Norah as she entered through the back door of her
mother's house.

"Mmm," Norah said, taking in a deep breath of the
delicious aroma. "That smells so good."

"Hey, daughter," Linda McKade said as she turned
from her position at the stove to look at Norah. "Things go
okay over at the Caldwell Ranch?"

Norah nodded and walked over to the coffee maker.
"Yep." Reaching in the cabinet above, Norah grabbed a
mug, placed it on the counter in front of her, and then
proceeded to make herself a cup of coffee. "You've sort of
got yourself a new neighbor."

"Really?"

"Mmm-hmm," Norah said as she poured creamer into
her cup and stirred in a spoonful of sugar. "He's Eli's
great-nephew."

"I didn't know Eli had a great-nephew," Linda said.

"Me either," Norah told her mother. "He said he used
to spend a couple of weeks every summer at Eli's ranch
when he was a kid."

"Wait, did he have a sister?"

Norah sent her mother a puzzled look. "Yeah."

"Oh," Linda said in recognition, dragging the word
out slightly. "I remember him now."

"You do?" Norah deepened her puzzled expression.

"Yeah," Linda told her as she placed the cooked
sausage onto a plate. "I remember seeing them one time
when I stopped by to visit with Mary. He was a lanky

thing."

Lanky? Norah lifted the mug to her lips and took a careful sip of the steaming hot liquid to hide her grin. He was hardly lanky now. Time had done his body good— that and whatever gym membership he had.

"Oh, by the way, I have more eggs for you to give Abby Daniels," Norah said.

"That's great," Linda replied. "I'll be seeing her tomorrow so I can take them to her then."

Norah took another sip of her coffee. "Have you heard from the boys?"

"Zane called just a little bit ago," Linda told Norah. "He said that Luke had to get nine stitches and a tetanus shot." Linda turned the stove off and turned to Norah with a large plate of bacon and sausage.

Norah bit the inside of her cheek. "A tetanus shot?" She leaned back against the counter and rested her coffee cup next to her. "So does that mean he…?"

"Passed out?" Linda finished for her and nodded.

A tiny burst of laughter escaped from Norah and she quickly apologized. "Poor Luke. He has got to be one of the toughest men I've ever known, but show him a needle and he's done for."

"I know," Linda said. "He's been like that ever since y'all were kids and I never did figure out where that fear came from."

"I guess the world will never know," Norah said and let out a soft laugh. "Well, I better get out to the barn. Our horses are probably pretty upset that they're still in their stalls." She pushed herself away from the counter and made her way across the room to the door.

"Andi mentioned that she was heading out that way after she collected the eggs from the hen house," Linda said to Norah. "Not sure if she made it that far yet or not."

"Okay," Norah said. "Thanks."

The screen door's hinges creaked as she opened it and stepped out onto the porch. She let go of the handle and the door slammed shut behind her, rattling slightly as it settled back into place. Jogging down the steps of the porch, Norah stepped onto the grass and crossed the gravel driveway to the barn.

Her thoughts went to handsome, sexy Chase answering the door with sleepy eyes and tousled hair. Seeing him this morning was something she hadn't been prepared for—mentally or physically. The image alone of his tall, muscular frame leaning against the open doorway with his tanned arms crossed over his broad chest and those green eyes staring back at her made her whole body buzz and tingle.

"What's that smile all about?" Andi asked.

"Huh?" Norah said, coming out of her Chase induced daydream and looked to Andi.

"That smile you're wearing," Andi said and pointed to Norah. "I know that smile."

Oh crap. *Had* she been smiling?

"I wasn't smiling," Norah said, picking up a lead rope from the hook on the wall and walking past Andi to one of the last stalls.

"Yes you were," Andi retorted. Her mouth turned up in an amused smile and she placed a hand on her hip. "And whatever was making you smile like that also affected your hearing, too."

"I have no idea what you're talking about." Norah opened the stall door and came back out with a young, sorrel gelding.

"I said 'Hi' to you at least four times," Andi told Norah, tossing her unneeded lead rope to the ground as she followed Norah out of the barn and to the pasture.

"So…what's his name?"

With a nonchalant roll of her eyes, Norah let the horse loose in the pasture with the others. "Okay, I'll admit I'm in a good mood. But who says it's because of a guy?"

"Oh don't play coy with me, Norah McKade," Andi said as she and Norah made their way back to the barn. "Does this have anything to do with that guy from the bar last night?"

Oh it has everything to do with that guy.

The corner of Norah's lips turned up as she worked on hanging the lead ropes back in the tack room and straightening a few things up.

"Please don't make me drag information out of you," Andi said, her voice tinged with annoyance. "I hate it when you make me do that."

Norah let out a small laugh. "Okay, okay." She finished adjusting one of the saddle blankets and turned to face Andi. "That guy from the bar last night…?"

"Yeah," Andi prompted.

"He's the new owner of Eli Caldwell's place."

Andi gasped. "Shut up. How'd that happen?"

Norah started to fill Andi in on her morning with Chase, having to pause when she got to the part about calling the Sheriff's Department on him because she and Andi couldn't control their laughter. The same thing happened again when she got to the part about her almost falling on her butt after she missed that last step on the porch.

The sound of gravel crunching beneath tires sounded from behind them, and Norah looked up to see Zane's pick-up truck coming up the driveway.

"I'll have to finish the story later," Norah said to Andi.

"Please," Andi said, swiping the back of her hand underneath her eye to wipe away the tears of laughter. "I can't wait to hear what happened next."

Moments later, Zane's truck pulled to a stop. "How's your arm?" Norah asked, directing her question to Luke.

"It's nothing," Luke said, then held up his bandaged arm as he walked around Zane's truck. "A few stitches. It was stupid really. I told Zane I was fine but he insisted I go to the ER."

"You cut your arm on a rusty nail, Luke," Zane said, wrapping his arm around Andi's waist as they climbed the porch stairs. "You needed a tetanus shot."

"Don't," Luke said, holding up his hands. "Just. Don't."

Zane, Andi, and Norah chuckled as they walked up to the house with Luke.

Once again, Norah's mind went to Chase as she stared off in the direction of his ranch. She let out a sigh as she rested a hand against the side of the house and slowly removed her boots one at a time by the back door.

This sucked.

There had been something there with Chase; she could feel it deep down inside her bones—something more than just a physical attraction. She liked him—liked him a lot for having just met him. But knowing that he had no intentions of sticking around made those feelings she held for him seem almost pointless.

"Norah!" Luke called from inside the house. "Are you coming or what? We're all about to starve to death."

"I'm coming," Norah answered Luke, glancing one last time across the open land before she turned away and entered the house.

CHAPTER TEN

A piercing scream came through the earpiece of Chase's cell phone causing him to jump slightly and quickly pull the device away from his ear. He held the phone down, resting his elbow on the center console of his SUV, and pressed the speaker button.

"Madelyn Grace, *do not* pull your sister's hair!" Sarah yelled. "I don't care who started what. Be nice to each other."

Chase smiled, keeping one hand on the steering wheel and his eyes on the road before him.

"Sorry about that," Sarah apologized.

"It's fine," Chase reassured.

"Okay, so how did things go this morning?"

Taking in a deep breath, Chase let it out forcefully and began to recount the visit with the realtor to his sister.

He'd been rather excited to meet with the realtor and find out just how much his great-uncle's ranch was worth—especially after he'd spoken with her on the phone and she'd made it sound like he could make a nice profit off of it. Although that had been before Chase had actually seen the place in the shape it was in now.

"This isn't exactly how you described the property," had been the first words out of her mouth after her introduction.

Strike one, Chase had thought to himself. And the rest of the visit didn't get any better. With all of the repairs that needed to be completed to the house, the barn, and the other various things around the property that had been neglected, Chase was looking to make next to nothing for the sale.

Strike two. And three.

"Well," Sarah said. "You still have the land. That's got to be worth something."

"It is," Chase told her. "But it's not the full package deal that most people are looking for." He rested the phone in the cup holder and ran his hand through his hair. "I could sell it as is, *should* sell it, and just call it a day."

"But," Sarah said dragging the word out. "I hear a 'but' in that tone of voice."

Chase forced out a sigh. "But the business man side of me sees the potential profit I could make."

"Ah," Sarah said. "I know that voice. Sounds a lot like Dad." She chuckled.

Chase joined in her amusement but cringed at the same time. Being compared to his father wasn't a favorite of his. "It does."

"Well, I'm sure you'll figure it all out," Sarah told him. "If you wanted to spruce the place up, I'm sure there are people around there that you could hire to do that."

"Yeah," Chase said, his voice trailing off. *Or I could just stick around and do the repairs myself.*

He'd been battling with the idea ever since the realtor left, and he couldn't find one good reason why he shouldn't just handle things himself. It just made sense. He was more than capable of doing the necessary repairs, and he'd be saving some money by doing them himself instead of hiring someone.

Plus, sticking around town meant there'd be a very good chance he'd run into a certain beautiful blonde.

And if he were truly going to be honest with himself, he was rather enjoying his time here in the country—even though he'd been dreading it at first. All of these childhood memories were flooding his brain, and he just wasn't ready to push them aside and leave.

"Chase?"

"Yeah?" he replied to Sarah. "Sorry, what were you saying?"

"I've got to run," Sarah said. "I've got to make the girls some lunch and then it's off to ballet."

"Sure," Chase said. "Oh, hey, before I forget…I need to take care of removing Uncle Eli's and Aunt Mary's belongings out of the house. I was just going to have an estate sale but I thought maybe you and Mom would want to come see if there was anything you'd want first."

"Yeah that'd be great," Sarah said. "I'll have to get back to you on when I can make it out there. I'll coordinate with Mom and maybe we can make the trip together."

"Sounds good," Chase replied. "Talk to you later."

He ended the call just as a small diner came into view.

"Finally," he said out loud to himself. "A place that serves food."

Parking his SUV near the front entrance, Chase pulled the keys out of the ignition and stepped out of the vehicle. As he walked to the door he gave himself a slight once over and was thankful that his great-uncle had a working washer and dryer. He might have been stuck wearing the same clothes from last night and this morning, but at least they were clean and so was he.

The bell rang over the door as Chase entered the tiny diner. He found an empty booth towards the center and sat down on the vinyl bench.

"Afternoon, hon," the waitress said. "What can I get ya?"

He looked up to see an older woman standing at his table with a pen and a notepad, ready to take his order.

"You still serving coffee?"

"All day every day," she told him, smacking on her chewing gum as she grinned at him.

"Perfect," Chase said. "I'll have a cup, black, and a menu, please."

"No problem, sugar," the waitress told him. "Comin' right up."

As Chase waited, he casually drummed his fingers on the tabletop while dozens of thoughts ran through his mind. He needed to make a plan and stick to it so that this repair project didn't get out of hand. The first thing he needed to do was to figure out what all had to be completed; then he could figure out the budget, and the time schedule. And he needed to have all this in place before presenting the idea to his father.

Darren O'Donnell wouldn't be too keen on the idea of Chase being out of the office for said amount of time, but if Chase made his case sound worthwhile, then that might smooth things over just a bit. Plus, it's not like he *had* to be in the office to get his work completed. He had one project he was working on—a design for a potential client—but that wasn't due for another six weeks.

"Here you go, hon" the waitress said as she placed a menu on the table in front of Chase.

"Thanks," Chase said with a nod.

"I'll give you a minute to look that over," she told him. "And I'll be right back with your coffee, but if you need anything before then just holler. My name's Belle."

As Chase thanked the waitress once more, he heard the bell over the door ring and looked up to see Norah.

"Well bless my stars," Belle said, walking to Norah with

open arms. "If it ain't my beautiful niece."

"Hey, Aunt Belle," Norah said, stepping into Belle's arms and hugging her back.

"What brings you here, darlin'?"

Norah followed Belle to the counter and took a seat on an empty stool as Belle made her way over to the coffee pots.

"Mom asked me to stop by and drop off a few boxes for the church yard sale."

"Well thank you," Belle told Norah as she turned around with one of the pots. Grabbing a ceramic mug, Belle proceeded to fill it with the smooth, dark liquid.

"Thanks," Norah said as she reached for the steaming cup.

Belle shook her head and slid the mug away from Norah. "Uh-uh, honey. This ain't for you."

"Oh," Norah said, gently folding her hands onto her lap. "Sorry."

"I'll get you a cup in a sec," Belle said. Her lips twisted into a mischievous grin. "But first I've got to take this over to that hot thang occupying my center booth."

Amused by her aunt's behavior, Norah turned to see this "hot thang" her aunt spoke of and froze.

It was Chase O'Donnell. And he was staring right at her.

"Look at him checkin' me out," Belle said.

Norah looked back to her aunt just in time to see her send Chase a wink and shimmy her hips. She bit the inside of her cheek to keep from laughing at the older woman's antics.

"That's Mom's new neighbor," Norah told Belle as she nodded her head towards Chase and crossed her arms on the counter.

"Looks like I'm going to have to make a trip out to

your mama's place in the near future," Belle said. "I may just get lost along the way…or better yet, my car might just break down in front of his house, and I'll need to use his phone to call for help." She waggled her eyebrows.

"You are too funny, Aunt Belle." Norah shook her head. She didn't have the heart to tell her aunt that he most likely wouldn't be there for that scenario to happen. "Who knew you were a cougar?"

"I'm just tryin' to stay young, darlin'," Belle told her as she walked from behind the counter to deliver Chase his coffee.

Norah laughed and shook her head again. She looked over her shoulder to Chase just as he looked up from his menu and accepted the ceramic mug from Belle. From the look on his face Belle must've been laying it on pretty thick. Poor Chase. He really didn't know what he was getting into. But he appeared to be playing along with it as he smiled and handed Belle the menu, saying something to her in the process that made her laugh. They spoke for another few moments before Belle patted his hand then walked away from him and back to Norah.

"So," Norah said to Belle in a teasing, upbeat tone. "Have you got yourself a hot date?"

Belle let out a soft chuckle and poured Norah a cup of coffee. "No…but I got you one."

Norah's eyes widened. "Come again?"

"Here." Belle pushed the cup of coffee across the counter towards Norah. "Take this and go sit with that fine young man."

Looking over her shoulder again, Norah watched as Chase gestured for her to take the vacant seat across from him.

She turned back to Belle and smirked.

"You're welcome, hon," Belle told her with a wink.

Picking up her coffee, Norah made her way over to Chase's booth and slid into the seat across from him.

"I didn't expect to find you here," Norah said.

Chase shrugged slightly. "I had to eat sometime today and, let's be honest, the kitchen back at the ranch wasn't exactly stocked full of groceries." He let out a soft laugh. "Of course I would still be here even if it *were* stocked full of groceries."

Norah took a sip of her coffee and then grinned. "Is that your subtle hint that you don't cook?"

"Yeah." He laughed again and nodded his head. "The extent of my culinary skills is ramen noodles."

"Oh good Lord," Norah said, joining in on his laughter for a moment before letting out a soft sigh.

Chase leaned forward then, rested his elbows and crossed his arms on the table as he looked at her. "You know, I've gotta be honest with you," he said, the sound of his voice sending a shiver down her spine. "I'm rather enjoying these brief meetings we keep having."

She took her bottom lip between her teeth and smiled. "We do keep running into each other, don't we?"

His answering sly grin made her stomach flutter.

"Must be fate," Chase teased.

She chuckled softly. "Must be."

"So what brings you here today?" Chase asked. "You just stopping in for a cup of coffee?"

She took a careful sip of the hot drink and shook her head. "Actually, I was just dropping off something."

"I see," Chase said as he too took a sip from his mug and stared at her with blatant interest.

"What?" she asked.

The corner of his mouth turned up. "I'm just wondering what your answer would be if I asked you to stay and join me for lunch."

Norah considered him. "I don't know," she told him, her voice light and airy.

"You have other errands to run?" he asked.

"No."

"Any important ranch things to take care of?"

"Not right now."

And there was that bad-boy grin of his again. "Good. Then you don't have an excuse to tell me no."

Norah sent him a sweet smile. "I guess not." She turned away from him, gained Belle's attention, and placed a lunch order. When she turned back to him, he was still giving her that blatant stare. Her heart leapt.

"So," Chase said, toying with the napkin wrapped utensils as he leaned against the backrest of the booth. "It looks like I'm going to be sticking around for a while."

"Oh yeah?" That surprised her. It excited her too, but she tried to hide that fact. "What changed your mind?"

"Let's just say that the meeting with my realtor didn't go as I had planned," Chase said. "There are a lot of repairs that need to be done to the ranch before I can put it on the market."

"I see." Norah paused. "Well, if you're looking to hire a handyman, I can get you in touch with the right people."

"I appreciate that," Chase said. "But I was actually planning on doing most of the work myself."

"Oh," Norah replied. "Still, if you change your mind or find you need help with something, just let me know."

"I'll do that," Chase answered her with a smile.

She lifted her mug and took another sip of her coffee. As she placed the cup back on the table she caught Chase's eye and held his gaze—those green eyes of his staring at her with wonder.

"So, it's been quite some time since I've stayed here

in Buford," Chase said. "Why don't you fill me in on what sorts of things there are to do for fun around town?"

Norah had to think about that one for a moment before she answered him with, "Not much, really. Most of the time when people want to go out for the night they just head for the bar."

Chase grinned at that. "Okay then. Let me rephrase my question." He leaned forward again. "What sorts of things do *you* like to do for fun? Something tells me that your definition of a night out doesn't involve going to your place of work."

"You'd be right," Norah said with a soft laugh. "Normally I'll call my friends and go wherever the party is that night." She gave him a slight shrug. "Most of the time it's just a bunch of us hanging out in someone's field around a bonfire. It doesn't sound like much when I describe it like that, but we have fun." She toyed with her coffee cup, spinning it in a slow circle on the table before cupping it with both hands in front of her. "What about you? What do you do for fun?"

"I'll do the bar scene with my friends from time to time. But I'm mainly a couch potato, especially when it's football season." Chase blew out a soft breath of air and sat back in the booth. "But I've been so busy lately that I haven't had any time for fun."

Belle appeared at the table then and handed them their lunch orders.

"All work and no play ain't a way to live your life, handsome," Belle chimed in.

"Aunt Belle," Norah chided. Belle had always been one for being forward, but it surprised Norah that Belle had been so opinionated with a man she didn't even know. Norah was just about to shoot Chase an apologetic look, but when she moved her eyes from Belle to him, he was smiling.

"Don't 'Aunt Belle' me, child," Belle said to Norah. "I'm just giving this young man some helpful advice."

"And I appreciate the advice very much, Miss Belle," Chase replied. "You're also absolutely right."

"Oh I know I'm right," Belle said and shot Chase a wink. She turned to Norah then and a playful smile spread across her face. "Why don't you take him out, hon, and show him around town, bein' that he's new and all?"

How humiliating. It was one thing for her aunt to set her up behind her back. But for Belle to do it right in front of Norah with the so-called love interest present was too much.

"What do ya say, handsome?" Belle turned back to Chase. "How'd you like for my niece here to give you a tour of the town?"

Norah could feel the slow heat of embarrassment creeping up her neck and to her cheeks. The urge to crawl under the table and die was present, too. She had no idea why her aunt was being so darn pushy. With a slight roll of her eyes, Norah looked from Belle to Chase and this time she did shoot him an apologetic look and mouthed the word, "Sorry."

His lips twitched into a brief amused smile and although he was answering Belle his eyes never left Norah's. "I think I'd like that."

CHAPTER ELEVEN

"Thank you for lunch," Norah said as she and Chase made their way out into the afternoon sun. Walking down the concrete steps, Norah stopped when her boots hit the gravel of the parking lot and she turned to face him.

"You're welcome," Chase said. "I'm glad you didn't turn me down."

The corners of her mouth turned up slightly and she hesitated for a moment before speaking. "I should get going." She gestured to her truck.

"Yeah, me too." He reached in his front pocket and pulled out his keys. "I've got a long drive ahead of me."

"The ranch isn't *that* far," Norah teased.

He chuckled at that. "I've actually got to head back home to take care of a few things, and I need to get some stuff from my apartment."

"I see," Norah said. "And where's home?"

"Dallas," he answered.

"Yeah, that is a hike," she told him. "And you're heading back there now?"

Chase nodded and grinned—that sly crooked grin that made her knees weak. "Missing me already?"

She let out a burst of air that was a combination of a laugh and a snort. "Easy there, O'Donnell. I was more worried about who's going to take care of your livestock."

Chase brought his hand to the back of his neck. "Oh shit, the horses. I don't suppose I could ask—"

"Yes," Norah said. "I'll take care of them for you."

"Thanks, Norah. I should be back late tomorrow morning."

"No problem."

"I don't suppose you'd be interested in giving me that tour of the town when I get back?" Chase asked. "Maybe we could throw in some dinner as well?"

She took a moment to consider his request and then teasingly answered him with, "Just as long as you're not cooking."

The sun had faded behind the tree line, casting flickers of light against the hood of his SUV as he drove through his parents' neighborhood. As his childhood home came into view, Chase silently rehearsed what he was going to say to his father about his need for time away from the office. He pulled into the drive, parked behind his mother's black sedan, and then made his way up the stone path to the front door.

"Hello?" Chase called out as he let himself in. "Mom? Dad?"

"Oh my goodness," Chase's mother said as she walked from the kitchen to the foyer. "What a nice surprise. I wasn't expecting you."

Susan stretched her arms out and Chase bent down to accept his mother's embrace.

"I know, I should've called," Chase told her as he slowly pulled away from her.

"Oh my, Chase," Susan said as she took hold of his chin and angled his face to see his bandaged wound. "What on earth happened here?"

"It's nothing," Chase told her as he gently pulled her hand from his chin. "I'm not interrupting your dinner or anything, am I?"

"Pshh," Susan said, waving him off. "You are never

interrupting anything, son."

She gestured for him to follow her to the kitchen and he complied with her request.

"Is Dad here?" Chase asked, walking behind his mother.

"He's in his office," Susan told him. "Are you hungry? I'm making shrimp Alfredo with garlic bread."

"I could eat," Chase said as he took a seat on one of the empty counter stools. "How's work?"

"Busy," Susan told him as she poured a glass of red wine and held it out to him.

"No thanks."

Walking back to the stove, Susan took a sip of the deep burgundy liquid and stirred the contents of a large pot. "I've got the Lawrence wedding coming up next weekend, and we were also invited to attend." She let out a deep sigh. "So it's going to be a hectic day."

"Mr. Lawrence finally marrying off that spoiled daughter of his?" he asked with a laugh.

"Oh stop," Susan said as she grabbed the handles of the pot with her potholders and walked it to the sink to drain the noodles. "You know," she said to Chase through the thick steam, "the invitation was made out to Mr. and Mrs. Darren O'Donnell *and family*."

"And?"

"And I was thinking it might be nice if you attended the wedding as well." She shook the strainer a few times and dumped the noodles back in the pot.

"And why would I want to go to Janie Lawrence's wedding?" His mother was up to something. He could tell from the breezy tone of her voice.

"I just thought that maybe you might meet a nice girl and—"

"Nope," Chase said and shook his head. "Uh-uh.

We're not doing this."

"Doing what?"

"Setting me up or trying to set me up with random single women at Janie Lawrence's wedding."

"Oh come on, Chase," Susan said and brushed her dark, shoulder length hair away from her face. "Is it bad that your dear old mother just wants to see you settle down?"

"I'll settle down when I'm ready."

Letting out a soft sigh, Susan rested her hands on the smooth granite surface and looked at Chase. "You're not getting any younger, son."

"I'm only thirty," Chase countered. "And what does my age have to do with this?"

"Okay, well *I'm* not getting any younger," Susan retorted. "I want grandkids before I'm too old to enjoy them."

"You have grandkids," Chase said with a laugh. "Maddie and Chelsea. Or did you forget about them?"

"I want *more* grandkids," Susan said and held her hand up to stop Chase from speaking. "And don't even tell me to talk to Sarah about that because she's already told me that she and Keith aren't having anymore. So that just leaves you."

Chase laughed as he stood from the counter stool and walked around the island to his mother. "I'll see what I can do." He rested his hand on her shoulder and placed a soft kiss on the top of her head. "But I'm not going to that wedding."

She swatted at him with a dish towel as he exited the kitchen. "I'd like a grandson, please."

"I'm on it," Chase answered her as he made his way down the hall to his father's office. Childhood photos of him and his sister lined the walls, each of them framed in dark wood to match the rest of the woodwork in the house, and he glanced at them as he walked by. When he came to his father's office door, he knocked softly before he slowly pushed the door open.

"Chase," his father said looking up from his computer screen. "What brings you here? And what the hell happened to your head?"

"Just a small accident," Chase said as he entered the wood-paneled room and took a seat in one of the chairs across from his father's desk.

"It looks like you got in a fight," Darren said in a chiding tone.

"I didn't get in a fight, Dad." This conversation wasn't off to a good start. Chase paused for a moment as he made himself comfortable and let out a soft sigh before he spoke again. "Do you have a few minutes? I need to talk to you about something."

"About what?" Darren asked as he typed away on the keyboard. "Oh, before you get started, how's it coming on the design for The Channing Group?"

"I'm working on it," Chase answered.

"You've got to do your best work on this one," Darren said and gave his computer mouse a few clicks before he leaned back in his executive style chair to look at Chase. "Because if things go well with The Channing Group then we have an in with Michael and Michaels."

Chase leaned forward at the mention of Michael and Michaels. Known to every architect in the area, Michael and Michaels was *the* top real estate development group and was responsible for the majority of buildings throughout the city. Getting involved with that company would do huge things for his father's firm and in return would do huge things for him as well.

"That's fantastic news," Chase said.

"I know," Darren replied. "And all of this is riding on you and how well things go over with your design." The facial expression he wore matched his no nonsense tone. "So don't screw it up."

"I know, Dad," Chase said and gritted his teeth. In all the years he'd worked for his father, Chase had yet to screw anything up, but Darren always had to throw that in the mix whenever a big client was involved. It pissed Chase off completely that his father had such little faith in him, even though he successfully delivered every time.

"So," Darren said, folding his hands over his stomach. "What did you need to talk to me about?"

Well, that had gone just as he had expected it to. Chase had barely gotten his first few sentences out before Darren had started in on him. There'd been a fair amount of yelling and a fair amount of name calling, but eventually Chase got his point across and his father agreed. Reluctantly.

He had six weeks. Six weeks to complete his design proposal for The Channing Group, make the necessary repairs to the ranch, and spend as much time with the beautiful blond country girl who had been on his mind since she landed in his arms the night before.

Even now as he sat in his quiet apartment, staring at his laptop as he attempted to get a few things done, Norah was present in the forefront of his mind. What would she be doing right now? He looked at the time and realized she was most likely working at the bar. The image of her in that tight little black top and those blue jeans with the hole in the knee burst into his brain. He replayed the memory of their first encounter over and over again, making it impossible to concentrate on his work. He closed his laptop and stood up from his desk, raking his hands over his face and through his hair as he made his way to the bathroom.

A nice hot shower would relax him and hopefully clear his mind so he could get some sleep. Little good it did him, though. The warmth of the water hitting his bare skin only reminded him of Norah's body pressing into his as she fell back into him. He cursed his brain for teasing him and making him want something he couldn't have. But a turn of the shower knob subdued his hormones as cool water replaced the warm. He quickly finished up and stepped out of the shower, dried off with a towel before he slipped on a pair of boxers and made his way to his bedroom.

Tossing the covers back, Chase lay down with a huff and tossed a hand behind his head while he rested the other on his stomach. He stared at the ceiling for the longest time, willing himself to go to sleep. But sleep never came.

"Screw it," Chase said and sat straight up and threw his legs over the side of the bed. He quickly put on some clothes, grabbed his belongings he'd packed earlier, and left his apartment. If he wasn't going to sleep, than he was going to drive.

CHAPTER TWELVE

Norah narrowed her eyes in confusion as she neared the Caldwell Ranch. From the road she could clearly make out the form of three horses grazing in the pasture.

"Now how did you guys get out there?" she asked out loud to herself.

She soon answered her own question when she spotted Chase's silver SUV parked next to the house.

I thought he wasn't coming back until late this morning?

Well, this was a pleasant surprise. She wasn't going to deny that seeing Chase would make her morning. The man had seemed to make permanent residency in her brain, and she welcomed him in most eagerly.

Parking her truck next to Chase's SUV, she got out and looked around to see where he was. She decided to check the house first, and when she received no response, she made her way out to the barn. The single, large door was slid to the side, leaving a wide entrance. She stepped through the opening and glanced around briefly before she found Chase.

Holy hell.

Apparently he was oblivious to her presence, but she sure as heck wasn't oblivious to the fact that he was shirtless. She was drawn to the way his muscles flexed under his tanned skin as he worked on cleaning out the horse stall. A thin coat of sweat covered his shoulders and she noticed that he had a tattoo in the center of his right shoulder blade. From where she was standing it looked like a bird with its wings spread—an eagle, maybe?—but she'd need a closer look to be sure. Her gaze traveled down the length of his body and she smiled to herself when she noticed he'd traded in his pretty boots for more sensible work ones.

Chase turned then and stepped out of the stall. He rested the blade of the shovel on the hard, packed dirt floor before he noticed Norah.

She jumped. Damn. He'd caught her checking him out.

"Have you been standing there long?" Chase asked as he walked over to a hay bale and picked up his t-shirt. He removed his navy blue baseball cap and wiped the sweat from his brow with his shirt before he replaced his cap.

"No I just…" Norah briefly looked away from him and behind her, gestured to her truck and then looked back to Chase. "When did you get here?"

Chase smiled. "Surprised to see me?" He tossed his shirt back on the hay bale.

Her eyes darted over his torso, noticing the thin strip of dark hair that started at his belly button and disappeared into his jeans. She quickly looked away.

"Well, yeah," Norah told him as she cleared her throat. "Considering that you told me you weren't coming back until *late* this morning and asked me to take care of things for you."

He shrugged. "I decided to drive back last night. It was kind of a spur of the moment decision."

"I see," Norah said and looked around the barn before she settled her gaze back to Chase. "It looks like you've got things around here covered and that you don't really need my help."

"Yeah, well, uh," Chase said, resting his hands over one another on the tip of the shovel handle. "I was hoping to be all done with everything by the time you showed up." His lips curved just slightly. "So since I've freed up your morning, what do you say you give me that tour of the town?"

Norah pursed her lips and crossed her arms over her chest. "You're sneaky," she teased as she shook her head.

"That a yes?"

She nodded. "But I've got a better idea."

"All right, O'Donnell," Norah said. "Hop on."

With a grin, Chase stepped around Norah to the side of the large bay gelding. He accepted the reins from her and slid them over the horse's head. Keeping the leather restraints in his hand, he took hold of the saddle horn, placed his foot in the stirrup, and hoisted himself onto the animal's back.

"Good?" Norah asked.

Chase settled into place before looking down to Norah. "Yeah. This feels strangely familiar."

"Told you it would all come back to you," Norah said and gave him a pat on the leg. "Now how about you be a gentleman and give me a hand."

He smiled at that as he removed his left foot from the stirrup and held a hand out for her. Riding double had been her idea, and at first he thought she was kidding or just trying to get a rise out of him. Well, she'd succeeded in getting a rise out of him; only, it probably wasn't the kind she expected. The thought of her hands being inches away from his fly sent a jolt of red-hot desire straight through him.

"You know," Chase told her, the mischievous tone of his voice deepened into a sexy rasp as she swung up onto the horse behind him and gently rested her hands on his sides. "If you wanted to put your hands on me, all you had to do was ask. You didn't need to come up with this whole riding double scheme."

A short laugh escaped from her lips. "Don't flatter yourself," Norah said. "I can't ride Missy and leave Buckshot here all alone. That just wouldn't be right. So our only option is for both of us to ride Doc."

"Mmm-hmm," Chase said. "Sure."

"All right," Norah said with a matter-of-fact tone.

He felt one of her hands leave his side and then a sharp smack against his arm.

"How's that for putting my hands on you?" Norah taunted.

"I'd be lying if I told you I didn't like it," he teased and turned his head to the side to see her reaction.

"Oh my God." She let out an uncomfortable sounding laugh as she rolled her eyes. "Can we please just get going?"

He smiled and let out a chuckle as he turned forward, adjusted his baseball cap, and gripped the reins. "Where to, trail boss?"

"That way," Norah said. "Towards that line of trees."

Resting the reins against the gelding's neck, Chase urged the horse to the right. A chorus of whinnies and neighs sounded from behind, and they turned to see the gray mare prancing along the fence.

"Looks like somebody's jealous," Chase said.

"She'll be okay," Norah said. "Once we're out of sight she'll forget all about us. If you're comfortable, you can take Doc into a canter."

"Sure," Chase said. He gently nudged his heels into the gelding's sides and clicked his tongue against the roof of his mouth twice. The horse picked up his pace and moved into a trot before he settled into a graceful lope.

Norah's hands moved from Chase's sides to lie flat on his stomach.

Sweet mother of God. Her arms tightened around his waist for no other reason than to stay on the horse—Chase was sure about that. He was also sure that her breasts were now crushing against his back.

"Isn't this fun?" Norah asked him breathlessly as they rode away from the yard.

Fun was not the word he'd use to describe his current situation. Torture would've been more accurate. The combination of her body plastered against his and the gentle rhythmic movement of the horse beneath them had both his mind and his heart racing.

He felt her lean forward as she tightened her hold and pressed into him even more.

"Chase, did you hear me?" Norah asked.

Her mouth was so damn close to his ear that he could actually feel her breath brush across his earlobe. The sensation sent all his nerve endings into a frenzy, and every bit of control he had over his thoughts went right out the window. He needed to pull himself together, be a gentleman and douse the raunchy scenarios he'd been playing out in his head.

"Whoa," Chase said to the horse—said to himself too—and pulled back slightly on the reins.

The gelding tossed his head a few times before slowing his pace and then they were walking, which gave Chase a chance to get his head clear and out of the gutter.

"I'm sorry," Chase said to Norah. "I did hear you but I, uh, was caught up in the moment."

Smooth.

He silently cursed himself for sounding so lame.

"And to answer your question," he said, "yes, that was fun."

"You know, you ride pretty good for someone who hasn't done this in over a decade," Norah said as she slid her hands from his stomach back to his sides.

"Thanks." He swallowed hard with the movement of Norah's hands. "So now are you going to tell me what brings us out here?"

"I just thought you might want a refresher on the property," Norah said. "It might come in handy to know the layout of the land for your potential buyers."

As Norah began to point out things throughout the property, Chase let his eyes wander over the scenery before him. Miles and miles of tall grass interspersed with wild flowers rolled in waves with the gentle breeze. The never-ending powder blue sky surrounding them hadn't a single cloud. It was absolutely breathtaking. Peaceful. Comforting.

Mother Nature had truly outdone herself.

They rode for a while with Norah talking and Chase commenting here and there, but he mainly just listened to her speak; her love of the land was evident in her voice as she spoke with pride and adoration. He could see how easy it would be to fall in love with this place. This lifestyle. Her.

Whoa! You just met her and you're already thinking of the "L" word? Slow it down, O'Donnell.

"And over there, where that wire fence is," Norah said, bringing Chase out of his thoughts. "That's the border between your ranch and my family's ranch."

"Nice," Chase said. "So what kind of ranch do you all run? Cattle?"

"Horses," Norah replied. "Quarter Horses to be exact. We breed and sell them, and my brothers will also occasionally break them for our clients. They also do some farrier work on the side."

"It sounds like you all like to keep busy."

"You could say that."

"So, if you don't mind my asking," Chase said. "How'd you end up ranching *and* bartending?"

"Well," Norah started, "I was born into ranching. And as for bartending..." He felt her shrug. "I needed the extra cash and Red was hiring."

"That would be a good reason to get a second job."

"What about you?" Norah asked. "What line of work are you in?"

"I'm an architect," Chase answered.

"Skyscrapers?"

"No. No skyscrapers. We mainly design office buildings."

"Who's 'we?'"

"My dad and me," Chase explained. "He owns his own firm back in Dallas, and I work for him."

"Are you originally from Dallas?"

They were interrupted momentarily by the gelding letting out a loud neigh to the other horses that were now in clear view.

"I live there now," Chase said. "But growing up we lived in the suburbs just outside of the city. Our house was very *Leave it to Beaver* like most of the houses in the neighborhood."

"It sounds pretty," Norah said as they rode into the yard. The gray mare reached her neck over the fence to greet them.

"Do your parents still live there?"

Chase reined the gelding to a stop and removed his foot from the stirrup so Norah could dismount. He silently groaned as she slipped away from him. "Yep."

"What about your mom?" Norah asked, taking the reins from Chase while he, too, dismounted. "What does she do for a living?"

"She owns a flower shop," Chase answered. God he felt bow legged and he sure as hell hoped he didn't look it.

The corner of Norah's mouth turned up into a playful smirk. "Bet that came in handy with girlfriends."

"It did actually." Chase chuckled. "What about your parents?" he asked as they walked the horse to the barn. "They both do the ranching thing?"

Norah shook her head then walked to grab two brushes from the tack room. "Just my mom. She's the brains behind the whole operation and runs the entire ranch."

"And your dad?" Chase asked. He removed the saddle from the horse and placed it, along with the blanket, on the saddle tree in the adjacent room.

"Couldn't tell ya," Norah told Chase and tossed him a brush. "He left when I was just a baby, so I don't know anything about the man."

"Oh," Chase said, clearly shocked by her statement. "I'm sorry, I—"

"You don't have to apologize," Norah said and looked over the horse's back to Chase. "It happened twenty-five years ago. It's fine. Really."

He nodded once as his simple way of letting her know he wouldn't pry any further.

A heavy silence filled the air as Chase followed her lead and ran his brush against the gelding's dark coat. After a few minutes, Norah stopped brushing and gave the horse a few gentle pats on his neck.

"Now don't you look so handsome," Norah said as she ran her hand up and down the white blaze on the gelding's face.

"Why thank you, Miss McKade." Chase grinned and stepped around the horse to look at her. "You're lookin' mighty fine yourself, if I do say so."

She laughed, which was nice because it seemed to cut some of the tension that lingered after he'd brought up her father.

"Thank you, *Mr. O'Donnell*," she said in a mocking tone. "But I was talking to the horse." She took hold of the lead rope and led Doc out of the barn to the pasture.

Chase tossed the brushes into the tack room and then jogged to catch up with Norah. "I had a nice time with you today." He stepped ahead of her and opened the gate.

Norah turned to him and looped the halter and lead rope over her shoulder as Doc trotted into the grassy area, dipping his head to the ground to graze. "Same here."

A smile lit up her face as Chase stared at her, making her blue eyes sparkle. He took a slow step away from the fence and reached his hand out; gently running his fingertips along her arm from shoulder to wrist.

"Norah, I'd really like to—"

Her cell phone rang a happy, upbeat country tune, and she jumped slightly.

"I'm sorry, I—" She shook her head as she reached in her pocket and looked at the caller ID. "I have to take this."

Chase didn't move. He smiled and nodded as she answered her call.

"Mmm-hmm," Norah said into her phone. "Yeah. Okay, I've got it. Yes, I'll be there soon."

He didn't like the sound of that. Their time together had been too short, as far as he was concerned, and he wasn't ready to let her go. Not just yet.

With a heavy sigh, Norah ended her call and shoved her phone back in her front pocket.

"That was my brother," she explained. "He needs my help with something and, of course, it can't wait." She gave a slight roll of her eyes.

"Of course," Chase repeated in a mocking tone, but smiled so she knew he was only kidding.

"I have to get going," Norah said. "Walk me to my truck?"

Chase nodded and walked the short distance with her. He took the halter and lead rope from her shoulder before he took her hand in his. "Like I was saying before," Chase said. "I had a nice time today; if you don't have any plans, I'd really like to see you later."

The corner of her mouth lifted. "I think I can do that." She brought her hand to her hair and tucked it behind her ear. "I'm free after seven."

"After seven it is then."

CHAPTER THIRTEEN

Norah looked up from setting the dinner table to see her brother Luke walk through the back door, clean shaven and wearing a freshly ironed pearl snap shirt and his good boots. There was no doubt in her mind that he'd made plans for later. She smiled to herself and shook her head.

"Hey, Luke," she said and continued setting down the ceramic plates at each chair.

"Hey, Nor," Luke replied with a nod as he walked around the kitchen island. "What'd you make tonight, Mom?"

Linda McKade hefted a large roasting pan from the oven with the use of two crocheted potholders. She set it down on the stovetop, kicked the oven door closed, and let out a sigh.

"I made a roast with fresh veggies," Linda said to Luke.

"It smells amazing." Luke walked over to Linda and greeted her with a peck on the cheek while sneaking a piece of the roast.

"Hands off, mister," Linda scolded Luke and swatted his hand.

Luke laughed and quickly ate the piece of roast he'd taken as he walked past Norah to the fridge.

"Oh my God, Luke," Norah said. She choked a cough for dramatic effect and waved her hand in front of her face. "Did you bathe in your cologne?"

"Joke all you want, little sister," Luke said. He removed a pitcher of sweet tea from the fridge and then poured himself a glass. "But I've yet to hear any complaints from my lady friends."

"Oh, gross," Norah said in a disgusted tone and rolled her eyes. "No one wants to hear about your lady friends and what they think, especially when we're about to eat."

Luke let out a soft laugh and took a sip of his tea. His cell phone rang and he placed his glass on the counter as he checked out the caller ID. "Speaking of my lady friends," he said and waved the phone at Norah. "That'd be one of them now." He smiled as he answered the phone with a "Hey, you" before making his way out the back door.

Norah shook her head at her brother and then returned her attention to the table. She narrowed her eyes as she counted the place settings.

One. Two. Three. Four. Five.

Well that covered her family. So why was she holding a sixth plate?

"Mom?" Norah asked, drumming her fingertips on the sage green ceramic.

"Yeah, sweetie," Linda answered from the stove.

"Is someone joining us for Sunday dinner?"

"Mmm-hmm," Linda answered Norah as she carved the roast. "I invited our new neighbor to have dinner with us."

Norah's heart hit the pit of her stomach. Her eyes widened and her breathing stopped for a moment.

Oh, you have got to be kidding me.

"You did what?"

"I invited our new neighbor for dinner," Linda repeated and looked to Norah with concern. "Why? What's wrong?"

"Nothing I...I just didn't hear you is all."

Well, this was just great. She was all prepared to see Chase *after* her family dinner, and quite looking forward to it. But now?

Now she was nervous. She wasn't nervous so much about actually seeing him but rather about how she would act around him. It wasn't a hidden fact that she liked the guy, or that he liked her as well. But keeping it a hidden fact while they were in the presence of her family was probably in her best interest, mainly because of her loving yet overly protective two older brothers. Zane and Luke had always done their best to protect their baby sister, and even more so now since her last break-up had left her embarrassed and heartbroken.

With trembling hands, Norah set the plate on the table and added the silverware next to it. The sound of tires on the driveway came from outside and Norah peeked out the window to see Chase's silver SUV come to a stop.

"That Zane and Andi?" Linda asked.

"No," Norah replied as Luke stepped off the porch and approached Chase. She watched them shake hands and speak for a moment, and when they began to make their way to the house, she stepped away from the window.

"Look who I found in the driveway," Luke said as he opened the back door for Chase. "I'll be back in a minute." He pointed to his phone and let the door close behind him.

Her heart slammed against her ribcage, creating a deafening *ba-bum, ba-bum* in her ears, and she wasn't sure if it was from being caught off guard or from seeing Chase. Damn he looked good. The sleeves of his white button-down shirt were rolled up to his elbows, which contrasted nicely with his tanned skin and showed off his toned arms. His jeans were dark blue and—*Sweet mercy*— they fit him just right and accentuated his long, muscular legs. And she'd bet everything that he smelled just as good as he looked.

"Thank you for joining us, Chase. Please." Linda gestured for him to walk over. "Come on in and make yourself comfortable."

"Thank you, ma'am," Chase said with a nod to Linda as he rounded the table to Norah. "Hello, Norah."

"Hello, Chase." And there went her knees. She gripped the back of the chair she was standing behind for support.

This is ridiculous. Get a hold of yourself.

"Would you like to have a seat in the living room while we wait for dinner?"

"Sure," Chase said.

When Norah was positive they were out of earshot she turned to Chase. "What are you doing here?"

"What am I...? Your mother invited me for dinner."

"I know that," Norah said. "Now."

"She didn't tell you?"

Norah shook her head.

"Is it a problem that I'm here?"

"No," Norah said then added, "I just imagined our next meeting a little different."

"Oh really?" Chase asked and casually tucked his fingers into the front pockets of his jeans.

Her eyes followed his action and, without thinking, zeroed in on his zipper. When she realized just where she was staring she quickly brought her eyes up to meet his and found him giving her a wickedly, sexy grin.

"And just how did you imagine our next meeting would go?" he asked. His voice was so deep and so smooth that she felt like she could melt from just the sound of it.

Calm yourself, woman.

"Well for starters," Norah said. "When you asked me

to have dinner with you, I honestly didn't think you meant like this with all of my family." She gave him a playful smile.

"This is definitely not what I had in mind."

"That's good to know."

His expression grew serious as he took a tiny step towards her.

He was so tall, almost a whole head taller than her, and her head fell back slightly as she looked up at him.

"My plans most certainly only involved you and me."

And wasn't *that* statement full of innuendos.

"Do you know just how incredibly sexy you look when you're cheeks turn pink like that?" Chase asked, inching closer to her.

Had she blushed? Her whole body felt like it was on fire, so it was hard for her to tell.

"Would I be totally out of line if I told you that I missed you this afternoon?" He was now standing so close to her that their bodies almost touched.

"No," she answered. Jesus. Her heart felt like it was about to burst from her chest.

"I've spent so much time with you over the past two days that it almost feels weird to not be with you."

She took in a deep breath and—*damn*—he *did* smell good. Whatever cologne he was wearing was an intoxicating mix of fresh out-of-the-shower and deep woods.

"Yeah," Norah breathed. "It was a little disappointing having to leave this morning."

He leaned in even more. "Only a little?"

Her eyes moved from his down to his mouth and, on instinct, she licked her lips.

"Norah," Linda called from the kitchen.

She jumped. Breathing hard, she took a step away

from Chase but held onto his gaze. He was breathing hard too, the dramatic rise and fall of his chest making it easy for her to tell.

"Zane and Andi just pulled up," Linda called again.

"Be right there," Norah said, not breaking eye contact with Chase.

He'd almost kissed her. Hell, she'd almost kissed him back.

In her mother's living room.

With her mother one room over and the rest of her family about to enter the house.

Way to keep things on the down low, Norah.

"We should probably get going," Norah told Chase.

He gave her a slight nod and added a reluctant sounding, "Probably."

With a soft shake of her head and a slight curve of her lips, Norah gently took hold of Chase's arm and led him from the room.

The back door opened just as they entered the kitchen and in walked Andi followed by Zane. When Andi caught sight of Chase her eyes widened and immediately went to Norah.

Norah held Andi's stare and shook her head with the slightest movement, hoping her sister-in-law wouldn't give her away.

"Come on in and take a seat," Linda said. "Zane, Andi, this is our new neighbor."

Zane outstretched his hand to Chase. "Nice to meet you. Chase is it?"

"That's right," Chase replied to Zane.

As Chase lifted his hand to shake Zane's, the back of his fingers grazed Norah's hip, instantly sending a shiver down her spine. She hadn't realized she'd been standing so close to him but, of course, now she was fully aware of just *how* close she was and shifted away. She moved then to take her seat at the table and was surprised when Chase pulled her chair out for her.

"Thank you," she told him. It was such a sweet gesture and, unbelievably, the first time a man had ever done that for her.

Chase nodded and took the seat next to her.

All throughout the meal Norah's stomach felt like one huge knot. She half listened to the casual talk, which was mainly her family asking Chase question after question. As they chatted, her thoughts drifted back to earlier. She'd wanted Chase to kiss her. She'd wanted to feel his lips against hers, to feel his hands curve around her hips and pull her close to deepen that kiss. Oh Lord. If the man kissed as well in real life as he did in her fantasy then she would be in sheer bliss.

"Norah?" Zane said.

"Hmm?" Norah replied. "I'm sorry I wasn't paying attention."

"Chase here was just telling us about all the repair work he's going to be doing at his ranch," Zane told her. "Luke and I have a full day tomorrow, so I was suggesting that you might be able to take him to Merle's and get him set up with everything he needs."

"Sure," Norah replied to Zane and then looked to Chase. "I'm free tomorrow morning."

"Works for me," Chase said and shot her a grin.

She held his gaze for a moment, and her eyes darted to his lips briefly before she turned back to her food. Oh yeah. Total, sheer bliss.

CHAPTER FOURTEEN

"Thank you for dinner, Ms. McKade," Chase said. "Everything was delicious."

"I'm glad you liked it," Linda replied, then took a sip of tea from her glass. "You'll have to join us again sometime."

Chase glanced out the corner of his eye to Norah before he turned his attention back to Linda. "I'd like that. Thank you, ma'am."

Zane cleared his throat and stood, resting his napkin on the table as he held his hand out for Andi. "Well, Mom, we hate to rush off, but I've got an early start tomorrow."

Goodbyes were said, and in a few short moments, Chase was sharing only the company of Norah and her mother.

Linda began to clean off the table, but Norah stopped her by resting a hand on her shoulder.

"Why don't you go rest, Mom, and I'll take care of cleaning up?" Norah suggested.

"Oh, sweetie," Linda said as she gathered the plates and began to walk them over to the sink. "I'm not going to have you clean all this up by yourself."

"I can help," Chase offered.

Both women stopped to look at him, and for a moment, he thought he'd said the wrong thing.

"That's not necessary, Chase," Linda said.

"But it's the least I can do to repay you for the meal," Chase said to Linda before turning to Norah. "That is, as long as you don't mind me sticking around to help."

Norah's lips curved slightly. "I don't mind."

Linda looked from Chase to Norah and hid a knowing smile. "Well, I'm not gonna pass up on good help," she said. "I think I'll go take a bubble bath and then head off to bed and read for a bit." She walked over to Norah and gave her a gentle hug. "Thank you, sweetie, and don't forget to lock up on your way out."

"I will," Norah replied.

"Goodnight, Chase," Linda said.

"You too, ma'am." He was all set to shake Linda's hand and was a little surprised when she instead reached up and gave him a gentle, motherly hug. Although it was unexpected, he returned the gesture. He then turned to Norah as Linda exited the room and asked, "What would you like me to do?"

Norah placed the dishes in the sink. "How about you start washing these while I put the leftovers away?"

"All right," Chase said and sauntered over to the sink. As it filled up with warm, sudsy water, Chase stole glances at Norah while she moved about the kitchen. She looked beautiful; that was nothing new, though, because he always thought that whenever he saw her.

He watched as she took the tupperware filled with the leftovers over to the fridge. His eyes roamed over her from head to toe, and he felt his heart rate quicken. Opening the refrigerator door, Norah bent over and began to move items around in order to make the containers fit. But Chase wasn't paying too much attention to that. He was more interested in the way the denim of her jeans stretched perfectly across her derriere—which was just as perfect. It was equally as pleasurable as it was agonizing to watch her. After a few moments, Norah stood upright and closed the door. Chase turned his head quickly as to not get caught and realized that he was still washing the same dish.

"Wow, O'Donnell," Norah teased as she stood next to him. "You're probably the slowest dishwasher in the whole county."

He chuckled.

"I'll rinse and dry," she said and took the clean plate from his hands.

They worked side by side in silence, the moment feeling strangely intimate for two people who weren't in an intimate relationship.

"Your family is very nice," Chase said just as Norah said, "I hope I didn't ruin your plans by offering to clean up."

They laughed.

"You didn't ruin my plans," Chase said, handing her another dish. "My plans were to be with you. And here I am. With you." The corner of his mouth lifted as he watched her smile. His eyes zeroed in on her mouth, and before he knew it, he found himself leaning towards her.

As Norah held onto Chase's gaze, she could see the want pooling in his green eyes. She recognized it so well because—*hell*—she felt the same. So when Chase's gaze fell to her mouth she didn't hesitate. He leaned in towards her, and when Norah parted her lips, she was rewarded with one of the tenderest kisses she'd ever experienced. His mouth brushed against hers with fleeting, feather light motions. Her body, stiff from the anticipation of the kiss, softened beneath the gentle caress of his lips.

Eyes closed, Norah heard a dish plop into the sink water and then felt Chase's body shift towards her. She dropped the towel and mimicked Chase's movement, bringing her hands up to rest on his shoulder and neck. A tiny gasp escaped from her as she felt Chase's wet hands against the back of her shirt, resting on the small of her back. But they didn't stop there.

As Chase deepened the kiss, Norah felt his hands slide into the back pockets of her jeans as he pulled her to him and pressed his pelvis into the cradle of her hips.

Oh my.

Everything about him was solid; his arms, his chest, his abs, his...

Her heart was racing. Her breathing kicked up a notch. Her head was spinning and she couldn't think straight. The only thing present in her mind was that she wanted more—more of his lips, more of his hands, more of...him. But when one of Chase's hands left the back pocket of her jeans and slowly snaked up to her ribcage, she quickly remembered where they were and knew this couldn't go any further. She moved her hand from the back of his neck to his chest and gently pushed away from him.

"Chase," she breathed.

"Hmm?" he replied, feathering kisses along her jaw and gently brushing her hair behind her shoulder so he could continue his way down her neck.

A tiny moan escaped from her lips.

"Chase," she breathed again. "Stop."

He did just that and looked at her. "Did I do something wrong?"

Norah let out a soft, brief laugh. "No," she told him. "You were doing all the right things."

He grinned.

"But we can't do this here."

Chase slid his hand down to Norah's hip and gently stroked his thumb back and forth against her jeans. He casually glanced around the room before he returned his gaze to Norah. "I kind of forgot where we were," he said with a chuckle and rested his forehead against hers.

The backdoor swung open then and Norah jumped at the sudden noise and quickly stepped away from Chase.

"Forgot my cell phone," Luke said as he jogged past them to the counter and grabbed it.

When Luke turned around to Norah and Chase, she could see it on his face that he knew exactly what had been happening between them right before he barged in.

Crap.

"What's going on here?" Luke asked, waving a finger between Norah and Chase.

"We're doing the dishes," Norah answered him.

Luke stared her down. It was the oldest trick in the book, the one that he and Zane always used against her when they wanted to get information out of her. And she hated it.

"What are you looking at?" Norah asked him with a miffed tone.

Luke lifted his hands in a silent defeat. "Nothing," he told her and attempted to hide an amused grin in the process. He pocketed his phone then grabbed up the dish towel Norah had dropped on the counter. "Don't let me keep you from *washing the dishes*," Luke said and handed her the towel.

As Luke walked away and towards the back door, Norah let out a soft sigh of relief and shot Chase a smile.

"Oh, hey," Luke said. He stopped in the open doorway and turned to look at them.

Oh God. What now?

Norah turned her attention to her brother.

"You might wanna use that towel to wipe away those soap bubbles from your butt."

Her mouth dropped in shock as she turned awkwardly

to check the back of her jeans. Sure enough there were soap bubbles hanging from her back pockets along with a wet handprint on her shirt right beneath her breast.

Luke grinned and tipped his hat. "Night, y'all."

Norah covered her face with her hands as the door shut behind Luke. "That was so embarrassing." She pulled her hands down to cover her mouth as she let out a laugh.

Chase joined in on her laughter for a moment. He then leaned against the counter and crossed his arms over his chest as he let out a sigh.

"That killed the mood," Norah said to Chase in a teasing tone as she proceeded to wipe away the soap bubbles from her jeans.

"Temporarily," Chase said with a grin and reached for her, pulling her into his arms.

It felt so nice being held by him. His masculine arms made her feel secure, cherished, and protected, like he would never let anything bad happen to her.

"Why don't we finish up here and head back to my place?" Chase suggested and brushed his fingertips against her forehead and down to her jaw.

Norah bit the corner of her bottom lip as she considered his proposal. "You go on ahead," she told him. "I'll finish up here and meet you there shortly."

Chase pulled back slightly and kept his hand on the side of her neck just below her ear as he looked at her. "You sure?"

Norah nodded. "Positive."

"All right," Chase said, then pulled her close for one sweet, long kiss. "I'll see you soon."

Holding onto the counter, Norah watched as Chase exited the house. When the door shut behind him, she let out a heavy, contented sigh. Her body was still tingling from her brief interaction with Chase, and it was making it hard for her to concentrate on even the simplest task. But she managed to pull herself together long enough to finish up with the dishes and get everything put away. After locking the door, Norah started down the porch steps and her eyes zeroed in on a familiar truck parked next to hers.

"You have got to be kidding me," Norah said to Luke as he stepped out of his truck. "What the hell?"

"Now hold on a minute," Luke said as rounded the front of his truck. "I just want to talk to you."

"Don't you have a lady friend to entertain?" Norah asked, hoping he picked up on the fact that she was annoyed with him.

"She can wait," Luke said. "Right now I need to have a big brother talk with my little sister."

"If you're going to give me a speech about the birds and the bees you're a little late." She gave him a smart-ass smile.

"Ha ha," Luke replied and leaned against the front of his truck. "So what's the deal with you and Chase O'Donnell?"

"Come on, Luke." Norah let out an exasperated sigh and fell back against the side of her truck.

"You dating him?"

"No."

"Sleeping with him?"

"Luke!"

"Calm down," Luke said. "Look, I know I'm prying into your love life here, but can you blame me?"

Norah looked to him and dipped her head before answering him with a soft, "No."

"I'm just trying to look out for you." Luke crossed the short distance to lean against Norah's truck with her. "He said himself that he's only gonna be here for a short time, and I just don't want to see you go through that heartbreak of having to let him go."

"You make it sound like I'm going to fall head-over-heels in love with the guy," Norah told Luke, her voice thick with irritation. "And after what I went through with Wade I am most certainly not looking for any kind of commitment right now. I just want to have some fun. Is that so wrong?"

Luke seemed to ponder that for a moment. "It's not wrong, Nor, but I think you're playing with fire if you think you can just keep things casual with him."

"And why's that?" she asked and lifted her chin in defiance.

"You have too much heart to have a relationship that's based solely on being attracted to one another and sex," Luke said. "I think you could deal with it at first and be fine with it, but in the end…" He shrugged. "I think you're going to want more than he's willing to offer."

Norah sat there in silence as she let Luke's words sink in.

"Plus there's that whole I'll-have-to-kick-his-ass-if-he-breaks-your-heart thing," Luke said and shoved her shoulder with his. "The cut on my knuckle still hasn't healed yet from taking care of good ol' Wade."

Norah smiled at that and nudged him back. "You're a good brother," she told Luke. "And I appreciate you looking out for me."

"Anytime," he replied and gave her a genuine smile before he pushed himself away from her truck and walked over to his own.

As Luke pulled out of the driveway, Norah entered her own truck and sat there for a long moment. She was supposed to be heading over to Chase's house right now. Actually, she should have been there already. But now, after her talk with Luke, she wondered if it was even a good idea to go through with it. She'd never been the kind of woman who slept with a guy she wasn't dating. So why start now?

She furrowed her brow as that question ran through her mind. But why *not* start now? Relationships had failed her in the past, especially the last one, and a change of pace was exactly what she needed. No commitment. No strings attached.

She could do this.

Taking in a deep breath, Norah shifted her truck into gear and headed for Chase's ranch.

CHAPTER FIFTEEN

Chase was sitting at the kitchen table, staring at the condensation pooling around the bottom of his glass, when a pair of headlights illuminated the living room.

He grinned.

As he pushed himself away from the table the chair made an audible scrape against the worn, linoleum floor. Chase stood and made his way to the back door and watched as Norah parked her truck next to his SUV. The headlights went out, but Norah was nowhere to be seen. What was only a matter of minutes felt like an hour, and it was long enough that Chase started to wonder if maybe he had rushed things by kissing her in her mother's kitchen like that. Maybe he'd scared her off with his forwardness? Maybe that was why she was later than he'd expected in showing up to his house? But he replayed the memory of the kiss, and she'd *welcomed* it—most eagerly if he recalled correctly.

Any doubts he'd been having over the past few minutes were put to rest when Norah stepped out of her truck and began to walk towards him. The sweet yet sultry smile on her face gave him the reassurance that he had indeed not scared her off.

"I was beginning to think you weren't coming," Chase said and gave her a boyish grin as he opened the door for her and stepped aside.

Norah brought her hand up and tucked her hair behind her ear as she walked past him into the house. "I would've called."

"I'm glad you didn't," Chase said.

The scent of her skin and how warm it felt beneath his touch was still fresh on his mind. And as much as he wanted to just take her in his arms and kiss her over and over again he'd promised himself that he'd be a gentleman. He watched her as she moved into the room, stopped by the table and looked around.

"Can I get you something to drink?" Chase offered as he walked past her to the fridge. "I have water, beer, and tea, although I have to warn you that it's store bought and not homemade."

She smiled at that. "A beer sounds good."

"All right," Chase said, then pulled out two longnecks and twisted off the caps.

Norah stood with her back to him and appeared to stare at something in the china cabinet with deep interest.

"Here you go," Chase said and handed over her beer.

"Thanks," she said, then took a sip from the bottle. "I've always wondered who these pictures were of." Norah waved her hand over the old photos and pointed to a particular one. "That's you, isn't it?"

Chase took a sip of his beer and nodded. "Yep, that would be me. Missing teeth and all." He chuckled.

"You were cute," Norah said with a gentle smile.

"Were?" Chase joked.

She let out a soft laugh and turned to him. "And still are, happy?"

"Almost." Setting his beer down on the table, Chase closed the short distance between him and Norah and placed his hands on her hips. "I don't know what it is about you, Norah," he said, deepening his voice into a throaty rumble. "But I just can't seem to get enough of you."

Norah placed her own beer on the table next to his. She then brought her hands to the back of his neck and slid them up so she could run her fingers through the hair on the back of his head.

"So what are you gonna do about it?" Norah asked, her voice breathless and sexy.

That comment shocked the hell out of him. Of all the responses he'd imagined her saying, *that* wasn't one of them.

Instantly turned on by her directness, Chase cupped her jaw in both of his hands and reeled her in for a kiss. He herded her against the wall, and only then did his lips leave hers. Her fingers curled into his hair harder as he trailed hot, wet open mouth kisses along her jaw and down her neck.

Norah moaned, and Chase thought he'd lose it. The sound of her pleasure vibrated in his ear and traveled straight down to his manhood. He felt her hands pulling at the hem of his shirt, attempting to free it from his jeans. He, too, moved his hands and snaked them up and underneath her shirt, feeling that warm, silky skin he'd been craving since he'd left her earlier.

Buttons were undone. His shirt hit the floor.

Chase grabbed Norah's shirt by the hem, pulled it over her head, and tossed it to the floor with his.

Damn.

Never before had she had a sexual encounter like this— raw and passionate. Chase's hands were everywhere, lighting her on fire and making her crave more of his touch. The feel of his roughened hands and warm lips on her skin was almost enough to make her explode.

She needed more.

As fast as her trembling fingers would work, Norah

quickly undid Chase's shirt and pushed it from his shoulders. God, the man was incredibly built—lean yet muscular. Her shirt went next, and she froze as Chase stared at her. His eyes roamed over every inch and every curve of her body, and when they returned to hers, they were smoldering. She couldn't believe how much that one look turned her on—just knowing that *she did that*, that *she* put that look in his eyes.

And then Chase's lips crushed against hers, and she let out a soft gasp as he lifted her to him. With his hands cradling her butt, Norah wrapped her legs around his waist and continued to kiss him as he walked them into the living room. She felt the sensation of falling, and the next thing she knew her back was pressed against the sofa cushions.

That slight fall to the sofa was enough to jostle her mind into thinking that maybe this *was* all happening too soon and that—*ugh! She didn't even want to think it*—Luke was right. She barely knew Chase, and here she was ready to get it on with him. This wasn't her—as much as she wanted it to be. Even with her little pep talk to herself in her truck as she sat in Chase's driveway just a short while ago, she knew she wouldn't be able to go through with this.

"Chase, wait," Norah said, rushing the words and gently pushing at his chest.

Chase quickly pulled away and hovered over her. "What's the matter?"

She slid out from underneath of him and went to where he'd dropped her shirt.

"I'm sorry, Chase," she told him as she flipped her shirt right side out and slid it over her head. "I can't do this."

He stood from the sofa and started to walk towards

her. "Are you okay? Did I hurt you?"

"I'm fine," she said and held up her hand to stop him. "I just…can't. I'm sorry."

"Stop apologizing," Chase said. "You've got nothing to be sorry about." He started to walk towards her again.

"I shouldn't have come here tonight and given you the wrong impression," Norah told him as she held her hand up again. "I didn't mean for this to happen."

"Norah—"

"Goodnight, Chase," Norah said and hurried out the door. She made her way out to her truck, hopped in and slammed the door shut behind her. Throwing the truck into gear, Norah sped out of the driveway with Chase's reflection in her rearview mirror.

Chapter Sixteen

"Okay, what the heck is going on with you?"

Norah looked away from the beer tap to see Andi staring at her with a concerned expression.

"I'm fine," Norah said and returned her attention to the mug of beer in her hand. She topped it off and slid it across the counter to the waiting customer with a, "There you go."

"No you're not," Andi said as she walked the short distance to the cash register with Norah. "You're acting weird. I wouldn't call it sulking, per say, but it's close."

Norah let out a heavy, exasperated sigh as she turned to her sister-in-law. "I did something really stupid last night."

Andi's expression changed to one of realization, and she tenderly rested her hand on Norah's shoulder. "Oh, sweetie." She lowered her voice and leaned in closer to Norah. "We've all had those regrets of sleeping with someone we shouldn't have."

Shaking her head, Norah turned to Andi and, in the same low voice, said, "I didn't sleep with him."

"You didn't?" Andi asked, clearly confused. "Then what *did* you do?"

Norah gave Andi the short version of what had, or in this case hadn't, happened with her and Chase last night.

"So," Andi said, dragging the word out. "You're upset because you didn't sleep with him?"

"I'm embarrassed that I led him on like that." Norah took a drink order from a customer and filled it before she turned back to Andi. "I have no idea what I was thinking.

That's not me. I'm not a sleep-with-a-guy-I-just-met kind of girl."

"Does Chase know that?" Andi asked.

Norah shook her head. "I ran out of there like a scared, confused teenage girl. And he's called me at least three times today, but I never answered the phone. I just don't know what to say to him."

"I'd start thinking of something to say," Andi said as she nodded her head in the direction of the door.

Norah knew without even looking that Andi was telling her Chase had just entered the bar.

Wonderful.

She silently berated herself for not answering his phone calls now. Talking over the phone instead of face to face would've been a whole lot easier.

"Hello, Norah."

Her body stiffened as she instantly became nervous. Simultaneously, a shiver ran down her spine at the sound of his smooth voice. Norah slowly turned around to face him, trying to act nonchalant.

"Chase," she replied as she grabbed up a bar towel and wiped up a nonexistent mess. "What can I get you?"

Chase folded his arms onto the countertop as he leaned against it. "I'll take a beer, but I was hoping maybe we could talk first."

"Chase—"

"Please, Norah," Chase said. "I wanted to talk to you this morning when we went to the hardware store, but you never showed up. And you haven't answered any of my calls…"

The pleading look in his eyes made her feel just awful. She'd been a jerk about this whole situation and an even bigger jerk for blowing him off all day. With a slight nod, Norah rounded the corner of the bar and gave a shout to Andi that she'd be back in a moment.

Chase followed and when they were in a secluded corner of the bar they turned towards each other.

"I'm sorry," they both spoke at the same time.

Norah watched as Chase drew back with a bewildered look. "What do you have to be sorry for?" he asked.

"I could ask you the same," she said, just as confused as he was.

Chase looked down and tucked his fingers into his front pockets as he leaned against the wall next to her. "I came on a little strong last night," he said. "I wasn't trying to scare you off, which I clearly did, and for that I'm sorry."

Norah relaxed a little and let out a sigh. "You don't have to apologize for that, Chase." She crossed her arms over her chest. "I was right there with you on the too-much-too-soon train. *I'm* sorry for running out on you like I did and not even giving you an explanation of why."

"Did you want to tell me now?" he asked.

"I just…" She let out another sigh. "I've never done…*that* with anyone I've not been in a relationship with, let alone someone I've just met." Looking down to the floor, Norah crossed and uncrossed her ankles. "It might make me sound like a prude, but I do have to have some standards for myself."

She felt Chase's fingers touch beneath her chin as he lifted her face so she could look at him.

"That doesn't make you a prude at all," Chase said softly.

She smiled at the kindness in his eyes. "I'm not going to deny that I'm attracted to you, because I clearly am. I just think that maybe we're getting ahead of ourselves here."

"What do you mean?"

"You're only in town for a short time," Norah told him. "I think it might be in our best interest to slow things down and keep this...*thing* between us platonic."

"Platonic?" Chase asked.

He watched as Norah nodded her head. Slowing things down? He could do that. Keeping things on a friends only level? *That* he wasn't so sure of.

"Is that really what you want, Norah?"

Her hesitation to answer him was the only confirmation he needed. There could still be more between the two of them if he played his cards right.

"It's for the best," Norah finally answered.

"If that's how you feel," Chase said and pushed himself away from the wall with a nod. "Then friends it is." He gave her a reassuring smile.

"Just like that?" Norah asked as she uncrossed her arms.

His smile widened. "Just like that." Reaching his hand out, Chase gently stroked her arm from her shoulder to her wrist. He then took hold of her hand. "I like spending time with you. And if you want to spend that time just as friends, then that's what we'll do."

Even though he wanted more from their relationship, he was being honest with her. He hoped that his honesty had shown through his words, and when Norah's face softened into a smile, he knew they had.

"Thank you, Chase."

"I'll let you get back to work," he told her and let go of her hand. "But I'll see you around." And with that, Chase headed for the door, not worrying with his beer. Sticking around tonight was out of the question. He'd promised her that they'd be friends and friends only. And he couldn't very well keep that promise if he had to keep looking at her in that tight little black top. This friends thing was going to take a lot of work.

CHAPTER SEVENTEEN

The midday sun was hot on his bare back as Chase knelt on the porch steps, banging the last few nails into place when a car horn sounded from behind him. Turning his head, Chase looked to see Norah's truck pulling into his driveway and a wide smile spread across his face. He rested his tools on the wooden planks, stood and made his way down the steps.

"Howdy, neighbor," Chase greeted with an exaggerated southern drawl and tipped the brim of his baseball cap as Norah exited her truck.

"Howdy," Norah replied with a laugh. "Did I catch you at a bad time?"

"Nope," Chase answered her. "I was just finishing up. What brings you out my way?"

Closing her door, Norah made her way to the truck bed and said, "I come bearing gifts."

"Oh yeah?"

"Mmm-hmm," she said. "I was in town and Merle mentioned that the paint you ordered came in. So since I was heading back out to my mom's ranch anyway, I offered to bring your supplies to you."

"Well, that was nice of you." He followed her to the back of her truck, pulled the tailgate down, and began unloading everything she'd brought him.

"Don't you ever wear a shirt when you work?" Norah teased and shoved his shoulder as she grabbed for the paintbrushes and rollers.

"Not when it's this hot outside," Chase told her and with a sly tone added, "You know you like it."

"You're so full of yourself." She laughed.

It took them a few trips, but they soon had everything from the bed of her truck sitting on the grass by the front of the house.

"The porch came out good," Norah said as she walked over to the steps and tested them with her foot.

"You won't fall through," Chase said with a chuckle. "I promise."

Norah made her way onto the porch and Chase followed, watching her as she ran her hands over the new railing. "The place is really coming along nicely, Chase." She turned to him and gave him a gentle smile.

"Thanks," he said and leaned against one of the porch posts.

"Just think, four more weeks and you'll be all done." Her smile faltered for the briefest moment before she turned away from him and looked out upon the land.

The past two weeks had been the best Chase had had in a very long time. Sure, he'd spent most of that time doing ranch chores, fixing the place up, and working on his design proposal. But every moment in between he had spent with Norah, mostly hanging out with her at the bar while she was working. Even though he was completely worn out from putting in a full day's worth of work, he'd shower up and drive the forty-five minutes just to see her. And they'd spent time outside of the bar together as well; they'd gone horseback riding and even gone fishing on one of her days off. For two people who weren't supposed to be in a romantic relationship, they sure acted like it— minus all the intimate stuff.

"Well, I guess I should be heading out now," Norah said with a sigh as she turned to look at Chase. "My mom's probably wondering where I am."

"I wouldn't say that," Chase said as he walked with

Norah to her truck. "I think she's got a pretty good idea of where to find you."

Norah let out a soft laugh as she opened her truck door. "You're probably right." She was just about to hop into the driver's seat but stopped and reached for something. "I almost forgot," she said as she pulled out a gallon size container and handed it over to Chase.

He laughed. "More of Belle's sweet tea?"

"Yep," Norah said and laughed with him. "I don't think she's fully recovered from hearing that you were drinking store bought tea."

"I'll have to thank her next time I see her," Chase said. "Thanks for delivering it."

"No problem," Norah said and started to enter her truck again but stopped once more and turned to him. "So, my friends called earlier and said that there's going to be a bonfire tonight down at Tim Miller's place. I was thinking about going, and I didn't know if maybe you wanted to come with me?"

The corner of his mouth lifted into a slight grin. "Sounds good to me."

The night air flowed through the open windows of the truck as Norah drove through the grassy field towards the flickering orange light surrounded by pick-up trucks.

"Is this what you all call *kickin' it in the sticks*?" Chase teased with a smile.

"Oh hush, city boy," Norah told him and shoved his shoulder with her hand as she found an empty spot and parked.

"Now seriously," Chase said with that same teasing tone. "Are we planning on tipping cows before or *after* we drink moonshine?"

"Shut up!" Norah laughed and pushed him again. "If you don't stop making fun, I'll tip *you*."

He laughed, deep and throaty, and just the sound of it made her insides curl.

You wanted to be just friends, so calm your hormones down, woman.

They exited the truck and Norah walked around to the bed, reached over the side and opened the cooler to pull out two longnecks. She handed one over to Chase as they walked towards the group of people hanging around the bonfire.

"Norah!"

"Hey, Jess," Norah said and stumbled backwards as her friend engulfed her in a hug.

"I'm so glad you came!" Jess said, then turned her attention to Chase. "Who's your friend?"

"Jess, this is Chase O'Donnell. He's taken over the ranch next to ours," Norah said. "Chase, this is my friend Jessie Davis."

"Nice to meet you," Chase said and shook Jess's hand.

"You too," Jess replied. She turned to Norah and mouthed the words, "Oh my God."

Norah smiled. "So who all's here?"

"Tim's over there with Parker and Dustin," Jess said and pointed to a souped up F-150. "Dustin got some new do-hickey for his truck, and he's showing it off." Jess rolled her eyes and laughed. "Everyone else is just hanging around the fire, although I think some people have snuck off to the pond, your brother being one of them."

"That'll be enough talk of my brother and his shenanigans," Norah said to Jess with a soft laugh before turning to Chase. "You wanna head over to the fire?"

"Sure," Chase said.

They met up with a group of people and, after a few introductions, easily joined in on the conversation. She hated to admit that she'd been the tiniest bit nervous about inviting Chase to come with her tonight. Hanging out in a random field and listening to the radio play through open truck windows wasn't everyone's idea of fun. But Norah was pleased to see that Chase seemed to be having a nice time and was getting along with her group of friends.

"I'm gonna grab another beer," Chase said as he leaned in towards her so he didn't have to yell over the music. His breath tickled her ear and made her skin break out in goose bumps. "Did you want another?"

"Sure," she replied, a little more breathlessly than she'd intended to.

Chase smiled that wicked, sly smile of his that always made her knees go weak, and made his way through the grass to her truck.

She was still recovering from Chase's grin when she heard a familiar voice next to her.

"Well if it isn't Norah McKade."

Norah's skin crawled as she pasted on her best smile and turned to see the face that went with the voice.

"Kelly Martin," Norah said and attempted to hide her disgust. "What brings you to Buford?"

"Heard there was a party going on." Kelly shrugged and leaned against the truck next to Norah. "So who's your new boy toy?"

Norah rolled her eyes and scoffed. "He's not my boy—" She let out a sigh. "Is there something you want?"

A devilish grin tilted Kelly's mouth. "You know, I heard the strangest rumor going around," Kelly said in an all too innocent and sweet voice. "Seems our perfect little

Norah isn't so perfect after all."

"What are you talking about?" Norah asked, her level of irritation growing by the second.

"Don't you mean *who* am I talking about?"

Oh God. How the hell did she…?

"Brandy Ellison is my cousin," Kelly said to Norah. "And *was* Wade Coleman's fiancé until you decided you wanted to screw him."

"Whoa, Kelly," Norah said, anger replacing the irritation. "I think you need to get your facts straight before you start accusing me of things."

"Oh really," Kelly said. She pushed herself away from the truck and glared at Norah. "So you can honestly stand there and tell me straight to my face that you weren't sleeping with Wade?"

"I didn't—"

"You've got all these people fooled into thinking you're such a nice person," Kelly interrupted. "But really? You're just a worthless piece of trash. I mean, who knew you'd stoop so low just to get down and dirty with a guy?"

"You really don't know what you're talking about, Kelly, so I think it's best if you just shut your mouth and mind your business."

She needed to get out of there and fast before she did something stupid like smack that holier-than-thou look right off of Kelly's face.

"That's really good advice, Norah, and I think you should work on following it yourself," Kelly taunted. "But along with keeping your mouth shut, maybe you should work on keeping your legs shut as well."

Norah's jaw dropped. "You are such a bitch."

"Better a bitch than a home-wrecking whore."

As Kelly got in her final dig, Norah tightened her jaw and balled her fist. She was just about to take a swing when she heard footsteps behind her. She turned and found Chase standing no more than three feet away with a puzzled expression on his face, holding a beer in each hand.

"Norah?" Chase asked in a soft and clearly confused voice.

Embarrassment washed over her. She opened her mouth to speak but the words just wouldn't come out. So she turned and walked away.

CHAPTER EIGHTEEN

Muffled voices and a woman's giggle sounded from behind him as Chase leaned over the bed of the truck and grabbed two more beers from the cooler. He turned as he shut the lid and saw two individuals emerge from the tree line.

"Chase!" A male voice called out.

Now who could that be?

Chase squinted his eyes against the darkness to make out the figure walking towards him.

"Luke," Chase replied.

The young woman Luke was with smiled at something he'd whispered in her and headed towards the group of people standing near the bonfire.

"How ya doin', Chase?" Luke asked as he closed the distance between them and reached his hand out.

"Doin' good," Chase said and shook Luke's hand. "You?"

"Can't complain," Luke replied with a grin and nodded to the woman walking away. "What brings you out this way? You know Tim?"

Chase shook his head slightly. "Norah invited me."

"I see," Luke said and adjusted his cowboy hat. "Can I ask you something?"

"Yeah," Chase said. "Sure."

"What's going on with the two of you?"

And there it was, the question he knew someone was bound to ask at some point.

"Nothing," Chase replied with a shrug of his shoulders.

"Nothing, huh?" Luke asked, wearing a skeptical look. "You know, you all sure do spend a lot of time together for there to be nothing going on."

"I know how it looks," Chase told Luke. "But your sister and I are just friends. That's it."

"Okay," Luke said and seemed to loosen up just a little. "It's really none of my business but at the same time it kind of *is* my business, you know? Because Norah is my baby sister."

"Yep," Chase said. "I've got a sister of my own, so I know how that is."

Luke's lips curved into a crooked grin. "Good. You seem like a stand-up guy, Chase, and I've got no quarrels with you," he said and slapped a hand down on Chase's shoulder. "But if you hurt her, I'll break your jaw. I don't care what kind of relationship you have with her."

Chase nodded and shook Luke's other hand. "Understood."

That was a first for him. Getting *The Talk* for a woman he wasn't even dating. Although he couldn't fault Luke for doing what he did. He was just playing the part of the protective older brother and looking out for Norah's best interest. Hell, Chase had given that very same speech to the guys Sarah had brought home when she was doing the whole dating scene. But in his case he'd been the protective younger brother.

He held both longneck beers in his one hand as he made his way back to the fire, and as he approached Norah he took one of them in his other hand to give her. She stood with her back to him as she talked to a short, curly haired brunette who wore a smug look on her face. From what he could tell, it didn't look like they were having a great conversation and Chase was all prepared to jump in and save her.

"You are such a bitch," Norah said to the woman.

"Better a bitch than a home-wrecking whore," the woman replied as she crossed her arms over her chest and lowered her eyes over Norah in disgust.

What the hell had he walked in on?

He noticed Norah's fist balled up by her side but then she spun around, seeming to be distracted by something, and locked her eyes on Chase's face.

"Norah?" Chase asked, confusion clouding his mind.

He stood there and stared at her as she opened her mouth and closed it. And then she was gone and he was still standing there wondering what in the world had just happened.

"I wouldn't waste your time with that one," the woman said to Chase.

"And why's that?" Chase asked as he turned to the curly haired brunette with narrowed eyes.

She smiled in a way Chase assumed was supposed to be sexy though it most definitely wasn't, and walked towards him. "Because I think I'd be better at giving you what you want." The woman reached her hand out and ran her fingertips down the buttons of his shirt.

"Is that so?" Chase asked and watched her hand before he looked up to meet her eyes.

She bit her lip and nodded with a, "Mmm-hmm."

"Okay," Chase said and leaned down to her. "Then why don't you take these?" He handed her the beers he'd been holding and, deepening his voice into a sexy rumble, added, "And crawl back under whatever bridge you came from?"

The brunette scoffed and mumbled something Chase couldn't quite make out as she stormed off. He then headed in the direction he'd seen Norah go, trading the bright light of the bonfire for moonlight. Coming upon the tree line, Chase found a narrow, worn path through the trees and followed it until he came to a clearing. A small pond stood in the center of the clearing; the moonlight gleamed on the still water. As he took in his surroundings he saw someone sitting on a downed tree next to the pond's edge.

Norah.

A stick snapped beneath his boot as he made his way over to her and she spun around at the sound. Her cheeks were wet from her tears and she quickly looked down and away from him.

"How much of that did you hear?"

"Just that end part," Chase told Norah and stepped over the log she'd occupied to sit down next to her.

She sniffed and swiped her fingertips beneath her eye. "God, I'm such a baby." Norah shook her head and looked down at her boots. "I shouldn't have let her get to me like that."

Chase lifted his hand to gently rub her back but stopped himself. "Well, she wasn't the nicest person, now was she?" he told her and leaned over as he rested his elbows on his knees and folded his hands together. "You wanna talk about it?"

Tucking her hair behind her ear, Norah looked out to the pond. "Not really, but…" She blew out a breath of air and turned to him. "What she said, about me being a…" She paused. "A 'home-wrecking whore?' That's not entirely true."

"I didn't think it was," Chase reassured her. But that last part of what she'd just said stuck with him and he had to ask. "What do you mean by 'entirely?'"

Norah turned to him, her eyes red from crying. "A few months ago I was dating this guy…Wade." She took in a deep breath and let it out slowly. "I'd never seen him before the night he showed up at the bar with a bunch of his friends. We ended up talking and, long story short, ended up sort of dating. He didn't live in town, so it was one of those things where we'd talk on the phone throughout the week and see each other on the weekends." She turned away from him and ran her fingers through her hair. "This went on for almost four months, but one day I get a call on my cell phone from his number. But instead of it being Wade, it was his fiancé, wondering why the hell my number was in his phone and how I knew her husband-to-be."

Holy shit.

Chase couldn't believe how quickly the anger inside him built. He had no idea who this Wade guy was, but he had the strong urge to find him and beat the living hell out of him for putting Norah through this pain.

"I still, to this day, can't believe that *I* was the other woman," Norah said softly, staring back at the ground. "I ruined a relationship."

"Whoa," Chase said, and took her chin in his hand as he turned her to look at him. "*You* didn't ruin anything. That sorry excuse for a man was the one who ruined his own relationship." He moved his hand from her chin and gently rested it on her shoulder. "Do not blame yourself for that guy's actions. I've only known you for a couple of weeks, but I can say that I know you are not that kind of woman."

A tear fell from her eye and he swiped it away with his thumb as he cupped her jaw with his other hand.

"Don't cry anymore."

She forced a smile. "Trust me, I don't want to," she said with a soft but short laugh and rested her hand over top of his. "I'm just so embarrassed because Kelly apparently knows the whole story. And she hates me anyway so what if she goes around telling—"

"Screw Kelly," Chase interrupted and pulled his hands away from her face. "So what if she tells people? Anyone who knows you will think she's lying. She looks like the type who loves some drama, and I can say I know that from only talking to her for thirty seconds."

"You talked to her?" Norah asked. "What did she say?"

Chase told Norah about Kelly hitting on him and his reaction.

Norah laughed through her tears. "Oh my gosh, I would've loved to see her face."

Chase smiled and stood. He reached his hand out and pulled Norah to stand next to him. "It was priceless."

"Thank you, Chase," Norah said and looked up at him through thick lashes. "Can I…?"

She opened her arms and Chase pulled her in for the hug she was silently asking for.

"Do you mind?" she asked and leaned her head against his chest. "Friends hug, right?"

"I don't mind at all," Chase replied in a soft voice and rested his cheek against her hair. He lifted one of his hands and stroked the blond strands of hair that fell against her back. The soft, floral scent of her shampoo wafted into the air and into his nostrils. That and holding her close in his arms was beginning to be a little too much for him to handle. He pulled back and her head fell back slightly as she looked up at him. His gaze fell to her mouth as he brought his hand to her cheek and tenderly grazed her skin with the back of his fingers. A few more inches and his lips would meet hers.

But that's not what she wanted. She'd asked for a hug—a simple, comforting hug. From a friend, which is all he was to her. Nothing more. Nothing less.

He smiled at her as he pulled away from her embrace. "Come on," he told her as he reached for her hand and wrapped it in his. "I'll walk you back to the party."

CHAPTER NINETEEN

"Does anybody work in this damn place?"

Norah shot the man at the end of the bar a dirty look as she continued to fill a pitcher of beer.

"Keep your shirt on, slick," she shouted over the music. "Someone will be with you in just a second."

The bar was packed, but that was normal for a Saturday night. Everyone was there to let loose and have some fun after a hard week's worth of work. What wasn't normal was her sudden lack of help behind the bar.

Where the hell was Andi?

"Seriously, babe," the man called out again to Norah. "I've been waiting for ten minutes. Come on."

"And you're going to wait another ten minutes if you don't leave me alone and let me help the customers who were here before you," Norah shot back as she handed over the pitcher of beer along with four mugs to the lady in front of her.

Filling the rest of the orders as fast as she could, Norah handed over the last drink and took advantage of the small break to go find her missing sister-in-law.

"Andi?" Norah called as she entered the back room. "Andi, are you back here?"

"In here," Norah heard Andi say in a strangled voice.

Norah turned and made her way over to the bathroom, pushing the door open with a, "What the hell are you—*Oh God!*"

Andi was kneeling on the tile floor with her hair in her hand and her head hovering over the toilet.

"Are you okay?" Norah asked as she quickly walked

over and brushed her hand across Andi's forehead. "Jesus, you're burning up."

"I feel like death." No sooner than she'd gotten the words out, Andi leaned over the toilet and vomited. "Please just kill me now," Andi begged, her voice echoed off the porcelain.

"Oh, sweetie." Norah grabbed some paper towels and wet them in the sink. "I'd love to help you out but I think Zane would have some objections to me putting you out of your misery." She placed one of the paper towels on Andi's forehead and the other on the back of her neck.

"Come on," Norah said as she helped Andi stand. "Let's get you on the sofa and I'll call Zane to come pick you up." With one arm around Andi's waist, Norah helped her sister-in-law over to the sofa. She gently laid Andi down and covered her with a blanket before she grabbed the wastebasket and set it on the floor next to the sofa for Andi.

Pulling her cell phone from her pocket, Norah punched the numbers on her phone and called Zane. Even though the situation was completely not Andi's fault, she couldn't have had worse timing. With Red out of town for the weekend visiting his sister, it meant that Norah was going to have to work the bar all by herself tonight. Good thing she worked in a place that served alcohol because she was surely going to need some of it before the night was over.

She headed back out to the main area of the bar and went behind the counter. A swarm of thirsty customers bombarded her as soon as she got back there, and she quickly worked to fill their orders. She had her back turned to the bar, placing cash in the register, when she heard a familiar voice and she smiled.

"Hey, stranger," Chase said.

Norah turned and rested her hands on the counter before she let out a long, tired sigh. "Hey, Chase. What can I get you?"

He'd occupied one of the barstools and casually leaned an elbow on the bar top as he gave her a concerned look. "You okay? You look stressed."

"That obvious, huh?" Norah said and ran her fingers through her hair. "Andi went home sick. Zane just picked her up, and Red's out of town for the weekend." She blew out a breath of air. "So I'm by myself tonight."

Chase glanced around the packed room and then turned back to Norah. "Yeah I can see how that would stress you out," he said. "You want some help?"

Norah let out a soft laugh, grabbed a glass and filled it halfway with whiskey before she slid it across the counter to the man standing next to Chase.

"I'm being serious, Norah," Chase told her.

"Chase, I can't ask you to do that."

"You're not asking," Chase said as he slid off the barstool. "I'm offering."

She held his gaze for a moment as she thought it over. "Okay, come on." She waved him to come behind the bar.

He grinned and rounded the corner.

"If you could take care of serving beer," Norah told him, "I can take care of mixed drinks and liquor."

Chase let out a chuckle and nudged her arm with his elbow. "Don't worry so much. I got this."

She didn't have time to question him as a break in the music sent all of the line dancers to the bar. There was so much going on that Norah didn't have a chance to check on Chase to make sure he was doing okay. Customer after customer, Norah filled orders and took their money. It was only when the customers on her side of the bar dwindled that she heard the commotion coming from Chase's end.

Norah turned and found Chase standing across the counter from a group of women who were clearly infatuated with the new bartender. What happened next surprised the hell out of her. When one of the ladies ordered a fruity mixed drink, Chase took hold of a liquor bottle and, with a flick of his wrist, flipped it into the air. As it came down, Chase grabbed the neck of the bottle and poured its contents over the ice in the glass. He topped it off with a splash of juice and a lime wedge, and then slid it across the counter. Norah then saw Chase turn his head to her as he worked on filling another order.

"What's the matter?" Chase asked over the crowd of voices and music.

"Nothing," Norah replied with a soft laugh and a shake of her head.

"Hey, can I get three longneck Coors?"

Turning to the man across the counter, Norah nodded and told him, "Coming right up."

"Well," Chase said as he walked across the worn wooden floor. "That was the last of them."

Norah collapsed against the counter with a heavy sigh. "What a night." She watched as Chase walked back around the bar and tossed a few empty beer bottles into the trash. "So those were some pretty fancy moves you were showing off earlier, O'Donnell," Norah said with a flirty smile.

"You noticed, huh?" Chase laughed as he pulled the full trash bag from the wastebasket and tied the drawstring.

"Where'd you learn to do that?" Norah asked him as she placed a fresh trash bag into the wastebasket he'd just emptied.

Chase shrugged. "I saw that movie *Cocktail* back in the day and thought it'd be cool to learn how to do that," he said. "Figured it'd be a fun way to pick up women."

"Well does it work?" Norah asked him with a smile.

"I don't know," Chase said and turned to her. "You tell me."

She shook her head and let out a soft laugh as she walked out to the floor and began to wipe down the tables. Chase followed behind her and placed the chairs onto the tabletops. With the two of them working together, they soon had the place all cleaned up.

As she made her way back to the bar, Norah placed the broom behind the counter then lifted her hands above her head and stretched.

"God, I'm exhausted," she said, then reached into the cooler and pulled out two longneck bottles of beer. Popping the tops off, Norah walked over to Chase and handed him one before she pulled down one of the chairs and sat.

"Thanks," Chase said as he accepted the beer and pulled down a chair as well. He let out a sigh as he leaned back in it and took a long drink from his bottle.

"You know," Norah said, "I really appreciate you stepping in and helping me out tonight."

Chase's lips curved into a soft smile. "You don't have to thank me, Norah."

"Yes I do," she said. "And I'm going to make it up to you."

Chase stopped mid drink and raised an eyebrow.

"Easy there, O'Donnell," she told him with a laugh and kicked at his chair leg with the toe of her boot. "I meant more along the lines of helping you out with stuff around your ranch."

He shook his head. "I can't ask you to do that."

"You're not asking. I'm offering," Norah told him, repeating the same exact words he had told her just a few hours ago. "You still have to paint, right? I'm good at painting. I can help you with that."

"Norah—"

"Nope," she said, cutting Chase off. "You're going to take my help and that's final."

Chase grinned. "Bossy much?"

"You know you like it," she told him and smiled back.

"I do," Chase said, his voice sexy and smooth.

She stared at him for a long moment, and then felt a warm buzz run through her body.

It's just the alcohol, she told herself, but she knew she was lying.

Chase stood from his chair a moment later, rested his beer on the table and walked across the dance floor to the jukebox. He leaned against the glass as he appeared to check out the song selections and, after a few seconds, pressed two buttons for his song choice. Dierks Bentley's "I Wanna Make You Close Your Eyes" played through the speakers as Chase made his way back over to Norah.

"What are you doing?" Norah asked as she looked up at Chase and his outstretched hand.

"What do you think?" he asked and wiggled his fingers.

Placing her hand in his, Norah allowed Chase to pull her from the chair. She rested her beer on the table and the two of them made their way out to the dance floor. Once there, Chase turned and tenderly wrapped an arm around Norah's waist and pulled her close as he began to sway them back and forth to the music.

"Interesting song choice," Norah said, leaning her

head back to look up at Chase.

"You don't like it?" Chase asked.

His warm breath brushed across her lips and sent a tingle down her spine.

"I didn't say that," Norah told him. "I do like this song. And I like *this*. It's been a while since a guy's asked me to dance."

"That's a shame," Chase said. "I'd take any opportunity I could to be close to you."

"Chase," Norah said softly before she let out a sigh and looked down.

"Can I ask you something?" The deep timbre of his voice made the skin on her neck prickle as he leaned into her ear.

She nodded.

"What's the real reason you don't want things to go further between us?"

Norah lifted her head, her cheek brushed against the stubble on his jaw as she pulled away to look at him. "It's just better this way, Chase. Easier."

"For who?" Chase asked. "Because I don't find this easy at all."

Norah stopped dancing but still held onto him. "What are you saying?"

"I'm saying that I made a promise to you that we'd be friends," Chase told her, and he gently brushed his fingertips along the side of her face and rested the palm of his hand against her jaw. "But I'm still hoping for more."

Norah closed her eyes and found herself nuzzling into Chase's hand. When she realized what she was doing she stopped herself. "I just...can't, Chase."

"Can't?" he asked. "Or won't?"

"Both," Norah replied and stepped away from Chase as the song came to an end. "This is all I can give right now. Please don't ask me for more."

Chase nodded, stepped towards her, and then placed a gentle kiss on her forehead. "I'll help you lock up."

His hand slipped from her waist and the warmth that'd pulsed through her body faded as she watched Chase walk away.

CHAPTER TWENTY

Gravel crunched beneath her tires as Norah pulled up to Zane and Andi's house. Grabbing the container of soup she'd made that morning from the passenger side floorboard, Norah stepped out of her truck and made her way up to the house.

"Hello?" She knocked on the door before she turned the knob and opened it.

"We're in here," Zane called out from the living room.

After wiping her boots on the doormat, Norah passed through the kitchen and stood in the opening between the two rooms. Zane was seated on the sofa with Andi's head resting on a pillow that was in his lap, looking a little bit better than she had last night.

"How are you feeling?" Norah asked Andi, her voice soft and full of worry.

"I'm okay, I guess," Andi said in a tired and scratchy voice.

Zane gently rubbed his hand back and forth on Andi's shoulder and she let out a soft sigh.

"I made you some soup," Norah said and held up the container for Andi to see. "It's chicken noodle with veggies."

"Thanks, Norah," Andi replied.

Norah nodded. "I'll just put it here on the counter for now." She carefully sat the hot soup down on the counter and then turned back to Andi. "Well, I just wanted to stop by to bring you this and see how you were doing. I'll get going so you can get some rest."

She gave Andi a soft smile and started to turn but stopped when Zane called for her.

Zane gently lifted Andi's head so he could stand from the sofa and then helped her get back into a comfortable position before he crossed the room to Norah.

"What's up?" Norah asked quietly.

"Dr. Moore did me a favor and stopped by this morning to check Andi out," Zane said. "He gave me a prescription for some meds, but I haven't exactly had a chance to leave to get it filled."

"You want me to stay with her so you can go?" Norah offered.

"Would you mind?" Zane asked. "I hate to leave her when she's this sick."

"Of course I don't mind," Norah told him. "Go on. I'll take care of her."

"Thanks, Norah." Zane crossed the room, whispered to Andi and gently placed a kiss on her head before he made his way out of the house.

Norah went to the sofa, sat down at the unoccupied end, and adjusted the blanket around Andi's stocking clad feet. "Can I get you anything?"

"No, I'm okay for now," Andi said. She took in a deep breath and then let it out slowly. "So what's new with you?"

Letting out a soft laugh, Norah shook her head and said, "Here you are sick as can be and you want to have small talk?"

Andi gave her a weak smile. "I don't get to see you much these days, besides when we're working at the bar. You're always off somewhere with Chase."

Norah chewed on the inside corner of her lip. "Yeah. I guess I am."

"So," Andi prompted. "Spill. What's going on with

you guys?"

"I honestly don't know," Norah said with an exasperated sigh. "I'm so confused."

"About what?" Andi asked. "You like him, don't you?"

"I do," Norah said. "But..."

Andi raised an eyebrow. "But what?"

"I'm a little scared," Norah said and looked down at her hands resting in her lap.

"Scared of what?" Andi narrowed her eyes and gave Norah a puzzled look. "Of Chase?"

"No. God no. I'm not scared of Chase," Norah rambled. "I'm..." She paused, looking for the right words to describe how she felt. "I guess I'm just scared of getting burned again."

"Norah," Andi spoke softly.

"I know, I know," Norah said. "It's stupid to think that."

Moving slowly, Andi propped herself up onto her elbow and looked to Norah. "It's not stupid. But you can't let the past influence your future. If I'd not given Zane a chance just because of all the stuff Vince put me through, well, we wouldn't be together. And I wouldn't be as happy as I am."

Norah had to admit that Andi did make a good argument. And her history with men was a far worse story than Norah's past with Wade. So if Andi could put all of the horrible stuff behind her and move on to a future of happiness, why was Norah having such a hard time doing the same?

"You're right," Norah said to Andi. "You're absolutely right. *God.* I can't believe the mess I've made of this whole thing. You know, I would've been fine if I hadn't let Luke get to me."

"Oh Lord," Andi moaned. "Please don't tell me you took relationship advice from Dr. Love."

A little embarrassed, Norah laughed and gently pushed at Andi's feet. "Don't say it like that. You make it sound like I called into one of those relationship hotlines or something."

"Well, what did he say to you?"

Norah took in a breath and told Andi about Luke's advice. "And after we had our little chat I was so confused about what I wanted to do. I wanted things to move forward with Chase but..." She stopped and shrugged.

"Look," Andi said. "If you want to be with Chase, then be with Chase. Luke did have some good advice, but I think a lot of that was him being the overly-protective brother that he is. In the end though, you're the one who has to decide what's best for you. So do what makes you happy." Andi's mouth turned up slightly into a teasing grin. "Or whoever makes you happy."

"Stop it." Norah chuckled and pushed against Andi's feet again. "And thank you."

"Anytime," Andi said and rested her head back against the pillow as she cleared her throat. "All this small talk has kind of made me thirsty. Would you mind getting me a glass of water?"

"Sure," Norah said, then stood up from the sofa. As she walked from the living room into the kitchen, she thought about Chase. What the heck was she going to say to him? For some reason, she thought coming right out and telling him that she was rethinking this whole just being friends thing wasn't the best approach. A thought popped in her mind just then and she grinned to herself. Maybe in this case, actions could speak louder than words.

Chase was getting all the paint supplies set up when Norah's truck pulled into the driveway. At the sound of her door slamming shut, he turned his head and squinted against the sunlight bouncing off the hood of the truck. He adjusted the brim of his baseball hat and froze as he saw Norah emerge from the blinding light.

She walked towards him wearing a hot pink tank top and a pair of Daisy Duke cut-offs. Her tanned legs gleamed in the sunlight, and Chase couldn't help but wonder if they felt as soft and smooth as they looked.

"Pretty hot, huh?" Norah said as she adjusted the straw cowboy hat on her head and looked down at him.

Yeah, Chase thought to himself; he quickly realized that she wasn't referring to her clothing choice but instead was talking about the weather.

"Yeah it is pretty hot out here," he agreed and cleared his throat as he stood.

"I'm surprised to see you're wearing a shirt," Norah said and reached out to tug on the hem of his white sleeveless t-shirt.

"Yeah, well, I didn't want you getting distracted or anything," he said with a grin before he silently berated himself. He'd promised himself that, out of respect for her and her wishes, he'd hold back his feelings for her and chill with the flirting. And here he'd gone and blown it within the first minute of her being here.

Way to go, O'Donnell.

"Hmm," she said. "That's a shame."

And the look she gave him, a seductive half smile with lust filled eyes, sent a jolt from his stomach straight down to his feet.

Was she…flirting with him? No. That couldn't be right. Not Norah. The woman who'd time and time again told him that she preferred to keep their relationship strictly in the friend zone.

He cleared his throat and looked to the house.

"So, I've, uh, already done the prep work and cleaned it," he told her. "I think we can have it all done within a few days." He paused and glanced over her from head to foot from the corner of his eye. "As long as we don't have any distractions or run into any problems."

"Well, let's get started then," Norah said and selected a paintbrush before she turned back to Chase. "Where do you want me?"

Chase was glad his better judgment was present instead of his spontaneity, because telling her "in my bed" was a wildly inappropriate answer to give her. Or was it?

He cleared his throat again.

"Umm, that's up to you," Chase answered. "You afraid of heights?"

"Nope," she told him as she ran her thumb against the blunt end of the brushes bristles.

"Okay," he said. "Well, you can have the ladder and I'll stay here on the ground."

Norah smiled. "Are you afraid of heights, O'Donnell?"

"Not hardly," Chase told her. "It just makes the most sense for you to go up instead of me."

"And why's that?"

Chase walked over to the house and adjusted the ladder so it was firmly set against the wood siding. "Because I have a better chance of catching you if you fall off of this thing."

"Good point," Norah said with a small laugh.

He walked back over to the paint supplies, opened one of the cans, and poured some of its contents into a separate container.

"Here you go," Chase said and handed her the portion of paint. "I'll stand here and hold the ladder while you climb."

She accepted the paint with a "thanks" and slowly made her way up the ladder.

Chase stared at the metal rung in front of him. It was all he could do to keep himself from watching her climb up that ladder. He held onto it and relied on the gentle vibrations through his hands to know that Norah was doing okay. When the vibrations stopped, Chase called out, "You good?"

"Yeah," Norah called back.

"Okay," Chase said. "'Cause I'm letting go."

"And you promise you're going to catch me if I fall, right?"

"I promise," Chase answered with a chuckle.

"I want you to look me in the eye and promise me."

"Norah—"

"Come on, Chase," Norah pleaded. "It'll ease my nerves a bit."

Damn it. Chase took in a deep breath and let it out slowly before he turned his head up to look at her. He'd meant to look directly to her eyes but instead found himself glued to just how perfect her butt looked in those damn shorts. Try as he might, that was an image that he was never going to be able to forget. When he finally met her face, she was smiling at him.

"You promise?" she asked.

And now a part of him—the devilish part of him—sort of wished that she *did* slip from that ladder so he could catch her in his arms and be the hero.

"I promise."

CHAPTER TWENTY-ONE

Apparently she was doing this whole flirting thing wrong.

Had to be.

It was the only reasonable explanation for why Chase hadn't picked up on the fact that she was interested in him.

Maybe she was trying too hard?

For the past four days she had made little comments with hidden innuendos and had done her best to make it obvious she was checking him out. And then there was the somewhat revealing clothing she chose to wear around him, which was another effort to help catch his eye and let him know what she was thinking.

But none of that was working with Chase.

Of course, there was always just telling him that she'd changed her mind and wanted something more between them. But for some reason she just couldn't muster up the guts to tell him that. Maybe she was just too much of a chicken to admit that she'd been wrong this whole time.

"Lookin' good," she heard Chase say, his voice drifted up to her from where he stood on the ground.

Okay, so maybe she *wasn't* doing something wrong after all. She stopped her brushstrokes against the house and held onto the ladder as she looked down to him.

"Liking what you see, O'Donnell?" she asked him, adding a generous amount of flirtatiousness to her voice.

"Yes, ma'am," Chase answered her with a grin from beneath the brim of his baseball cap. "You weren't kidding when you said you were good at painting."

Oh.

She tried to hide her disappointment as she looked back to the house and continued with her task.

"I'm all done down here," Chase said. "Let me know when you're done and ready to come down. I'll hold the ladder for you."

"Okay," Norah answered him, not bothering to look his way.

After brushing the last few strokes of the sunny yellow paint against the house, Norah tossed her paintbrush into the container of paint and started to make her way down the ladder.

Or at least, that's what she'd meant to do.

With her mind still focused on Chase and his inability to pick up on her come-ons, Norah tossed the brush against the rim of the paint container instead of inside of it. It flopped off of the top and spiraled down to the ground. Norah instinctively reached out to grab it, causing the ladder to unbalance.

"Oh no!" she shouted.

The brush would've landed in the grass if Chase hadn't scurried over to the ladder to steady it, but instead it slapped right on top of his navy ball cap and slid down the brim before falling to the ground.

Norah sucked in a shocked breath of air.

She hurried and made her way down the ladder, careful to hold onto the paint container in her hand so she didn't have any more accidents. With a few last steps remaining, Norah jumped from the ladder and set the container on the ground before she looked to Chase.

His expression was blank, almost dumbstruck.

"Chase?" Norah asked cautiously.

"What. The. Hell?" Chase asked, speaking the words slowly and quietly.

"I am so sorry," Norah said. "I didn't mean—"

"I told you to let me know when you were ready to come down," Chase said. "What were you thinking?"

"I—"

He cut her off. "You could've fallen and seriously hurt yourself."

"But I didn't," she told him, trying to smooth out the situation.

"Thankfully," Chase said and let out a relieved sigh as he took his hat off and ran a hand through his hair. "You're gonna kill me, woman." He then looked at his hat and his eyes widened at the bright yellow paint streaked across it. "Ah, damn it. This is my favorite hat."

Norah bit her lip to keep from laughing but couldn't contain it. She let out a short burst of laughter and quickly covered her mouth with her hand. "I'm sorry, I'm—"

Chase narrowed his eyes as he looked at her. "You think this is funny?"

"No," Norah quickly said but then changed it to, "Well, yes, it is kind of funny when you think about it." She laughed again.

"Oh, okay," Chase said with a nod as he placed his hat back on his head and quickly reached to the ground for the paintbrush.

He popped back up before she had a chance to dodge out of the way and slapped the brush against the front of her dark gray Rolling Stones t-shirt. Her mouth fell open as he drug the yellow paint between her breasts down to the knot she had tied at the hem of her shirt.

"You jerk," she gasped.

He gave her a smart-ass smirk as he dropped the paintbrush. "How's that for funny?"

"You ruined my shirt," she told him, her voice still full of disbelief as she tugged on the fabric to look at the damage done.

"And you ruined my hat," Chase said. "So now we're even. What do you know about the Rolling Stones anyway?" He gave her a half smile and knelt on the grass as he collected the paintbrushes.

She dropped the soft fabric and planted a hand on her hip. "Is that supposed to be a dig at me? 'Oh that country girl don't know nothin' about good music,'" she said, deepening her voice for that last part.

Chase chuckled and looked at her. "Was that supposed to be me?"

She smiled bashfully. "Maybe."

Chase grabbed all of the brushes and dropped them in an empty bucket before he walked back over to her. "Look, I'm sorry if I offended you," he said and shrugged his shoulders. "I'm just surprised. I thought you only liked country music."

"Well, I don't," Norah told him. "That's like me assuming you only like rock or rap or something."

"Well, which is it?" Chase asked her, the corner of his mouth turning up slightly. "Give it a guess. Let's see just how well you think you know me."

She gave him a playful smirk. "Okay." Crossing her arms over her chest, Norah brought one of her hands up to her face and tapped her finger against her chin as she thought about her answer. "I'm thinking you're more into upbeat tunes rather than the slow stuff. Right so far?"

"That's a good start," Chase said.

"And even though you like today's music you really prefer the older stuff."

"Right again."

Norah pursed her lips as she continued to tap her chin with her finger. "I'm thinking you're a seventies kind of man."

Chase applauded her. "Nicely done, Miss McKade."

"Why thank you, Mr. O'Donnell," Norah said and uncrossed her arms. "But I'll do you one better. I bet you I can go as far to guess who your favorite artist from that time is."

"Okay," Chase told her, clearly amused. "Let's hear it."

"Hmm?" Norah said as she pursed her lips again and moved her eyes to look at the sky. "Let's see there's Foghat, Aerosmith, The Who—" She stopped short and snapped her fingers as she looked directly at him. "I got it! ABBA."

"ABBA?" Chase said with a raised eyebrow and gave her a befuddled expression.

"Mmm-hmm," Norah replied with a teasing smile. "You know you rock 'Dancing Queen' when nobody's looking. Don't deny it."

Chase shook his head with a small laugh. "I think you are sorely mistaken. But good try though." He walked away from her and back to the mess of supplies scattered about the ground.

"Aw, did I hurt your feelings?" Norah asked, sporting a pouty face as she followed him.

"A little," Chase joked, sniffing as he wiped away a fake tear with the back of his hand.

"Aw. Cheer up, Chase," Norah said in a fun and almost girlish voice as she gently grabbed at his side. "Come on. *Come on.*" She continued her efforts to tickle a smile out of him, but it just wasn't working out for her.

"What *are* you doing, woman?" Chase asked, lifting his arm to watch her.

"Trying to make you laugh," she answered.

"I'm not ticklish," Chase told her and blocked her hand from grabbing at his side.

"I bet you are," Norah said. "You're just really good

at hiding it."

She laughed softly as she grabbed for his side again, but she was a bit caught off guard when Chase took hold of her wrist. Simultaneously, and before she even had time to move out of the way, Chase reached out with his other hand and grabbed at her side just as she had previously done to him. Norah shrieked and scrunched her body before quickly jumping away from Chase.

"Oh, are you serious?" Chase asked with a wide grin. "Look who *is* ticklish."

"Chase, don't you dare," Norah warned, giving him a stern look and pointing her finger at him.

He stalked towards her.

"I'm warning you," Norah said, walking backwards to keep an eye on Chase. The back of her leg hit one of the paint buckets and she instinctively looked down for the briefest moment before she returned her eyes to Chase. He was standing no more than a few feet away from her, staring at her with a hungry look in his eyes.

She took a slight step to the side.

He followed.

She took another step in the opposite direction.

He followed once more.

Her fun little game of let's-get-a-laugh-out-Of-Chase had quickly turned into a game of cat and mouse with Norah being the prey and Chase being the hunter.

Keeping her eyes on Chase, Norah slowly began to take another step but quickly faked it and bolted in the opposite direction. Her efforts to escape him were fruitless. Chase quickly caught up to her and swung both of his arms around her waist, picking her feet off of the ground as he pulled her to him.

"Chase!" Norah squealed as he tickled her. She laughed uncontrollably as she attempted to free herself from his hold.

He was laughing too. The deep sound of his voice was right against her ear, sending what felt like a current of electricity down her neck and spine.

Norah had no objection to being pressed against Chase the way she was. All she needed, though, was for him to stop tickling her long enough for her to take advantage of it. She swatted at his hands and attempted to wiggle free but only caused herself to lose balance. She fell to the ground and took Chase with her.

"Chase!" Norah shouted between laughs. "Stop! I can't breathe!"

Chase laughed breathlessly and removed his hands from her waist, resting them against the ground on either side of her body.

She focused on taking slow, deep breaths as she stared into Chase's green eyes. How she had been able to say no to that face time after time was a wonder to her. But even though the man was extremely attractive, that wasn't the only reason she wanted to be with him. She honestly and truly liked him for who he was and she was going to tell him exactly how she felt right now. Either that or she was going to kiss the hell out of him.

Where was that angel on his shoulder when he needed it?

Chase was fighting every one of his instincts right now, and it looked as though they were going to win. As he hovered above Norah, his gaze darted from her eyes to her mouth, and all he could do was think about kissing her. Well, that and letting his hands roam all over that silky skin of hers.

He was just about to throw in the towel with this

whole "friends'" deal of theirs when his cell phone rang, momentarily distracting him. He let it go, not even bothering to check the caller ID. Whoever it was would have to wait for a call back later on. After the fifth ring, silence filled the space between them as Chase continued to look at Norah. She was so beautiful lying there on the ground with her golden hair splayed about the grass. Her questioning blue eyes seemed to be trying to predict his next move.

They'd been lying in that exact position for a good few minutes, and she had yet to have any objections about it. In fact, she looked as though she *wanted* him to make a move.

Screw it, Chase thought to himself and slowly started to lean down to her.

His cell phone rang again, piercing through the silence like a siren. Chase dropped his head with an exasperated sigh.

"You should probably get that," Norah said softly.

As Chase reached in his pocket for the phone, Norah rolled away from him and stood. He watched her walk away towards the side of the house before he looked to the caller ID. He let out another exasperated sigh as he pressed the button to answer the call.

"Hey, sis," Chase said.

"Hey, Chase," Sarah said. "I just tried calling, but it went to your voicemail. Did I catch you at a bad time?"

Chase looked to Norah as his sister spoke. "Yeah, you kind of did. But what's up?"

"I talked to Mom, and we've decided to make the trip to the ranch tomorrow to go through Uncle Eli's and Aunt Mary's belongings," Sarah said. "Is that going to be okay with you?"

"Sure," Chase said, only halfway paying attention to

what Sarah was saying.

"I'm not exactly sure what time we'll show up," Sarah told him. "But I can give you a call when we're on our way if you want."

"Mmm-hmm," he replied.

"Chase, are you even listening to me?" Sarah asked.

"Yeah," he answered.

"Then what did I just say?"

"You're planning on coming by, and you'll call when you're on your way," Chase said as he stood and brushed the dirt from his shorts. "Look, I've gotta go, Sarah. I'll talk to you later. Okay?"

He ended the call as he walked up to Norah.

"Sorry," Chase told her. "Guess my sister doesn't know how to take a hint when someone doesn't answer the phone."

"It's okay," Norah said. "I went ahead and packed everything up. The only thing left to do is wash the brushes."

"Thanks," Chase said. "And thanks again for offering to help out. This would've taken me twice as long if I'd done it by myself."

"You're welcome," she said with a sweet smile.

"Did you want to come in for something to drink?" Chase asked with a nod and jerked his thumb towards the house.

She hesitated. "I'd really love to, but I have to get going. There are a few things I need to take care of before I go into work tonight. But maybe later."

He nodded again and tucked his fingers into his front pockets. "Later it is then."

"Of course, if you were planning on stopping by the bar tonight, we could make *later* happen sooner," she suggested.

Chase smiled and shot her a puzzled look. "I thought you didn't drink on the job?"

Norah gave a slight shrug of her shoulders. "I'd be willing to make an exception for you."

He wondered if that was the only thing she was willing to make an exception for.

"I guess I could swing by for a bit," Chase said and held onto her gaze, hoping to somehow read her thoughts.

"I sure hope you do," Norah told him before she bid him goodbye and walked away to her truck.

Chase waved to her as she pulled out of the driveway and then he was left with nothing but himself and his thoughts. Thinking about his relationship, or lack thereof, with Norah, Chase would definitely admit that she was in control of the ride. And even though she may have pulled tight on the reins to keep them from moving forward too fast, she was now loosening up and letting that pony ride. It was an extremely cheesy and corny thought, but Chase found it fitting for his cowgirl.

His cowgirl.

Who knew? Maybe after tonight she would be.

CHAPTER TWENTY-TWO

"Is there a reason you keep looking at the door?" Andi asked as she walked past Norah to grab a bottle of liquor from the shelf.

Norah filled a glass with ice and poured the concoction from the cocktail mixer into it. Tossing a straw into the pink liquid, Norah slid the drink over to the busty blonde in front of her.

"Is it that obvious?" Norah asked Andi as she turned with the blonde's cash and made her way to the register.

Andi nodded her head. "So did you finally tell the man just how you feel about him or what?"

"I tried letting him know, but nothing I did worked." Closing the drawer to the register, Norah turned and leaned back against the counter next to Andi.

"What do you mean?" Andi asked, perplexed. "You didn't just come right out and say 'Hey, I like you?'"

"Well, no," Norah said. "I couldn't bring myself to just blurt it out like that. So I tried being flirtatious and sexy, but that didn't work either."

Andi let out a small laugh. "You're something, you know that? Chase likes you. That much is obvious, and he's even told you. So stop wasting time and just get on with it. You'll be much happier if you do. Trust me."

"I know," Norah said softly. "And I will. I mean, I plan on telling him tonight."

"Well, here's your chance because there's lover boy now," Andi said and nodded towards the door.

Norah looked and saw Chase walking through the crowd of people. Her stomach knotted at the sight of him, but she wasn't sure if it was from being nervous about telling him her feelings for him or the fact that he looked sexy as sin in his dark t-shirt and blue jeans.

Maybe it was a little of both.

"Hey," Chase said as he approached the bar. He propped an elbow on the counter and casually glanced around the room before he turned back to Norah. "It's pretty busy in here tonight."

"You're tellin' me," Norah said. "Apparently a tour bus broke down just outside of town and it won't be fixed until tomorrow."

"So all of these people are staying in Buford?" Chase asked with a raised eyebrow. "Where?"

"From what I've heard, from a very lovely but very chatty woman, they're staying in a motel in the next town over," Norah said. "And they wanted to have a 'true honky-tonk experience,' so they ended up here."

Chase grinned. "A true honky-tonk experience?"

Norah let out a small laugh and shook her head. "I'll bet you they've seen *Roadhouse* one too many times and are expecting this place to be just like the *Double Deuce*. And I've got news for them, A, this place just isn't that rowdy, and B, I think Trace is a great bouncer, but between you and me, he's no Patrick Swayze."

She reached down in the cooler and pulled out a longneck beer. Using her bottle opener, she popped the top and tossed it into the trash before she slid the beer across the counter to Chase.

"I'll agree with you on both of those facts," Chase said with a chuckle. "And thanks." He lifted the bottle and tipped it towards Norah before taking a sip. "You still going to join me for one later?"

She gently bit the corner of her lip. "Yeah. Later being the keyword there. We're too swamped right now for me to have any down time."

"Not a problem," Chase said, then turned around to scan the room. "I think I'm gonna head over to the pool tables to kill some time." He turned back to Norah and shot her a gleaming smile and a wink. "See you in a bit."

Her heart produced a fluttering sensation. Oh, she needed to figure out what she was going to say and fast because she couldn't take much more of this. All of this sexual tension building within her was becoming frustrating.

Just stop being weird about it and tell him how you feel. No need to dance around it anymore.

She would. As soon as she was alone with him and had his undivided attention, she would tell him exactly what was on her mind.

Chase was racking up the balls on the pool table when he felt a hand rest softly, almost seductively, on his shoulder.

Well, that's new.

He turned with a crooked smile, expecting to see Norah, but he instead found a good-looking blonde staring back at him.

"Hey there, handsome," she cooed, gently rubbing her hand in a slow circle on his shoulder.

"Umm, hi," Chase replied as he looked to the woman's hand.

"You mind if I join in on your game?" the blonde asked, giving Chase a doe-eyed look as she ran her hand down his arm.

"Sorry, but I've already got a partner," Chase said and nodded to the man standing next to the table holding the cue stick.

"Actually, Chase," the man said, looking at his phone as he thumbed the buttons. "I've gotta get going."

"Oh, come on, David," Chase said. "We just started."

"I know but my girl is giving me what for right now and if I don't go smooth it over…" David shrugged sheepishly. "You know how it is. Sorry man." David walked around the table and handed the blonde the stick and slapped Chase on the shoulder. "Have fun."

"Yeah, thanks," Chase muttered.

"Looks like you and I are partners," the blonde said to Chase in a smooth southern belle voice. "By the way, I'm Lyla."

Chase looked to the blonde's outstretched hand and, with an exasperated sigh, placed his own hand in hers and shook it. "I'm Chase."

"Now that we got introductions out of the way," one of the other players said. "Let's play some pool."

Chase walked to the end of the pool table, leaned over, and rested the heel of his hand on the green felt. His focus was on the cue ball in front of him until he noticed his new partner standing across the table from him. Her white, midriff-baring tank top and denim mini-skirt were quite the distraction, and it was starting to piss him off. He knew what she was up to, and he wanted no part of it. All he wanted to do tonight was see Norah and hopefully get to spend some time with her, not fight off the advances of a twenty-something woman who looked like she was auditioning to be one of Hugh Hefner's girlfriends.

He pulled his focus back to the game and struck the cue ball, sending it gliding across the table into the other balls with a loud crack. Three of the striped balls fell into the pockets, and the blonde clapped her hands as she bounced up and down.

"Yay!" Lyla exclaimed. "Oh, you are so good at this

game, Chase."

"Thanks," he mumbled without looking to her as he moved around the table to get his next shot.

After sinking two more balls and missing the third, Chase stepped away from the table and went to take a drink of his beer.

"So are you from around here?" Lyla asked Chase, holding onto the cue stick as if it were a stripper's pole.

"Nope," Chase answered her.

"Me either," she said with a sigh. "I'm just here for the night. A few of my friends and I decided to check this place out, hoping we'd get to see some real cowboys."

"Ah, damn it," one of the other players called out as they missed their shot. "It's your turn."

Chase waited for Lyla to approach the table but she was still looking him over with a do-me-now look in her eyes.

"Umm," Chase said and pointed to the table with his beer bottle. "It's your go."

"Oh," Lyla said and laid her hand over her heart. "Silly ol' me."

She walked over to the table with a dramatic sway of her hips and leaned over the edge.

Chase looked around the room, trying to see where Norah was and what she was up to when he heard Lyla call for him.

"Could you help me?" she asked Chase, giving him an innocent look that he darn well knew wasn't innocent at all.

He pressed his tongue to his cheek before he took another drink of his beer and walked over to the pool table.

"What do you need help with?" Chase asked.

"I don't think I'm holding the stick right," Lyla said,

her lips forming a slight pout. "Could you show me?"

Chase explained to Lyla how to properly hold the cue stick and even went so far as to stand next to her and demonstrate it, but she still wasn't getting it.

"Oh, come on!" the player across the table yelled. "Quit dickin' around, man, and just show the girl how to hit the damn ball. I'm tired of waiting."

Chase looked to the man and flexed his jaw before looking to Lyla.

"Please," she said with a flutter of her eyelashes.

He was so going to regret this. With a heavy sigh, Chase walked behind Lyla and helped her get into the proper position. Attempting to keep as much air between them as possible, Chase rested his left hand on the table with hers and brought his right hand over her body to grab hold of the stick.

"Okay, line up your shot," Chase explained. "And then when you're ready just…" He brought the stick back and then wacked the cue ball, sending their ball into the side pocket.

Chase quickly stood and stepped away from Lyla, who was bouncing up and down with excitement.

"That was so fun!" she said.

And before Chase had time to even blink, Lyla threw her arms around him and planted a kiss smack dab on his lips.

What the hell?

"Thank you," she told him when she pulled away.

He couldn't believe what just happened. Okay, well maybe he could believe it but he didn't want to.

"I'm gonna go grab another beer," Chase said and leaned his cue stick against the wall.

"Don't be long," Lyla told him as she stared at him seductively.

Chase turned, fighting the urge to wipe his mouth, and maneuvered his way through the crowd in search of the woman he'd come here for.

"Excuse me," Norah said, quickly lifting her tray above her head to avoid it being hit by the people standing all over the place. She made it to her table and was dropping off the drinks when she happened to glance up and see Chase over by the pool tables.

He was resting next to one of the pub tables and drinking his beer as he stared at something, but what it was she couldn't tell. And she couldn't quite read the look on his face. He was either annoyed or deeply focused. Tucking her now empty tray under her arm, Norah took a few steps in Chase's direction, figuring she'd drop by for just a minute to say "Hi," but she stopped short when she noticed Chase talking to a rather scantily dressed woman.

She didn't want or mean to pry, but she felt glued to that spot there on the old wooden floor as she watched Chase interact with the woman. Norah recognized her as the busty blonde who'd been ordering fruity cocktails all night long and had been going on to her friends about how she wanted to "ride a cowboy."

Norah laughed to herself. Chase was hardly a cowboy, but that certainly wasn't stopping the blonde from laying down the moves. But if Norah knew Chase at all, then she knew he wouldn't give in to them.

Or would he?

Norah felt her mouth pop open as Chase stood behind the blonde and helped her with her shot. But the shock didn't stop there. A sickened gasp escaped from her mouth as Norah watched the woman fling her arms around Chase and kiss him. She wasn't sure what pissed her off more, the fact that the woman kissed him or the fact that Chase didn't do anything to stop it.

Fuming, Norah turned and made her way back to the bar. She set her tray down with a little more force than she'd intended and went straight to work filling drink orders.

"What's wrong with you?" Andi asked Norah as she handed a couple of beers and a cocktail over to the customer in front of her.

"I'm fine," Norah said without emotion as she slammed a glass filled with ice on the counter and poured an amber colored liquid over the top.

"No you're not, but it's okay," Andi said. "I get you don't wanna talk right now but if you change your mind just let me know." A woman at the other end of the bar yelled for service and Andi headed that way.

Norah was so busy filling orders, and still fuming over what she'd just seen, that she hadn't even noticed Chase standing across the bar from her. When she did notice, she froze and stared at him for the briefest moment before jumping back into her work.

"You need another beer?" she asked him flatly without looking in his direction.

"Yeah, thanks," Chase said and rested his hand on the lacquered bar top. "Why don't you take a break and join me for that drink?"

"I'm a little busy right now, Chase," Norah said, handing over another customer's order before giving Chase his beer.

"Maybe it'd be best if we just waited until closing time," Chase suggested. "I could stick around and help you like I did that one night."

"I don't think so," Norah told him.

Chase drew back and looked at her with questioning eyes. "You don't think so about me helping you out or sticking around after closing time?"

Unable to hide her frustration any longer, Norah slammed a glass down on the counter and looked to Chase. "Look, I told you I'm busy right now. I don't have time for this. So please just…" She held her hand up, palm facing out to Chase. "Just leave me alone."

"Okay," Chase said, the confusion on his face mixed with anger. He reached for the back of his jeans and grabbed his wallet. Pulling the bills from the opening, Chase slapped them down on the counter then pocketed his wallet back into his jeans. "I'm out."

And with that, Chase made his way through the crowded room towards the exit.

"So *now* are you going to tell me what's got you all in a mood?" Andi asked.

Norah wiped the counter and shook her head. "I just saw something tonight that I didn't really care to see."

"And that would be?" Andi pried. She hefted the full trash bag from the wastebasket and set it on the floor as she tied the drawstrings together.

"I don't really want to talk about it," Norah said.

Dropping the towel next to the sink and grabbing a clean one, Norah walked around the corner of the bar to the main floor. As she began to wipe down the tables, she thought more and more of what happened earlier with Chase. She really wished she'd just gone ahead and told him that she thought he was a piece of shit for messing with that blonde when for the past few weeks he'd been spending all his time with her.

But spending all that time with you as friends, her subconscious chimed in. *Which is what you asked for.*

Be that as it may, it still pissed her off to no end that he could simply throw her aside so quickly like that and move on to the next victim. Right in front of her. She couldn't do this. There would be no rest in sight for her until she talked to him.

"Hey, Andi," Norah said, walking back behind the bar and tossing the dirty towel next to the other.

"What's up?" Andi asked with a trash bag in each hand.

"Would you be okay closing up tonight without me?" Norah asked. "There's something I need to take care of."

Andi shot her a puzzled look but shrugged and said, "Yeah, I guess. I mean, Red's here, so I'm sure we can take care of everything just fine. Are you sure you're okay?"

"I'm fine," Norah said and grabbed her truck keys. "I promise. Thanks so much, Andi!"

Holding her keys in her fist, Norah jogged out to her truck and hopped in the driver's seat. The truck came to life with a rumble, and Norah quickly shifted it into drive and sped out of the parking lot, leaving a trail of dirt and dust behind her. She was about to give Chase O'Donnell a piece of her mind.

CHAPTER TWENTY-THREE

Chase was lying in bed, fully awake, arms tucked behind his head, and staring at the ceiling when he heard someone knocking at the back door. Curiously, he turned and looked at the alarm clock on the nightstand.

2:58 a.m.

The knocking continued, so Chase threw back the covers and climbed out of bed. Grabbing his jeans from the floor, he slipped them on and zipped them up, not bothering with the button. He then made his way from the bedroom and down the hall to the kitchen.

"Who is it?" Chase called out, but no one answered.

Eyeing the baseball bat he kept next to the door, he reached for the light switch. He flicked on the outside porch light just as he pulled back the curtain that covered the door's window. With a sigh, Chase let the semi-sheer fabric go and opened the door.

"Norah, what are you—"

"I need to talk to you," Norah said as she pushed past him into the house.

"Well, come on in," Chase muttered with a sarcastic tone as he closed the door behind her. When he turned around he found Norah standing by the table, arms crossed over her blue plaid pearl snap shirt, giving him an icy stare. "Can I get you something? Tea? Beer? A watch, maybe?" He walked over to the sink and grabbed a glass from the drying rack and filled it halfway with water. Leaning back against the counter, Chase took a sip as he stared at Norah.

"You're a real jerk, you know that?"

"Excuse me?" Chase said, setting the glass down on the counter next to him.

"You heard me."

"Yeah, I heard you. You wanna tell me *why* I'm jerk, though, because there's obviously something I'm missing here."

"You wanna know why?" Norah said with a huff and threw her hands in the air before she slapped them against her thighs. "Well let me enlighten you, Chase. I saw you with that woman tonight at the bar."

"What woman? What are you talking about?" His forehead wrinkled as he stared across the room at her with bewilderment.

"The one you were playing pool with," Norah said. "Or was the game tonsil hockey?"

Tonsil hockey? Seriously?

Chase let out a tired sigh and rubbed his eyes with his fingers. "You drove all the way out here at three in the morning to yell at me about that?"

Then it hit him. She drove all the way out here at three in the morning to yell at him about some woman who'd hit on him at the bar.

Holy shit. She was jealous. Crazy jealous.

Trying to hide his amusement, Chase crossed his arms over his bare chest and narrowed his eyes. "So it bothers you that another woman kissed me? Hmm? I never thought you'd be the jealous kind."

"I am not jealous of Big Boobs McGee," Norah shot back. "I'm just annoyed that you kissed her and were all over her."

"I hate to break it to you, Norah, but that's what people call jealousy," Chase told her. "But before you say anything else, let me ask you this. Why? Why are you jealous? We're only friends, or at least that's what you keep telling me."

Norah let out a short burst of laughter, no doubt a sign of her frustration, as she rolled her eyes and rounded the table. "Wow. On top of being a jerk you're also an idiot."

He bit the inside of his cheek to keep from smiling. "Well, how about you enlighten me some more then?"

"Okay," Norah said. She then opened her mouth and closed it again, her hesitation was as plain as day on her face.

Chase raised an eyebrow as he slowly started to walk towards her. "While you're searching for those perfect words, I want to clear the air here about that woman at the bar."

Norah was holding onto his gaze as she took one step backwards for every step he took towards her.

"I wanted nothing to do with her," Chase said. "And I want it to be known that I *did not* kiss her. She kissed me. As soon as that happened I left and went looking for you because you are the only reason I went out tonight. I wanted to be with you. I *always* want to be with you. And you know what else?"

Norah stopped abruptly as her back hit the wall dividing the kitchen from the living room.

"What?" she asked him breathlessly.

"I think we were kidding ourselves when we agreed to keep this platonic," Chase told her, his voice low and deep as he searched her face for a response. "Am I wrong?"

He was standing close enough to her where their bodies almost touched. So close that he could feel her escalated breath against his skin as he looked down to her.

"Well?" Chase whispered as his eyes briefly dipped to her mouth.

Norah shoved at his chest, sending him two steps away from her. "No matter what you think or what you say, Chase, it doesn't change that fact that you *let* that happen tonight. And the fact that you're still an idiot."

Feeling more frustrated and confused than he'd ever felt before, Chase threw his hands into the air and rolled his eyes. "Jesus Christ, here we go again with the idiot thing. Why am I an idiot? Because I let some stupid woman trick me?"

"Because for the past four days I've been trying my hardest to show you that I want something more between us," Norah said, raising her voice as the words spilled from her mouth. "But apparently you're too stupid to figure that out."

Chase took in a deep breath through his nostrils and let it out slowly through his mouth. "I knew you were flirting with me, Norah. And trust me, I wanted to give in. But I was keeping my promise." He ran a hand through his hair and rubbed the back of his neck. "Do you know just how hard it's been for me to be around you when all I can think about is touching you and kissing you? Do you know how many nights I've laid awake because I can't stop thinking about you?"

He scoffed. "Then you have the nerve to come to my house in the middle of the night to yell at me about another woman and to tell me that you've been trying to *show* me that you want me instead of just coming out and telling me. I'm a guy, Norah, I don't do subtle hints." Chase turned and walked a few feet away from her before raising his arms as he shrugged and looked back to her. "I just don't know what you want from me anymore."

Norah tightened her jaw as she stared at Chase. "I really hate you sometimes."

Oh for Christ's sake. He couldn't take much more of

this. He was just about to ask her "Why?" but stopped when she began to speak again.

"I drove here, mad as hell, ready to tell you that I never wanted to see you again. And now?" She released a heavy sigh.

"Now what?" Chase asked.

"Now all I want you to do is just shut the hell up and kiss me."

Chase didn't need any more prompting than that. He crossed the room in two long strides, framed Norah's face in his hands, and smothered her mouth with a blistering kiss.

All of the tension caused by her anger melted away as Chase kissed her, deeply and thoroughly. He barely let their lips part for more than a second before he dove back in with another scorching kiss. A hint of cologne on his heated skin wafted into her nostrils—warm, spicy, and all male. It was intoxicating. Almost as intoxicating as his kiss. Chase's tongue was smooth as whiskey as it glided against hers in wild abandon, leaving her trembling with want.

Norah slid her hands up his muscular back and dug her fingers into his skin. Oh man. If she'd thought he was hard-toned during their first brief encounter, then how the hell would she describe him now? All those long hours on the ranch and fixing up the place had worked his muscles into a rock solid mass. Pulling him closer to her body, Norah let out a soft gasp as she felt his arousal through his jeans poking at her abdomen.

"Sweet Jesus, Norah," Chase muttered against her lips. "I want you so damn bad." He feathered open mouth kisses along her jaw to her ear. "Please tell me we're on the same page here."

His warm breath hit her ear, sending a shiver down her spine.

"Yes," Norah breathed as Chase scattered kisses down her neck. She moved her hands to the back of his head and tangled her fingers in his dark hair. "I want you too, Chase. I've wanted you for so long. Please."

She felt his body shift and then his large hands were gripping her butt, lifting her to him. He pinned her against the wall as he darted his tongue out and tasted the exposed skin of her chest. She moaned and tightened her legs around his waist as one of his hands skimmed up her side and cupped her breast. Dropping her head back against the wall, Norah closed her eyes as he teased the hardened tip through the thin fabric of her shirt.

Oh man, that felt good.

Her skin prickled as Chase's hot mouth traveled across her chest, over her collarbone, and up to her mouth as he moved her away from the wall. With his hands still gripping her butt, he carried her through the living room and down the dark hallway. A few moments later they entered a bedroom, lit by one small table lamp on the dresser, and only then did Chase set Norah down.

The second her boots hit the floor she scrambled to get out of them, holding the heel of the one with the toe of her other. It was quite the task, but she managed to get out of them and kick them out of the way, all while kissing Chase and running her hands over the smooth plains of his chest. He was built wonderfully and she didn't think she'd ever grow tired of the feel of him beneath her hands.

Then Norah let out a throaty moan as she felt Chase's hand sneak underneath her shirt and snake up to her ribcage. She craved the feeling of his hands against her breasts, but it appeared as though the tight-fitting fabric had become a bit of a roadblock for Chase. He pulled back slightly and glanced down to her buttons before looking back to her with a wicked smile.

Her stomach jumped with anticipation.

"Have I mentioned," Chase said, his voice low and husky as he kissed her chin. "How much I love these pearl snap shirts?"

And without a warning, Chase took hold of the fabric on each side and pulled, hard.

Snap, snap, snap, snap.

"Oh my God," Norah gasped as her shirt ripped open. It had surprised the hell out of her. She'd never had anyone do *that* before. It also surprised her how turned on she was by it.

Not wanting to waste anymore time, she reached for the fly of his jeans but paused before grabbing the zipper. With her shirt now on the floor, Norah leaned into Chase, pressing her lace covered breasts against his torso. His hands fisted in her hair as he pulled her to him to kiss her. She allowed it, but only for a moment. Pulling away from his mouth, Norah kissed Chase's chin and down his neck to his chest. Simultaneously, she moved one of her hands from Chase's zipper and rubbed the palm of it against his rock hard erection through his jeans.

Chase sucked in a breath of air through his teeth.

She smiled against his chest and darted her tongue out to taste him, thoroughly enjoying how responsive he was to her touch. She then unzipped Chase's jeans before sliding her hand into his fly and taking hold of him.

Chase hissed and let out a deep, throaty moan as she stroked him. "Jesus Christ, Norah," he said in a strangled voice. His head fell back as she continued to tease him with her hand, loving how smooth and warm he felt. A few moments later though, Chase gripped her wrist and pulled her hand away before turning her face up to his.

His green eyes were wild with a ferocious hunger and desire—all for her.

"Bed," Chase said. "Now."

She wanted to jokingly make some smart-ass comment about his bossiness, but she didn't have time to do anything as Chase crushed his mouth against hers and lifted her to him once more. Seconds later, they fell onto the soft mattress and bounced upon impact. His mouth zeroed in on her neck, licking and kissing his way down to the slender curve then nipping his teeth against her skin. Her whole body shuddered as Chase gently sucked the tender spot to soothe the slight sting.

"I could spend days like this," Chase breathed in a husky tone against her neck. "Exploring every inch of you."

She quivered as Chase's hand moved south along her trembling stomach.

"Find every spot that makes you shudder."

He unbuttoned her jeans.

"Every spot that makes you moan."

He unzipped them.

"Every spot that makes you beg for more."

He slipped his hand beneath the denim and rubbed against her feminine folds through the lace of her underwear.

Oh sweet Jesus. The feel of his fingers sliding against her made every nerve in her body buzz and tingle. And although she loved what he was doing and the effects it was having on her, she needed more. She needed to feel him against her skin instead of through the now dampened fabric. Norah moved against his hand, prompting him to go further and give her that sweet release she was craving.

"Chase," she begged. "Please."

He gave her a cocky smile and, without hesitation, slid the delicate fabric to the side. Norah sucked in a breath of air and moaned, gripping onto the comforter as Chase found the entrance to her feminine core.

"More," she breathed, loving how his fingers soothed the ache within her.

She could feel her pleasure building as Chase continued to tease her relentlessly, reducing her to a trembling mass of want.

"*Oh my God.*" Her breathing escalated. "*Please. Chase.*"

His thumb stroked over her sensitive skin, and the tension that'd been building inside her broke. She cried out as she pulsed around him and clenched her thighs as heat flooded her veins.

"Whoa," she breathed when the sensation eased.

Grinning, Chase moved away from her, sliding down the bed and gripping her jeans in his hands. Seconds later they were gone, and she was naked from the waist down. She then watched as Chase stood from the bed and removed his last remaining articles of clothing. Her gaze traveled down the length of his body and...

Oh. My. God.

Her eyes widened slightly at the sight of him and her pulse kicked up a notch. Without thinking, she licked her bottom lip before tucking it between her teeth. When she returned her gaze to his, he was grinning again in a sinfully sexy way that made her abdomen coil. He reached for his wallet on the nightstand, opened it and pulled out a gold square packet. She watched him as he covered himself, unashamed that she was blatantly staring at him. And then Chase joined her on the bed, his palms flat by her shoulders as he hung above her.

He brushed his mouth against hers. "You okay?" he asked against her lips.

"No," she replied in a soft-spoken tone.

He pulled back to look at her curiously.

Norah's lips twitched. "But I'm sure I will be in a minute though."

Chase grinned and let out a short burst of laughter as his legs brushed inside hers. "I'd like to think you'd give me more credit than that." His tongue dove into her mouth as he pushed himself inside of her with one long, slow stroke.

Norah moaned and circled her legs around his waist, digging her fingers into his hair and his shoulders as he set the pace. She moved with him, grinding her pelvis against his as she skimmed her hands down his back to grip his butt. This was perfect. He was perfect.

As Chase continued with his slow and tantalizing strokes, he bent his head down and ran his tongue against the exposed skin of her breast along the lace edge of her bra.

She'd forgotten she still even had it on.

But that didn't seem to deter Chase one bit. He brought his hand over and moved the lace to the side, fully exposing her breast to him. He did the same for the other and brought his mouth down to her.

"Oh sweet Jesus." Norah moaned and arched into him as he sucked and licked the beaded tip while he teased the other with his fingers.

It was too much for her all at once.

And then Chase's lips moved to her neck, finding that spot that always set her off, and her abdomen began to tighten as her impending orgasm grew. The familiar tingling sensation moved through her limbs, leaving her aching and trembling.

"Chase," Norah gasped and gripped onto his shoulders as he began to quicken his strokes, thrusting into her harder and faster. "Chase! *Holy shit.*"

She felt herself go as she clung to him for dear life. Her body pulsed around him as he came, groaning against her neck as he collapsed on top of her.

They were both panting and breathing hard as they lay there unable to move. After a few moments, Norah brought one of her hands to Chase's head and ran her fingers through his dampened hair. He lifted his face to look at her.

"I'm sorry I called you a jerk," Norah murmured, still trying to catch her breath as she traced the outline of his jaw with her fingertip. "And an idiot."

Chase laughed, and the action did interesting things to their still entwined bodies. "Don't forget stupid."

"Okay," Norah said and laughed with him. "I'm sorry for that too."

Chase pushed himself up so he was barely hovering above her. "I think it's safe to say that you're forgiven." He nudged her nose with his before ever so gently pressing his lips to hers. "But if you're still feeling any remorse, I can think of some ways you could make it up to me." His lips moved slowly along her jaw to her ear, tugging gently on her lobe with his teeth.

"Chase," Norah said softly as she leaned into him.

She'd wanted to talk to him about what had just happened between them and what this meant. But then Chase kissed her. And then he kissed her again. And all her plans of talking vanished.

CHAPTER TWENTY-FOUR

Norah opened her eyes to sunlight shining brightly through a wood paned window.

Not *her* window, though.

Her eyes darted around the room.

Not her room either.

For a moment she'd forgotten where she was. But then she realized that she was lying on Chase's chest, and she remembered exactly where she was and what had happened. Taking in a deep breath, Norah stretched her aching limbs, and the memories of last night flooded her brain. She smiled slightly, thinking to herself that she'd never experienced anything like Chase. They'd made love not once, not twice, but three times over the course of the wee morning hours, finally collapsing from sheer exhaustion as the sun peeked over the horizon.

She rested her weight on her elbow as she lifted her head and found Chase staring at her, wearing a sleepy smile that pulled at her heartstrings.

"Good morning," he said, his voice deep and scratchy.

"Mornin'." She returned his smiled and ran a hand through her messy blond strands. "What time is it?"

Chase turned his head to look at the alarm clock. "11:36."

A heavy sigh escaped her lips and she buried her face into Chase's chest. "My brothers are going to kill me," Norah groaned, her voice muffled as she spoke against his skin.

Feeling Chase's hand take hold of her chin, she

allowed him to gently pull her face up to look at him.

"They'd have to get through me first," Chase said. As he leaned in to press his lips to hers, his hands slid down her body and pulled her to straddle his lap. Palms pressed firmly against her back, Chase trailed warm kisses along her neck and collarbone, making her skin break out in goose bumps as he blew gently across her heated flesh.

His cell phone rang from the nightstand. Again. And again.

"Aren't you going to get that?" Norah asked softly, shuddering when he hit the sensitive spot where her neck met her shoulder.

"I'll call them back," Chase muttered against her skin as he continued to taste her. His hands moved down her back and gripped her rear end as he stood from the bed.

"Where are we going?" Norah asked with a small, soft laugh.

"Where we won't have any more disturbances," Chase said and nipped at her bottom lip with his teeth.

"I can walk, you know." She toyed with his hair, running her fingers through the dark locks as Chase carried her into the hall bathroom.

"Now where's the fun it that?" he said with a teasing grin.

Pulling back the shower curtain, Chase turned on the water and stepped over the edge of the tub. The small room quickly began to fill with steam as he set her down and closed the curtain. He pulled her with him to stand beneath the spray from the showerhead, dipping his head down to kiss her as the water bounced off of his shoulders. Breaking the kiss, Chase reached for the bar of soap and rubbed it between his hands as he stared at her.

"I hope you don't mind smelling like *Irish Spring*," he said, setting the bar of soap down. His soapy hands started at her shoulders and worked their way down her arms, circling her wrists before dragging the tips of his fingers back up to her shoulders. This was lovely, having him wash her and feeling the gentle caress of his work-roughened hands against her skin. But as much as she was enjoying being the center of attention, she wanted to return the favor. She took the bar of soap and lathered it between her hands.

"And just what do you think you're doing?" Chase asked, his voice teasing and sexy as it bounced off the tile of the shower.

She smiled and placed her palms against his chest, making slow circles around his pecs to his shoulders. "I can't let you have all the fun. Now turn around so I can wash your back."

He complied with her demand and turned his back to her. Glancing over him from bottom to top, Norah caught sight of his tattoo and she leaned in closer to get a better look. She was right about it being an eagle, shaded in black with its wings spread wide, frozen forever on Chase's shoulder in a swooping position.

"This is nice," Norah said as she traced the design with her fingertip. "Is there a meaning behind it?"

He let out a small laugh and turned his head to the side. "Freedom," he told her. "I got it the day I turned eighteen. It was my subtle way of letting my parents know they couldn't tell me what to do anymore." He turned and placed his hands on her hips. "Fun teenage rebellion stuff."

"So you were a bad boy, huh?" she teased, rubbing her hands up his arms to rest on his biceps.

"What do you mean *were*?" Chase replied and backed her against the wall. "I still am."

Chase held onto Norah's gaze as he felt her hands move to rest gently on his hips. He zeroed in on her mouth as he slowly leaned towards her and…

The bathroom door swung open with such force that it bounced against the wall, making both Norah and Chase jump. He quickly spun around, standing in front of Norah in a protective stance. A lot of good that would do, though. Being naked and wet was hardly intimidating. He heard the toilet lid slap against the ceramic tank and a light trickle sound followed.

What the hell?

Drawing his eyebrows together in confusion, Chase turned to Norah and pressed a finger to his lips. He gripped the edge of the shower curtain and pulled it back slowly, peeking to see who the intruder was.

"Chelsea!" Chase said. "What are you doing?"

"Hi, Uncle Chase," the little girl said as she held onto the toilet seat and kicked her legs back and forth. "I had to pee."

He closed the curtain, shut his eyes for a moment and sighed heavily.

Shit.

He'd completely forgotten that Sarah was coming today. Oh God. That meant his mother was here too. And here he was naked in the shower with the woman he was intimately involved with.

Double shit.

"Umm," Chase whispered, rubbing his hand against the back of his neck as he took a step towards Norah.

She was staring at him wide-eyed and covering herself with her arms. "Umm, what?" she whispered back.

He hesitated for a brief second. "I sort of forgot that

my sister was coming today."

"You what?" Norah hissed.

"I'm sorry," Chase quickly apologized. "But it gets worse."

Her mouth popped open slightly as she gave him a disbelieving look. "How?"

"My mom's here too."

Her mouth fell completely open this time and she brought her hands up to cover her face. "This is bad, Chase! Why didn't you remember something like that?"

"It's not my fault," he said defensively. "She called yesterday while you and those damn shorts were distracting me."

"Shut up," she said with a soft laugh and pushed at his chest. "What are we going to do?"

He had a plan—a poorly devised plan but it'd have to do considering their predicament. And he was all ready to fill her in when he heard the toilet flush and the lid drop down against the seat.

The once warm and comforting water had turned ice cold in that split second.

Chase yelled.

Norah screamed.

Chelsea screamed too and then started to cry.

"It's okay, Chels," Chase called out and quickly turned off the water.

Footsteps sounded from the hall. "What happened?" Sarah cried, her voice growing louder and clearer as she entered the room. "Chelsea, are you okay?"

"She's fine, Sarah," Chase said from behind the curtain. "I think I just scared her when I yelled. Would you mind taking her out of here so I can—"

"Is she okay?" Susan asked.

Goddamn it. Now his mother was in here too? This

was absolutely mortifying.

"Yes, she's fine," Sarah said as she soothed her daughter.

"Chase?" Susan said.

He let out an exasperated sigh. "Yeah?" He then looked to Norah to mouth an apology but found her with her arms tightly wound around her shivering body. He reached his arm out and pulled her to him, wrapping both of his arms around her to keep her warm.

"Did you know there's a truck parked just outside?" Susan said. "I was thinking it might be a handyman you hired to help out around here, but I didn't see him anywhere."

Chase rolled his eyes and Norah let out a short burst of air, covering her mouth quickly with her hand.

"Chase?" Susan asked, slowly. "Is there...?"

"Can everyone just please get out of the bathroom?" Chase asked, adding just enough annoyance to his voice to get his point across.

"Come on, Sarah," Susan said. "Let's take the girls outside to see the horses."

The bathroom door closed and Chase let out a sigh of relief. He pulled back the curtain and grabbed two large towels. Wrapping one around Norah, Chase used the other to wrap around his waist as he stepped out of the tub.

"I can't begin to tell you how sorry I am that all of that just happened," Chase told her as he rested his hands on the upper part of her arms.

Norah sighed. "You're forgiven."

The corner of his mouth turned up as he pulled back to look at her with questioning eyes. "Really? Just like that?"

"Just like that," Norah agreed with a small laugh. But then she slapped at his chest and added, "But don't ever let it happen again."

"I promise," Chase said and kissed the tip of her nose before resting his forehead against hers. "So, what do you say? You wanna hang around here today with me? Keep me company?"

"You've got your family here," she said. "I think you have plenty of company."

"Yeah, but they're going to be busy going through all of this stuff in the house," he told her. "Plus, you know they're out there now wondering who you are. Might as well put their minds at ease."

"I don't know," Norah said with hesitation. "It'd be kind of awkward, don't you think? I mean, they literally just caught us with our pants down."

"Only if you let it be," Chase said. "We're adults and have nothing to be ashamed about. So? Will you stay?"

She seemed to think it over for a moment. "Mmm-okay," she said. "But only because I can't seem to say no to this face." She gripped his chin in her hand and shook his head gently from side to side.

"Really?" Chase said. "I'll have to keep that in mind." He waggled his eyebrows.

"You need to stop," she told him with a laugh and slapped at his arm.

"We'll see if you're still singing that same tune later," Chase said and gave her a mischievous smirk.

CHAPTER TWENTY-FIVE

"Uncle Chase!"

Chase stopped in the middle of the yard as two little girls bolted for him. His face brightened into a smile as he bent down and held his arms out.

"How are my favorite girls doing?" he asked.

They slammed into him, giggling, and Chase fell backwards to the ground taking both of them with him. He let out a playful groan for dramatic effect as the girls squirmed to free themselves from his arms.

"Uncle Chase!" Maddie said, bouncing on her knees as she spoke enthusiastically. "We got to see your horses! We saw a brown one, and a gray one, and then a really small one that was brown and white. And can we ride them?"

He laughed and sat up. "Slow down, Mad," Chase told the little girl.

"That's all they've been able to talk about," Sarah said as she walked over to them. "The whole way here."

"Oh yeah?" Chase asked, looking up to his sister before turning back to his nieces. "Well, we'll just have to see what we can do about that then."

Both girls squealed their delight and ran back to the barn.

"I see that pony is still here," Sarah said. "I guess he stills hates me because I couldn't even get him to come to me."

Chase brushed the dirt and grass off of his clothes as he stood. "He can't see you," he explained. "I found out he's blind now."

He started for the barn and Sarah followed, walking next to him with her arms crossed over her chest.

"That's so sad," she said. "How'd you find out? Did you have a vet come out to look at the horses or something?"

Chase shook his head. "Norah told me."

Sarah gave Chase a knowing smirk and nudged him with her elbow. "Your shower partner?"

Shoving her back playfully, Chase stopped a few feet away from the barn and turned to look at his sister.

"She's going to stick around today," he said. "I think it'd be nice if you all met and got to know one another. So, just do me a favor, please, and be nice."

"I'm always nice," Sarah said seeming a little put off by his comment.

"You are," he said. "But just don't go bombarding her with ten million questions and doing your interrogation thing." Looking to the house, Chase brought his hand up and rubbed the back of his neck before looking back to Sarah. "Things are… new between us, and I don't want you to scare her off."

"New?" Sarah asked with questioning eyes. "Like how new?"

"Like last night new," Chase told her.

"Oh," Sarah said. "Oh. *Oh* God. Okay, I didn't need to know that." She shook her head and exhaled softly. "All right, I'll back off with the questions."

"Thanks," he said just as Maddie came running from the barn.

"Come on, Uncle Chase!" She grabbed his hand and pulled hard, causing her feet to skid against the ground.

Chase chuckled. "Okay, okay. Let's go."

Norah was standing by the kitchen sink, staring out the window as she watched Chase interact with his sister and his nieces. Smiling, she brought her cup of coffee to her lips and took a long sip.

"So you must be the owner of that truck out there."

Startled, Norah jumped and turned quickly, causing the hot liquid to slosh over the edge of the cup. "Shit," she mumbled and set the cup in the sink as she wiped her hand clean with the dish towel.

"I'm sorry, sweetie," Chase's mother said. "I didn't mean to scare you. I thought you heard me come in the room." She carefully set the box she'd been carrying onto the kitchen table.

"No, it's okay," Norah said and placed the towel back on the counter. "And yes, that's my truck. I'm Norah McKade." She smiled and extended her hand across the kitchen table to Chase's mother.

"Susan O'Donnell," the older woman replied, shaking Norah's hand. She then opened the lid of the cardboard box and began sorting through the various items, pulling out old knick-knacks and photo albums. "I take it you're not a handyman?" Susan looked up from her sorting to give Norah a playful smirk.

Norah let out a small laugh. "No, ma'am, I'm not. But I have helped Chase with a few things around here. We just finished painting the outside of the house yesterday."

"Well, you all have done a fine job of fixing the place up," Susan said. "I couldn't believe how bad it looked in the pictures Chase emailed me."

"I know what you mean," Norah said. "I guess it all just became too much for Eli to take care of. Especially in the end."

Susan looked to Norah and raised an eyebrow. "You knew my uncle?"

"Yes, ma'am," Norah said. "My family owns the ranch next door. I knew him and Miss Mary my whole life."

The back door opened just then and Sarah walked in.

"Well the girls are in their glory right now," she said, crossing the room to stand next to her mother. "Chase just became the uncle of the century. I'm going to have a time of it getting them off of that horse."

Susan smiled and looked over to Norah. "Norah this is Chase's sister Sarah. Sarah, this is Chase's...well, Norah." She laughed.

"It's nice to meet you, Norah," Sarah said with a sweet smile.

"You too," Norah replied, feeling her nerves ease a bit.

Facing his mother and sister after the shower incident was something she had really wanted to avoid for two main reasons. One, it was completely embarrassing. And two, she felt that it gave the wrong impression of her. She really didn't want them to think she was just some floozy who was shackin' up with Chase while he was in town.

But Susan and Sarah didn't seem to think that. At all. In fact, the shower incident seemed a thing of the past or like it had never even happened in the first place. It appeared that she'd been given a clean slate to start fresh with them, and she was going to take it.

"Did you all want something to drink while you go through these boxes?" Norah asked, stepping forward and placing her hands on the back of one of the kitchen chairs. "I think Chase might have some sweet tea in the fridge."

"Oh, that would be lovely," Susan said. "Why don't you pour yourself a glass and join us? Give us some time to get to know one another."

"Sure," Norah said as she made her way over to the cabinet and pulled out three glasses. She then stepped over to the fridge and poured some tea for each of them before sitting at the table across from Chase's mother and sister and sliding them their drinks. "So what brings you all to Buford? Just stopping by to see Chase?" She took a small sip from her glass.

"Yes and no," Sarah said, thanking Norah for the tea. "He called me a few weeks ago about coming out to go through all of our great-aunt and great-uncle's belongings before he got rid of it all in an estate sale. I meant to come here sooner, but I just couldn't fit it into our schedule." She nodded sideways to Susan.

"I've been booked with wedding after wedding," Susan said with a soft sigh. "But I guess I shouldn't complain because it keeps me in business."

"Oh, yeah," Norah said. "Chase told me you own a flower shop."

"He did, did he?" Susan asked with a smile. "I wish I could say I know more about you, but Chase has been pretty tight lipped about things since he's been here. Tell me, what do you do for a living, Norah?"

Hmm? So Chase hadn't mentioned anything to his family about her at all? At first she was a little offended. But then she realized that up until last night all she and Chase were just friends, so there was really nothing to tell his family about.

"I work on my family's ranch, and I also bartend at the local bar," Norah said to Susan, tucking her hair behind her ear before resting her elbows on the table.

"Busy gal," Susan said. "And you still found time to help my son?"

With a small laugh, Norah nodded her head. "Yes,

ma'am."

"So do you all spend a lot of time together?" Susan looked to Norah then turned her attention to an old photo album, flipping open the cover and running her fingers over the black and white pictures.

"Oh look," Sarah said, leaning over Susan's arm and pointing to one of the photos. "Isn't that you?"

"Yes, it is," Susan said. "And look there's your Uncle Ted and your Aunt Lynn. Oh, we used to have so much fun coming here when we were kids. Did I ever tell you about the time…"

As Susan went on to share her childhood memories, Norah and Sarah caught each other's eye and Sarah gave Norah a wink along with a half smile.

Norah returned Sarah's smile, a part of her thankful that his sister had put an end to the conversation that was quickly becoming all about her and Chase. She didn't mind answering Chase's mother's questions, but she knew—just *knew*—that the dreaded *what's your relationship with my son?* question was coming, and Norah didn't have an answer for that.

Chase bounced through the back door of the house with Chelsea perched on his back while Maddie ran past him to her mother.

"Mom! Can we get a horse?" Maddie asked, clasping her hands in front of her as she hopped in place.

Sarah shot Chase a look.

"Don't give me the stink eye," he said as he removed Chelsea's arms from around his neck and helped the little girl down. "I told them no, but they kept asking. I finally just told them to talk to you."

Sarah smiled and rolled her eyes at Chase before she let out a sigh and turned to her daughter. "Maddie, sweetie, we can't get a horse."

"Oh, *please*," Maddie begged. "It can stay in the backyard and sleep in the garage."

Chase, Susan, and Norah laughed while Sarah gave her young daughter a gentle smile. "That sounds like a nice plan, sweetie, but we can't keep a horse at our house. We just don't have room for it."

"It can stay here at Uncle Chase's house then," Maddie suggested. "And we can come visit it all the time and ride it."

"Maddie," Sarah said, giving the young girl a look that was meant to silence her and put an end to the conversation. "No."

"Okay, well if it can't stay here than maybe it can stay at Uncle Chase's girlfriend's house," Maddie said. "He said she has lots of horses."

Three pairs of eyes darted to look at Chase. He felt as though he'd just been accused of a horrible crime or something.

"*Good* friend," Chase corrected his niece. "I said good friend."

He looked around the room to each of the women.

Sarah's lips twisted in amusement as she shook her head before she leaned in to listen to something Chelsea wanted to tell her.

Susan was beaming. The hopeful look on her face made it easy for Chase to know exactly what she was thinking: marriage and grandbabies.

And then there was Norah. She was staring back at him with that sweet yet sexy expression on her face that made his insides jump.

"Who's hungry?" Chase asked, slapping his hands

together as he quickly changed the subject and walked over to the fridge. "I can throw together some sandwiches. You all okay with turkey and cheese?"

He pulled out all the ingredients and set them on the counter as Norah came to stand next to him.

"Here," she said and reached for the bread, her fingertips grazing his hand as she took it away from him. "Let me help you."

Warmth radiated the spot on his hand she'd just touched and traveled through his body. His pulse quickened. Jesus. She hadn't even remotely done anything sexual, but here he was all hot and bothered from just her being in close proximity to him.

He quietly cleared his throat. "Thanks."

As the little girls jibber-jabbered in the background, Chase and Norah worked in unison.

"So," Norah said quietly. "I'm just a *good friend*, huh?"

He turned to look at her and found her giving him a sexy sideways smirk.

"No," Chase told her, lowering his voice to almost a whisper. "But what was I supposed to say to a nosey seven-year-old?"

"True," Norah said with a nod. She reached for the turkey and slapped a few pieces on the bread.

"Hey," Chase said.

She turned her head to look at him again; her blue eyes caught the sunlight shining through the window and gleamed.

"You know you're more than that, right?" Chase told her. He cocked his head to the side slightly and grinned. "You always have been."

And then he leaned in and tenderly pressed his lips to hers.

"Uncle Chase is kissin' his girlfriend!" Maddie shouted.

Chase pulled away from Norah and looked to his niece.

"All right, loud mouth," Chase said as he started for Maddie. "You asked for it."

The little girl squealed and ran as Chase went after her. It didn't take long for him to catch up to her. He swooped her into his arms and swung her around in a circle as her laughter trickled into the air.

"I'm getting dizzy," Maddie said breathlessly.

Chase laughed and set her down, holding her steady as she swayed a bit.

"Me next! Me next!" Chelsea pleaded and tugged on Chase's arm for him to lift her up.

He laughed again and happened to look up to see Norah staring at him, wearing a smile that warmed him to the core. Standing in the kitchen there with his sister and his mother, Norah looked right where she belonged—like part of the family.

A younger Chase would've been scared to death at a sight like that. He'd never considered himself a serious relationship kind of guy. Sure, he'd been in love before— or at least told himself he had—but he'd never let things go too far. The thought of settling down had never truly appealed to him, but maybe that was just because he'd never really found anyone he could see having a future with.

As he watched Norah interact with his mother and sister, his heart swelled with adoration and all of those old hesitations about love and forever slowly began to fade away.

CHAPTER TWENTY-SIX

"That's the last of them," Chase said, placing the last box in the back and closing the hatch of his sister's massive Suburban. He slapped his hand twice on the side of the vehicle and made his way over to the driver's side door.

"Thanks, Chase," Sarah said through the open window.

He nodded and peaked into the back seat, smiling when he saw both of his nieces' heads leaning against their windows.

"Out already, huh?" he said.

"Thank God," Sarah replied. "It'll be a peaceful drive home."

He laughed softly. "Well, I won't hold you up. Drive safe and shoot me a text or give me a call when you get there."

"I will," Sarah said.

"Chase, sweetie," his mother called from the passenger seat and waved him over to her side.

Walking around the hood of the SUV, Chase made his way over to Susan and rested his hand on the side mirror. "Yeah, Mom?"

"I just have to know," Susan said. "Are you dating that girl?"

"Mom," Sarah chided from the driver's seat.

"Don't you 'Mom' me," Susan said to Sarah in a similar tone. "You distracted me earlier so I couldn't ask, but now I'm going to, so hush."

Sarah held her hands up in defeat and gave Chase an apologetic smirk. "You're on your own, little brother."

"Well?" Susan prompted and looked back to Chase.

"Maybe I am," Chase teased then shot his mother a mischievous grin. "And maybe I'm not. That's for me to know."

Susan swatted at his arm. "Since I can't get a straight answer from anyone around here I'm just going to say this. Norah seems like a sweet girl and if you aren't dating her you should be. There, I've said my peace and now we can go."

"Duly noted, Mother," Chase said and removed his hand from the side mirror. "Drive safe, Sarah. I'll talk to you all soon."

Norah was standing by the front porch as Chase walked away from Sarah's SUV, waving as goodbyes were called out to her.

"That wasn't so bad, was it?" Chase asked as he walked up to Norah and stood behind her, resting a hand on her hip as he too waved goodbye.

"For being surprised? Yeah, I'd say it went pretty well," Norah said and leaned back against Chase's chest.

"They really liked you," he told her, wrapping both of his arms around her mid-section and pulling her close. He kissed her hair.

"I like them too," Norah said and rested her hands on his arms. "Your nieces are adorable. It's sweet how they think the world of you."

His kisses traveled down to her neck. "I missed you today," he said in a low voice against her skin.

She laughed. "I've been here with you all day."

"You know what I mean," he said. "Stay here with me."

He gently sucked on the tender slope where her neck met her shoulder, smiling when she shuddered and sighed. God he loved that he'd figured that out so quickly.

"Chase," Norah said, a hint of hesitation in her voice. "I'd love to but I should go home tonight. Plus, I don't have a change of clothes or anything."

Keeping her body close to his, Chase spun her around in his arms to face him. "Who said anything about needing clothes?"

With that, Chase bent down and swept her off her feet, cradling her to him as he carried her into the house.

"Where on God's green earth have you been?"

Norah stopped the brush against her horse's coat and looked behind her to see Luke entering the barn, wearing a stern look on his face that said she was in major trouble.

"Around," she answered him coolly and returned her attention to her horse.

"Don't cop an attitude with me, Norah," Luke said and walked over to her. "Where the hell have you been? You didn't show up at the ranch at all yesterday and didn't even answer your phone when Zane and I tried calling you."

"Take it easy, Luke," Norah said. "My battery died so I didn't see any of your missed calls until this morning." Setting the brush on the ledge of the stall, she reached for the hoof pick and walked back over to her horse.

"Well, that explains part of it," Luke said, crossing his arms over his puffed up chest. "But it still doesn't tell me where you were."

Norah scraped the pick against the bottom of her horse's hoof and looked up to Luke, narrowing her eyes as she quickly became agitated.

"No offense, but it's really none of your business where I was or what I was doing." She let go of the

Palomino's hoof and stood as she gave the animal a few gentle pats and praises.

"It becomes my business when you play a disappearing act like that," Luke spat out. "Jesus Christ, Norah, you had Zane and me worried sick, not to mention Mom and Andi as well. You've never just not showed up and not answered your phone. We all thought the worst."

Norah gave Luke an incredulous glare. "That's a bit dramatic, don't you think?" she said. "It was one day. And, in case you couldn't tell, I'm fine." She walked away from him and grabbed her saddle, blanket, and bridle from the tack room.

"Where do you think you're going?" Luke asked.

After adjusting the blanket on her horse's back, Norah lifted the saddle onto it and shifted it into place. "I'm taking Cheyenne out for a ride. I haven't ridden her in a few days, and she needs to stretch her legs."

"Well we're not done here," Luke said. He moved closer to her and placed his hand over hers to stop her from doing anything else.

"Umm," Norah said, snatching her hand from underneath his. "I think we are."

She took in a deep breath as she glared at her brother. The man had fully succeeded in pissing her off this morning, and she'd been in such a good mood too. Keeping an icy stare fixed on Luke, Norah heard Zane enter the barn but didn't turn to look at him.

"What's going on with you two?" Zane asked, fiddling with something in his hands as he walked to the tack room.

"Your sister thinks it's okay to disappear for over a day and not tell anyone where she's been or what's she's been up to," Luke said to Zane.

"And *your* brother," Norah countered, "thinks

everything is his business when it's not."

Zane walked out of the tack room and expelled a heavy sigh. "Okay, you two, put the gloves down and get back to your corners."

Luke backed away, bringing him side by side with Zane.

Norah shot him a nasty look before adjusting her saddle once more and then tightening the cinch to keep it in place.

"Look, Norah," Zane said. "I know you like your privacy and all, but I'm going to have to side with Luke on this one."

She paused for a moment before bending down to the hay bale and picking up her bridle.

"Why am I not surprised?" she muttered.

"I'm just sayin'," Zane told her. "This isn't like you."

She could feel both of their eyes on her back as she slid the bridle onto her horse's head. Liquid heat pulsed through her veins as the rage inside her grew until her fingers trembled. This over-protective bullshit was getting old and was doing a number on her nerves right now. The need to escape quickly consumed her. She took hold of Cheyenne's reins and began to walk the horse from the barn, without sparing either of her brothers a single look.

"Norah," Zane said just as Luke said, "You get back here, young lady, and tell us what the hell is going on with you."

Young lady? Oh hell no.

Keeping the reins in her one hand, Norah turned and walked back over to Luke, poking at his chest with her index finger.

"May I remind you that you are two years older than me," she said to Luke through gritted teeth. "And you *are not* my father, so stop acting like it. I don't need him, and I certainly don't need you keeping tabs on me and my whereabouts. Butt. Out."

She stepped away, taking a deep breath as she looked to Zane.

"Both of you."

Not wanting to give them a chance to speak, Norah quickly turned and made her way from the barn. Once she was in the yard, she looped the reins over her horse's head, gripped the saddle horn and swung herself up onto the animal's back. With a gentle nudge of her heels and a click of her tongue, the horse kicked up into a smooth canter as they made their way away from the barn, away from the yard, and—most of all—away from her brothers.

The night air held a faint chill as Chase stepped out of his SUV and shut the door behind him. He started to make his way across the parking lot towards the Rusty Spur but paused when his cell phone rang.

"Hey, Dad," Chase said after glancing at the caller ID and placing the phone to his ear.

"Why haven't you sent me the designs yet for The Channing Group?" Darren demanded.

What? No *Hi, how are you, son?* Chase let out a silent scoff and rolled his eyes. *Typical.*

"I have a few more things to do and then it'll be ready," Chase answered his father. "What's the rush? You'll have it way before it's due."

"The rush is," Darren said, his voice growing thick with what sounded an awful lot like irritation, "that The Channing Group has been very impressed with what we've done so far. They're so impressed that they've spread the word to Michael and Michaels."

Chase hadn't really been paying much attention to the conversation. His focus was more on the door of the bar and seeing Norah. But at the mention of their biggest potential client ever, Chase directed all of his attention back to the phone call with his father.

"Does that mean what I think it means?" he asked as his heart thumped with excitement and anticipation.

"It means," Darren said, "get your ass back to Dallas."

Norah was behind the counter when Chase entered the bar. A sense of calm swam over her at just the sight of him, which was much needed after her run-in with her brothers earlier in the day.

"Hey, you," she said as he walked over and popped a hip on a barstool.

"Hey," he said back, his face beaming with a bright smile that left her wondering what his good mood was all about.

"Is that smile just for me?" she asked him with a soft grin, crossing her arms over the counter and leaning towards him slightly. "Or is there something else going on that's got you all excited?"

He let out a small, soft laugh. "Both," he told her and nodded his head sideways towards an unoccupied corner of the bar. "Got a second to talk?"

"Sure," she said and then told the new girl Red had hired that she'd be back in a few minutes.

Chase held his hand out for her as she made her way from behind the bar. She accepted it and walked with him over to the far wall with the hallway that led to the restrooms.

"What's going on?" Norah asked.

Chase stopped and turned to face her, reaching for her other hand. "First," he said and drew her to him, kissing her soft and slow.

"Mmm," she said, smiling against his mouth. "What's second?"

Pulling away from her slightly, Chase stroked his thumbs against the back of her hands as he looked at her. "I have some pretty incredible news."

"Well, let's hear it," Norah said, feeding off of his excitement and giving his hands a gentle squeeze.

"Okay," he said and let out a calming breath before he began. "There's this real estate developer back in Dallas that my father has been trying to get in with for years, and it looks as though he finally got it."

"That's great, Chase!"

"This is so big, Norah," Chase told her. "I mean, this company is constantly putting up new buildings all around the city. If we land them as a client? *God.* Can you just imagine the things it will do for my dad's firm?"

"*And* you," Norah added. "You'll be the one doing all the designs, right?"

He nodded slightly and shrugged. "Well, yeah. There are two other guys in the firm but I'll most likely be the one working one on one with the Michaels'."

"The Michaels'?" Norah asked.

"The potential clients," Chase explained. "Jerry Michaels and his partner Michael... Michael and Michaels. I've met Jerry before, but I've never met his partner."

Norah gave Chase a sweet smile. "I'm so happy for you."

Removing her hands from his, Norah circled her arms around Chase's waist and gave him a gentle hug. She felt his hands rest on her back as she laid her head against his chest.

"Thanks, Norah," Chase said, pressing his lips to her hair and tightening his hold on her. "There's one more thing I need to tell you, though."

"Hmm?" Norah asked, loving how comforted she felt from Chase's tender embrace. And after the day she'd had she needed a whole lot of comforting. Hell, who was she kidding? What she needed was a whole lot of Chase O'Donnell.

She was just about to tell him that too, or at least make it very clear to him, but as Chase spoke she felt her heart tighten in her chest.

CHAPTER TWENTY-SEVEN

Chase could feel the subtle tense of her body the second he told her he was leaving town.

She slowly lifted her head from his chest and leaned her head back to look up to him. Her eyes studied him with unspoken questions.

"I know that look," Chase told her, lifting his hand to stroke his fingers gently along the side of her face. He rested his palm on her neck with his thumb beneath the hollow point of her ear.

Norah closed her eyes for a moment as she brought her hand up to rest over his, leaning into him as she stroked his wrist.

"I knew you'd eventually leave," Norah said, opening her eyes to look at him before turning them to the floor. "I guess I'm just a little shocked that you're leaving sooner than expected."

"Hey," he said.

She returned her eyes to his.

"This doesn't change anything," he told her. "I'm not leaving for a few days. Even then, I'll only be gone for about a week or so."

"Oh my gosh," she said and let out a soft laugh followed by a sigh. "You made it sound like you were leaving for good."

He smiled and kissed the tip of her nose. "I'll be back before you know it. There's still a bunch of stuff I have to do around the ranch before..." He paused.

"Before you move back to Dallas permanently," Norah said softly, finishing his sentence for him.

He stroked his thumb against her skin as he gazed into her eyes. Bending his head down, he rested his forehead against hers.

"Let's not talk about that right now," Chase suggested. "Let's talk about how we're going to spend the next few days."

"What'd you have in mind?"

He slowly slid his hand from the side of her neck, down to her waist, and to the small of her back before bringing her closer to him.

"I could think of a few things," he told her, deepening his voice into a sexy whisper as he pressed his lips to hers.

"Mmm," Norah replied. "I like what you're thinking."

He smiled and pulled away to look at her. "You working tomorrow night?"

"Unfortunately, I am," she said, wrinkling her nose before giving him a slight pout.

"Okay," Chase said. "Can I steal you for a few hours tomorrow afternoon then?"

She seemed to ponder that for a moment before smiling and replying with, "I think I could squeeze you in."

"Good," Chase said and kissed her once more. "I'll swing by your place and pick you up around two."

Norah was rummaging through her closet looking for a shirt to put on when a knock sounded from her front door. She quickly made her way over to the window and pulled the curtain back slightly. Chase's silver Chevy Tahoe sat in her driveway, looking pristine and shiny as it gleamed in the sunlight. Dropping her hold on the curtain, Norah walked from her bedroom and down the hall to the living room.

Chase knocked again.

"I'm coming," she called out. Reaching for the deadbolt, Norah unlocked both that and the lock on the knob before opening the door to a wide-eyed Chase.

"What's wrong?" she asked, puzzled by his expression.

"Do you always answer the door like that?" he asked and gestured to her half naked upper body.

She glanced down and laughed.

"No." Covering her white lacey bra with her arm, Norah stepped aside so Chase could come in.

"No need to cover up on my behalf," he told her and shut the door behind him before placing a hand on her hip and drawing her to him.

Resting her arms on his biceps, Norah leaned back to look at him with a teasing grin. "Well, if someone had told me where we were going, I would be ready by now."

The corner of his mouth lifted as he moved his hands to stroke her back.

Her skin tingled beneath his touch.

"Jeans and a t-shirt are fine," he said. "Whatever you're most comfortable in."

She raised an eyebrow. "Okay," she told him with uncertainty and backed herself away from his embrace.

As she walked away, she felt Chase's hand slap against her bottom.

"Oh!" She stopped, placing her hand over the sharp sting as she turned back to look at him.

"Hurry up before I change my mind about our plans," Chase told her with a sexy, wicked grin.

Smiling and shaking her head, Norah turned and continued to her bedroom.

"This is a nice place," she heard Chase say from the other room. "You been here long?"

After flipping through the shirts in her closet, Norah walked over to her dresser and pulled out a simple white v-neck t-shirt.

"Not quite a year," she answered him, slipping into the shirt and tucking the front of it into her jeans. "I'd like to buy my own place eventually, but for now this'll do. The rent is good and it gets me away from the ranch."

After adjusting her belt, putting on her boots, and running her fingers through her hair, Norah gave herself one final glance in the mirror and made her way out to Chase.

"I thought you liked your family's ranch?" Chase asked with his back turned to her as he scanned the framed pictures hanging on the wall.

"I do, but I like my privacy too," she said. "And I never got much of that when I lived at my mom's."

"Privacy *is* a good thing to have," Chase said with a grin as he turned to look at her. His eyes glanced over her from head to toe. "You look great."

"Thanks." She took the corner of her bottom lip between her teeth. "You ready to go?"

"We better," Chase said, taking in a deep breath as he held her hand and walked with her to the door. "Because I keep thinking of what's under that shirt, and if we don't leave now, I don't think we'll be leaving at all."

As Chase parallel parked his SUV, Norah stared out the passenger window to the strip of storefronts. Chase still hadn't dished on where they were going and hell if she could figure it out. There was nothing here but a law office, a vintage clothing store, a pawn shop, and…

Her eyes stopped on the store they were parked in front of. The large display windows were full of gorgeous ceramics, varying in all shapes, sizes, and colors. A sign in the corner of the window caught her attention and she read it silently with questioning eyes.

"Are you taking me to a pottery class?" she asked, turning to Chase with a raised eyebrow as she thumbed in the direction of the store.

"What?" Chase asked, sounding thoroughly confused by her question as he shifted the vehicle into park and turned off the ignition. He leaned over her to look out the window and let out a soft laugh. "No, that's not what we're doing." Moving back to his side, he reached for his door handle and pushed the door open.

Norah started to do the same on her side but stopped when Chase said, "No, no, wait a sec."

She dropped her hold on the handle and sat patiently as Chase got out and rounded the front of his SUV to her. With a smile, Chase opened her door and reached for her hand.

"Wow," Norah said, stepping onto the concrete sidewalk as Chase closed the door behind her. "Pulls chairs out *and* opens doors? Such a gentleman, you are."

He intertwined his fingers with hers as they began to walk.

"I try," he said and gave her hand a gentle squeeze.

She leaned into him and took in her surroundings as they strolled through town. "I haven't been here in ages," she said.

"Really?" Chase replied. "Glenburn's only an hour away from Buford."

"I know, but I just never have a reason to come here," she told him. "When my brothers and I go to rodeos we normally pass through, but it's been a while since we've done one of those."

"You rodeo?"

"Occasionally," she said. "Not so much anymore because I'm just so busy. But yeah, I've got one of the fastest barrel racing horses in the county."

"Brag much?" Chase teased.

"Shut up," Norah replied and playfully slapped his arm with her unoccupied hand. "She is. I'll have to show you sometime."

He stopped and pulled her around to face him.

"I'd like to see that," he told her, lowering his voice to a sexy rasp.

Her heart did a hop-skip-jump as he looked at her with want pooling in his eyes. But it wasn't just want showing there; it was also something more that she couldn't quite read. Desire? Lust? A different L word, maybe?

No. Not love. It was too soon for love. Way too soon. They'd known each other for less than a month and been intimate for less than a week. So…no. It could definitely not be love shining behind those sexy green eyes of his.

"Have you figured it out yet?" Chase asked, the corner of his mouth curling up into a grin that made her knees go weak.

Could he read her mind? Had he known that she'd been standing here arguing with herself over whether or not he was in love with her?

But then Chase moved slightly and glanced back to the building they were standing in front of. Norah looked around him and smiled.

"A movie," she said, feeling relieved that Chase hadn't been able to read her thoughts after all.

"I know it's not the most extravagant or original date

idea," Chase said, looking back to her and sliding his hands to her hips. "But it's a classic."

Standing on her tiptoes, Norah rested her arms over Chase's shoulders, crossed her wrists just behind his head and pressed her lips gently to his. "I love it," she said, pulling back to look at him. "What are we seeing?"

"Whatever you want?" Chase said and turned with her to view the list of movies being played.

"Whatever I want, huh?" Norah asked playfully. "How about...that one?" She pointed to one of the action films. The actor on the poster held an intense stare as he leaned casually against the hood of an electric blue sports car.

"I'm good with that," Chase said. "You want anything to snack on?"

"Ooh, can I get one of those giant tubs of popcorn with tons of butter?"

"That depends," Chase said with a soft chuckle. "You plannin' on sharing?"

She pursed her lips. "I guess I could," she teased. "And can we get one of those really embarrassingly big cups of that slushy drink that leaves your mouth all blue?"

"Sure." He laughed. "Anything else?"

"Nah I think I'm good," Norah told him with a nonchalant tone. "I don't want you to think I'm a pig or anything."

His head fell back slightly as he laughed again, and she joined him this time as they made their way inside the building.

Almost two hours later, Norah and Chase made their way out of the dark theater and into the bright light of the late afternoon sun.

"That was fun," Norah said, bringing her unoccupied hand up to tuck her hair behind her ear. "I haven't seen a movie in forever."

"Same here," Chase said and took a sip of the slush drink. "So, what do you feel like doing now?"

As they walked hand in hand down the sidewalk towards Chase's SUV, Norah pulled her cell phone from her purse and checked the time.

"Well, it's five o'clock, and it takes us an hour to get home." She blew out a soft breath of air. "And I've got to be to work at seven, so…"

"So home it is," Chase said.

"I'm sorry," Norah told him.

"Don't be," Chase said and let go of her hand so he could unlock his SUV. "It's not like I can't see you after work or anything."

She let out a short laugh. "At three a.m.?"

"Why not?" he asked with a grin as he reached for her door. "That never stopped us before."

Shaking her head slightly, Norah stepped around him to enter the vehicle. "You're a mess."

"Hey Norah, wait a second."

With her hand resting on the door and one foot on the running board, Norah turned to look at Chase.

He'd grown serious all of a sudden.

"What's the matter?" she asked, staring into his green eyes as she tried to figure him out.

He took in a breath and stepped towards her. "If I were to ask you a question right now, how honest would you be with me?"

"That depends on the question," she told him, giving him a soft, teasing smile.

He grinned. Closing the short distance between them,

Chase took her hand in his and looked down to it as he stroked his thumb against the back of her fingers. When his eyes found hers she was instantly reminded of the look they shared earlier as they stood outside of the movie theater.

Maybe Chase *did* love her.

Her heart hammered inside her chest as she thought about that. A flood of emotions ran through her, clouding her mind and making it hard to think straight.

The past few weeks with Chase had been amazing, more amazing than she'd ever dreamed.

Okay, well maybe not more amazing than she'd ever dreamed because she'd had some pretty incredible dreams involving Chase O'Donnell. But still…

She couldn't deny that there was more between them than friendship and an intense sexual attraction for one another. There was something deeper—deeper than companionship, deeper than desire, lust, and need. And then she realized…

Maybe *she* loved Chase.

She barely had a chance to let the realization sink in when Chase moved even closer to her and let go of her hand so he could rest his on her hip. Her breath caught in her throat.

Oh Jesus.

"What color is my tongue?"

She drew back from him and stared at him in bewilderment. "What?" she asked sharply.

"My tongue," Chase said. "What color is it?" He stuck it out for her to see.

She shook her head and blinked her eyes a few times. "Umm, blue."

"Thought so," Chase said with a sly grin. "Yours is too." He took another sip of the drink. Air slurped through the straw as he finished the last few drops.

Cocking her head to the side, Norah gave him a baffled look. "Is that it?"

"Yeah," Chase answered her and tossed the large cup in a trash can that was bolted to the sidewalk a few feet away from them. "Why? What'd you think I was going to ask?"

"I didn't know what to think," she said and gently shoved at his chest. "You made it sound like you had a serious question and got me all worried for nothing."

"I'm sorry," he said with a soft laugh. "I was just messing around. Forgive me?"

She allowed him to wrap his arms around her waist and pull her close to his body.

"You're lucky I like you so much," she told him. "But just remember this, O'Donnell...you get me all worried for nothing like that again and your tongue won't be the only part of your body that's blue."

He laughed again and tugged her closer. "Point taken," he said and dipped his head to kiss her.

She gave into him, kissing him as thoroughly as he was kissing her. And in that moment, she realized that even though he hadn't asked for her heart, she'd gone and given it to him anyway.

CHAPTER TWENTY-EIGHT

The next evening Chase sat in his kitchen with his laptop perched on the table in front of him. He was just typing the last few words of an email addressed to his father when the familiar sound of gravel crunching beneath tires caught his attention. Glancing at the time on his laptop screen, Chase quickly worked to finish his email and added the necessary attachments.

"Knock, knock," Norah said as she slowly pushed the door open and peered inside.

"Hey," Chase said, looking back to her briefly before returning his attention to his laptop screen. "Come on in. I'm almost done."

He heard the door shut softly and then a few seconds later felt Norah's hand rest lightly on his shoulder. After pressing the send button, Chase closed his laptop and turned slightly to pull Norah onto his lap. She sat down with her legs lying across his thighs and brought her hand up to his face, running her fingertips along the stubble on his jaw.

"You ready to go?" she asked.

"I guess I am," Chase answered her. "Where are we going?"

"You'll see," Norah said and gave him a quick kiss before standing up from his lap.

He took her outstretched hand and walked with her outside to her truck.

The sun was hanging low in the sky, casting a golden glow upon the land, as Chase opened Norah's door for her and then made his way around to the passenger side. He breathed in deep the second he was seated and closed the door.

"Is that what I think it is?" Chase asked, eyeing the picnic basket on the seat next to him. His mouth started to water as the truck cab quickly filled with the delicious aroma of fried chicken.

"It might be," Norah teased and swatted his hand as he tried to peek inside. "No cheating. You have to wait." She smiled as she shifted her truck into gear and then pulled out of his driveway.

A short while later, Norah turned down a grassy lane surrounded by trees on both sides. The truck bumped along the uneven land for a few minutes before they emerged from the trees and into a clearing with a small pond. The last rays of sunlight danced along the water as Norah parked her truck near the water's edge.

"We're here," she announced and removed her keys from the ignition. "Would you help me out by grabbing that quilt and setting it out on the grass?"

"Sure," Chase said, picking up the patchwork quilt that had been beneath the picnic basket. He stepped out of the truck and made his way around to the front, unfolding the quilt as he walked. Holding onto the edges of the fabric, Chase shook it into the air and let it gracefully settle onto the grass.

"Thank you," Norah said, sitting down with the picnic basket and opening the lid.

"So do I finally get to know what's in there now?" Chase asked as he joined her.

The corner of her mouth lifted as she pulled out the container of fried chicken and shook it at him. "You've got a good nose, O'Donnell."

He returned her smile. "Wasn't that hard to guess," he said. "But I bet you I can really impress you by saying that I know it's your Aunt Belle's fried chicken."

"You're partially right," Norah told him as she pulled potato salad and biscuits from the basket. "It's her recipe, but I made it."

He'd been helping her set the items on the blanket, but he stopped and just stared at her.

"What?" she asked, setting a paper plate in front of him with real silverware instead of the plastic stuff. "What's that look for?"

"You cooked for me?" Chase asked. The weirdest sensation filled his entire body, making him feel lighter than air but completely grounded at the same time. It seemed silly to feel like that over such a simple gesture, but it was the thought that went behind it that made it so special. He couldn't think of a time in the past when any of his exes had put an effort into doing something *just* for him. It was always about what they wanted to do, where they wanted to go, and so on and so on.

Boy, he really knew how to pick 'em.

"Yeah," Norah answered him, confusion and concern growing on her face as she looked at him. "Should I not have?"

"No," Chase said and shook his head. "I mean yes." He let out a sigh. "What I'm trying to say is…thank you. This was a really nice idea, and I love that you cooked for me."

When a soft smile spread across her face, Chase felt his heart melt. God he loved this woman.

There. He'd finally admitted it, to himself. He didn't just like Norah McKade; he freaking loved her. And he didn't give a shit if it was too soon to feel that way. Now that he'd owned up to his feelings, the strong urge to share it with her was making itself present. But for some reason, telling her seemed like a really bad idea. Maybe *he* didn't give a shit about falling in love so soon, but maybe *she* did, and he really didn't want to scare her off by pushing things on her that she wasn't ready to deal with.

After they'd finished eating their meal, Chase helped Norah clean up then leaned back against the quilt on his elbow, patting the space next to him for Norah to join him.

"Hold my spot," she said as she stood up from the quilt and made her way over to the truck. A few moments later she came back with a bottle of wine and two plastic cups. "Nothing like a bottle of cheap wine to help set the mood." She laughed.

Sitting up, Chase smiled and reached for the wine, letting out a soft chuckle when he noticed the screw on top.

"Don't make fun." She shoved at his shoulder.

"I'm not. I'm not," Chase said and removed the top from the bottle. He poured them each a generous serving and handed one of the cups to Norah.

She sat in front of him and straightened her shoulders as she held her cup out to him. "Here's to the past, the present, and the future," she said. "The last four weeks with you have been the best I've had in a really long time. You're an incredible person, Chase, and I'm really glad I met you. And as for the future…" She paused and fidgeted with her cup. "I hope things go well with your meeting with Michael and Michaels. I'd wish you luck but you don't need it."

The sun had now disappeared behind the horizon line, leaving the sky in a vast array of pastels all blended together into one unforgettable sunset.

Chase held onto Norah's gaze. "And what about the

present?"

She stared back at him for what seemed like a really long time. "I wish it would never end."

With a soft smile, Chase tipped his cup against hers and took a sip. He then took his cup, along with Norah's, and set them both on the ground before pulling Norah into his arms and lying back on the quilt with her. The crickets started in with their nighttime chorus and a few frogs chimed in as the sky slowly gave way to darkness.

"Can I ask you something?" Norah said, snuggling closer to Chase and resting her head against his shoulder.

He brought his hand up and ran his fingers along her blond waves. "Sure."

"Did you always want to be an architect?" she asked.

"Not always," Chase told her. "For a while I was really set on becoming a space cowboy."

He let out a small laugh when she poked at his side.

"All right, smarty pants," she said. "Let me rephrase my question then. How did you know you wanted to become an architect?"

"I didn't really," Chase answered her. "It was kind of decided for me."

He felt her shift and moved his eyes to watch her roll to her side and rest her head in her hand with her elbow against the quilt.

"You didn't want to be one?"

"It's not that," Chase said. "Don't get me wrong I like what I do, but I don't think it's what I would've chosen."

"Well, if you weren't an architect," Norah said. "What would you want to do?"

"Honestly?" Chase said, raising an eyebrow to her before resting his head against the blanket and looking up to the starlit sky. "A part of me always wanted to own a ranch. I loved coming out to my great-uncle's place and looked forward to visiting every year. He was always so proud of his work, and I respected that about him because he worked his butt off for everything. No matter how long the day had been or what had transpired throughout the day, he would always tell me that it was worth it and he wouldn't trade it in for any other lifestyle. I think it was seeing how my great-uncle loved being a rancher so much that turned me on to the idea of owning my own one day."

"So why'd you become an architect?"

Chase blew out a breath of air and turned his head to look at Norah. "My dad. He was always about me following in his footsteps. That's all I ever heard after he stepped out on his own and created his firm—that one day, when he was ready to retire, he'd hand the business down to me."

She had rested her hand on his chest and was now making lazy circles against his shirt with her fingertip. "Did you ever tell him that you had something else in mind for your future?"

"Nah." Chase shook his head. "I mean, I tried to once but it got brushed off as a foolish notion."

"What about your freedom tattoo?" Norah asked, giving him a playful smirk. "I thought you got that so you could *stick it to the man*." She lifted her hand from his chest and pumped her fist in the air.

He grinned. "I guess I needed a little more than just some ink on my shoulder. But seriously, my relationship with my dad hasn't always been the greatest. I guess I thought that maybe if I just did what he wanted me to do that it would make things better between us."

"Did it?" Norah asked.

"Eh," Chase said with a shrug. "Enough about me though. What about you? What were your big plans growing up?"

A soft breeze blew through the air and Norah reached her hand up to brush her hair behind her shoulder.

"I'm sure I had the typical little girl dreams of becoming a world famous ballerina at some point," she told him with a soft smile. "But for as long as I can remember I've always wanted to work with horses."

"Pretty lucky that you grew up on a horse ranch then," Chase said.

"Yeah, I suppose," Norah replied and then let out a sigh. "I love my family's ranch, but I'd honestly like to do more with rescues. There are so many good animals out there that are neglected or abused, and it would be wonderful if I had a place of my own to take care of them and give them the help and care they need."

"You ever work with rescues before?"

Norah nodded. "We've had a few come to the ranch. That's actually how I got my horse."

"Oh yeah?" Chase asked.

"Mmm-hmm," Norah answered. "When she came to us, she was nothing but skin and bones. Her coat was caked in dried mud and her tail and mane were all matted. We never did find out what her whole back-story was, but apparently her previous owner just abandoned her and three other horses for God knows how long. A part of me thinks she may have been abused at some point because she was so skittish for the longest time."

"And then you turned her around," Chase said, bringing his hand up to run his fingertips along her arm and down to her hand.

"It took a while, but she eventually warmed up to me when she knew I wasn't the bad guy," Norah said. "Patience can go a long way."

"It certainly can." Reaching his arm to her shoulder, Chase gently pulled her to him and rested his arms around her. He felt her breathe in deep as he stroked his hand up and down her back. "You okay?"

She nodded. "It just sucks that this is sort of our last night together." Lifting her head, Norah rested her chin on his chest and looked to his face. "Call me crazy, but I think I'm gonna miss you, O'Donnell."

There was absolutely nothing crazy about that statement. But she wasn't the only one that was going to be crazy by the time this next week was over. Having her with him every day and mostly every night had spoiled him. He just wasn't ready to let all of that go.

But he had to, at least for a little while. He traced the slender curve of her jaw with his fingertip. "I'm gonna miss you too."

CHAPTER TWENTY-NINE

Norah turned her head to the sound of bottles clinking together as she swept the worn wooden floor of the bar.

"Here," Andi said, holding one of the longneck bottles out to Norah. "Let's take a well deserved break."

Accepting the drink from her sister-in-law, Norah pulled out a chair and sat down. She brought the bottle to her lips and took a long drink, releasing in a heavy breath when she was done.

"You doin' all right there, Norah?" Andi asked before taking a drink of her own beer.

"Yeah," Norah answered.

"No you're not," Andi said, shaking her head and smiling. "You don't have to lie to me. I'm not one of your brothers."

Norah let out a small laugh. "I know. Sorry," she said. "And…no. I guess I'm not doing all right."

"You miss Chase pretty bad, don't you?"

The corner of Norah's mouth lifted just slightly as she nodded and looked down to her beer. She used her thumb to wipe the condensation from the silver label. "Is that completely ridiculous? It's only been five days."

"Five days can seem like forever when you've been spending all your time together for the past few weeks," Andi said. "Have you talked to him?"

"Yeah, we've talked," Norah said. "He's been really busy with meetings and getting ready for his presentation." She took another sip of her beer and propped her feet up on the chair across from her. "He sounds so stressed on the phone sometimes, and it kills me that I'm here and he's there and there's nothing I can do about it."

"He'll be back in a few days, right?" Andi asked. "I'm sure you could de-stress him when he gets back." She laughed.

Norah kicked at Andi's chair and laughed with her. "Enough of that," she said. "So what's new with you? Anything?"

Finishing her sip of beer, Andi nodded and rested the bottle on her lap, holding it between both of her hands. "There is actually," she said. "Zane and I have been talking lately about the possibility of starting a family."

Norah looked at her sister-in-law with a wide-eyed expression. "Seriously?"

Andi nodded. "But we're not going to *try* to have a baby, you know? We've decided to just stop trying *not* to have a baby. I don't want to stress over getting pregnant. It'll happen when it happens."

Removing her feet from the chair in front of her, Norah planted them on the floor and leaned in to give Andi a hug.

"I am so excited for you two," Norah said, giving Andi a gentle squeeze before letting go and sitting back in her chair. "You're going to make great parents. And, of course, I'll be an awesome aunt."

"I know you will," Andi said to Norah with a smile and looked to her bottle of beer. "I guess this'll be my last adult beverage for a while."

"I'll cheers to that," Norah said and clinked her bottle against Andi's.

As she drank the last of her beer, Norah thoughts swirled with the happiness she felt for her brother and sister-in-law and this journey they were about to embark upon. But Chase was ever present in the back of her mind.

With the news Andi had just shared, Norah wondered what the future held for her and Chase, or if there would be a future at all.

Spending the rest of her days and nights with Chase did sound absolutely heavenly, but a part of her wondered if she was just grabbing at straws. She and Chase hadn't really talked about what would happen between them after he permanently moved back to Dallas. A five-hour distance didn't seem like a lot when you talked about it, but it made all the difference when you actually had to drive it. She was starting to depress herself but stopped the feeling dead in its tracks. Why was she worrying about this now? If things were meant to be with Chase, then everything would work out in the long run. And if it wasn't meant to be?

Well, she'd not worry herself with that either right now.

Norah was lying in her bed, propped up against her pillows and reading a book in the dim light of her table lamp when her cell phone rang. Closing the book, she reached for the phone and smiled at the caller ID.

"Hey, you," she answered in a sweet and sexy voice.

"It's amazing how just the sound of your voice makes me feel a hundred times better in an instant," Chase said.

"Bad day?" Norah asked and set her book down on the nightstand.

"Just long and tiresome," Chase told her and sighed.

"Well, why don't you get some rest," Norah suggested. "I can talk to you tomorrow—"

"Are you kidding me?" Chase interrupted her. "I've been looking forward to talking to you all day, so I am not about to hang up with you now."

"Okay," Norah said as she smiled and snuggled into the pillows. "You wanna tell me how your presentation went?"

"It went great," Chase said. "They loved my designs and want to move forward with the project."

"That's wonderful, Chase!"

"I'm pretty excited about it myself," he told her. "But that being said, I do have something else to tell you."

A feeling of dread creeped into her stomach. "What's that?"

She heard him blow out a breath of air. "I'm gonna be stuck here another week."

And now her heart sank. "Another week?" Norah asked and tried to her disappointment.

"Yeah," Chase said. "My dad has lined up this major dinner meeting with Michael and Michaels for next Saturday night. It's at this fancy restaurant downtown and all of the men are bringing their spouses. So I was thinking…"

She listened but didn't hear anything on his end. "Chase?"

"Why don't you come stay with me in Dallas for the weekend?"

That surprised her a little bit, and she didn't know quite what to say.

"Norah?" Chase asked.

She blinked and shook her head. "Like for the whole weekend?" she asked.

"Yeah," Chase said, the sound of his voice making it obvious for her to figure out he was smiling. "And I'd like for you to attend that dinner meeting with me as my date."

"Chase, I…" She paused. "Are you sure?"

"Very sure," Chase said. "Call me crazy, but I think I

miss you."

She giggled—actually giggled like a love struck teenager. "I miss you too, you crazy fool."

"Then come spend the weekend with me," Chase said. "Do you think you'd have a problem getting off from the bar?"

"I don't think so," she told him.

"So is that a yes?"

She smiled. "It is."

"Great. Now that that's out of the way," Chase said and deepened his voice to a sexy rasp. "Why don't you tell me what you're wearing right now, Miss McKade?"

"Chase," Norah chided teasingly and added a soft gasp.

"You're not gonna tell me? I haven't seen you in a week, and I think I'm going through Norah withdrawal."

She let out a soft laugh. "Okay, okay." She paused for a second, briefly looking down to her tank top and shorts. A wicked little thought popped in her mind, and she worked to make her voice sound smooth and sultry. "I'm wearing a sheer light blue baby doll nightie with a satin bow smack dab in the center of my breasts. Oh, *and* matching panties with tiny satin bows on each hip."

"Holy shit, are you serious?"

"Maybe I am," she teased. "And maybe I'm not."

She heard him take in a deep breath and let it out slowly. "Okay, well that's an image that's going to stick with me for a very long time. I don't suppose you'd wanna?"

She faked a yawn into the phone and smiled. "I think I'm gonna call it a night."

"Oh. No. Come on," Chase said, letting out a combination of a laugh and a sigh. "You're seriously going to leave just like that?"

"I think you'll be fine," Norah said. "I'll see you next weekend and make it up to you."

"I'm going to hold you to that," Chase said.

I hope you do. "Goodnight, Chase."

"I'm here," Norah said, resting her cell phone between her ear and shoulder as she grabbed her bags from the passenger side of her truck.

"Glad you made it there safe and sound," Andi replied. "How was traffic?"

Norah scoffed and kicked the door closed as she shouldered her overnight bag. "Horrendous. Makes me love living in the country even more."

Andi laughed softly. "Okay, well have fun this weekend. I want to hear all about it when you come home."

"Will do," Norah said and started across the parking garage for the elevators. "And Andi?"

"Yeah?"

"Promise me that you won't tell the boys I snuck off to Dallas to be with Chase," Norah said. "I really don't think I can take any more of their lectures."

Silence came from Andi's side of the phone.

"Andi?" Norah questioned. "Oh no. Please don't tell me you told them."

"Not on purpose," Andi quickly explained. "And I only said something in front of Zane."

"Andi," Norah whined.

"He's my husband, and we don't keep things from each other," Andi said. "I really didn't mean to tell him. It just kind of came out when we were talking."

Norah let out an exasperated sigh. "Well, what did he

say?"

"Not much really," Andi said. "He was just kind of disappointed that you felt the need to hide stuff from him."

"Did he tell Luke?" Norah asked.

"He said he wasn't going to," Andi said. "I really think you should have just told both of them, even if things aren't so great with you all at the moment. I know you hate it that they watch over you so closely, but they mean well."

"I know they do," Norah said with a soft voice and stepped into the elevator.

After saying goodbye she tossed her cell phone into her purse and pressed the button for Chase's floor. She tapped her toe against the floor and practically bounced with nervous excitement as the elevator made the slow climb up. She needed to get a hold of her emotions before she saw Chase because if she greeted him with this much energy buzzing through her she was surely going to jump him the second she saw him. Taking in deep breaths, Norah worked to settle herself.

She was almost calmed when the elevator made a dinging sound and stopped. Her heart rate kicked up a notch as the doors opened. Stepping out of the elevator, Norah looked left then right and continued in that direction to Chase's apartment. She stopped in front of a glossy black door and looked down to the piece of paper she'd wrote his directions on along with his apartment number.

They matched.

Breathing in deep, Norah lifted her hand and knocked against the door.

CHAPTER THIRTY

Chase was going to wear a hole in his floor if he kept pacing. It had been the same figure eight path for the last twenty minutes—around the coffee table in his living room, around the small dining table, and back again. He checked the clock.

Any minute now.

He was starting to make another round when he heard three soft knocks sound from his door. His heart went into overdrive. Crossing the room, Chase unlocked the deadbolt and the lock on the handle before giving it a twist and opening the door. And there she was, her blond hair resting in waves around her shoulders and those blue eyes staring back at him seemed to mirror his exact feelings.

"Hey," Norah said, giving him a smile that made her eyes sparkle.

"Hey." He'd missed her like crazy these past two weeks and was ready to just pull her into his apartment and make up for lost time. But he didn't. Instead he returned her smile and stepped aside, gesturing for her to come in.

"How was your drive?" Chase asked as he took her bags from her and set them on the oversized chair in the living room.

"Not bad," Norah answered, her voice taking on a slightly high-pitched tone.

Chase turned to her with a grin and watched as she removed her shoes by the door. "Liar." He chuckled.

She looked to him and smirked. "Okay, it was horrible. I have no idea how you've made that drive multiple times over the past month."

He smiled and tucked his fingers into the front pockets of his pants as he watched her move about the apartment.

"So this is your place, huh?" she said, running her fingers along the glossy black stone countertop in his kitchen. "It's very nice."

"Thanks," Chase said, keeping his eyes on her as she moved from the small kitchen to the dining area. "I can show you around if you'd like."

"Sure."

He held out his hand and she walked over to him, lacing her fingers with his.

"Well, you've seen the kitchen and dining area," he said. "And this would be my living room."

Norah stood next to Chase and slowly took the room in, her eyes roaming over the black leather sofa and chair before settling on the sixty-inch flat screen mounted to the wall. "That's a pretty big TV you got there, O'Donnell."

Chase let out a small laugh. "I told you I'm pretty much a couch potato. And I love my football. Watching games on this baby makes me almost feel like I'm there."

"You guys and your football." She shook her head with a playful smirk then nodded her head to the right side of the room. "What do those two doors lead to?"

He followed her nod with a turn of his head. "That would be my office and the guest bathroom."

"I see," Norah said and looked to the other side of the room. "So that would make that one..."

"My bedroom."

"Oh," Norah said, dragging the sound out into three syllables. She briefly took the corner of her bottom lip between her teeth as she looked up to meet his eyes. "Do I get to see it?"

Chase didn't reply. He just gave her a sly, crooked smile and gently pulled her hand as he walked towards the room.

Once they were in, Norah let go of his hand and walked around the space, running her fingers along the navy blue comforter that covered his queen size bed.

"You know," Norah said, turning around to face him. "This place isn't as bachelor-paddy as I thought it would be."

Chase let out a soft snort. "Bachelor-paddy?"

"Don't make fun," Norah said, narrowing her eyes to him but smiling as the same time. "It's totally a real word."

"If you say so." He grinned and crossed the room to her. Sliding one of his hands to her hip, Chase moved the other one to cup her jaw. "I believe I forgot to give you a hello kiss."

She smiled and rested her hand over his hand that was cradling her face. "I was wondering when you were going to get around to that."

His grin widened as he bent down and pressed his lips to hers. Again. And again.

He felt her body shift, moving closer into him as she pressed her breasts against his torso. Jesus that felt unbelievably good. Moving his hand away from her face, Chase slid it slowly down the length of her body then slid both of his hands into the back pockets of her jeans and drew her to him.

Norah moaned softly into his mouth as he pulled her hips to him, letting his growing arousal do all the talking for him.

"Looks like somebody's missed me," Norah murmured, her voice sweet and sexy as she spoke against his lips.

He kissed her mouth then moved to her jaw and along her neck to that spot that made her whole body quiver. He gently nipped at it with his teeth and dipped his tongue out to taste her. A feeling of satisfaction swam over him when her body shuddered beneath his hands.

"You have no idea," Chase said between open-mouthed kisses on her heated skin.

She let out a shaky sigh as Chase moved his hands to the hem of her shirt and slid them underneath the soft fabric. Her skin felt so soft and smooth beneath his touch, but he wanted more than to just feel her with his hands. He wanted to feel the warmth of her body against his, but in order for that to happen he needed to rid her of her shirt and pesky—yet extremely sexy—bra and ditch his shirt too. Just as he was about to make that happen, she placed her hands over his as he pulled the hem of it over her stomach.

"Hold on there, O'Donnell."

Keeping the fabric of her shirt bunched up above his hands, Chase rested his palms on her ribcage as he feathered kisses along her neck. "Please don't tell me I have to stop."

She moved her hands to his biceps and took a small step away from him. "Only for a minute," Norah said and smacked a quick kiss on his lips before she walked towards the door.

"Where are you going?" Chase asked, thoroughly confused by her actions.

"I have a surprise for you."

That sparked his interest. "I'm not much for surprises," he teased.

"Oh I think you'll like this one." She stopped in the doorway with one hand on the frame and looked back to him with a sexy smile before disappearing into the next room.

Chase walked around to the side of the bed, ridding himself of his blue dress shirt and tossing it to the floor as he sat down on the mattress. Resting his elbows on his knees, Chase laced his fingers together and waited for Norah. He couldn't imagine what kind of surprise she had for him. Okay, well maybe he *could* imagine, and the image of Norah entering his bedroom wearing that skimpy little outfit she'd described to him on the phone was making him harder by the minute.

"Are you ready?" Norah called out from the other room.

"More than you know," Chase said and felt his eyes widen and his mouth fall slack as Norah entered the room. The lingerie wasn't quite like the outfit she'd described but hell if he was going to complain. She looked amazing. Pink lace covered her breasts and the sheer fabric of the rest of the nightie was split right down the center, exposing her taut stomach and a pair of matching panties with a tiny bow on the front of them.

"I'm gonna go out on a limb here and guess that you like my surprise."

Chase rested his hand on the back of his neck as he watched her walk towards him, his eyes roamed over her from head to toe. "You look…" He blew out a soft breath of air and shook his head as he reached for her. "Incredible."

The corner of her mouth lifted into a sexy smirk as she looked down at him and ran her fingers through his dark hair.

Resting his hands on her smooth skin, Chase slowly moved his palms up and around her thighs to her bottom as he leaned in and pressed his lips to her stomach. His fingers slid beneath the sheer fabric of her panties as he pulled her closer to him. Norah sighed softly and wound her fingers tighter into his hair as he darted his tongue out to taste her heated flesh.

God he'd missed this—missed the delicate scent of her perfume, the feel of her skin beneath his touch, her warmth. Her.

Two weeks away from her had felt like a lifetime. It'd been eating him up not being able to see her every day, have her near him or hear her voice. He had no idea how they were going to pull this off once he moved back to Dallas. But he pushed that thought aside, focusing on the present and that tiny satin bow that was right in front of his face. He kissed her stomach right beneath her belly button and continued kissing his way down as he moved his hands to hook his fingers in the sides of her panties. He was just about to start sliding them from her hips when she placed her hands over his.

"And just what do you think you're doing?" Norah asked him with a playful tone.

Chase looked up to her and flashed a sly grin. "Unwrapping my present."

Shaking her head, Norah removed her hands from his and gently pushed at his chest sending him backwards to the mattress. He smiled curiously as she crawled onto him, straddling his lap as she bent down to kiss him. Her hair blanketed them, and he used one of his hands to brush it away from her face and over her shoulder before cradling her jaw with his palm. Deepening the kiss, Chase moved both of his hands down to her butt and pulled her into him. Unable to help himself, he groaned against her mouth and pulled her even closer. If he didn't get inside of her soon, he was going to burst—quite literally.

Gripping her hips in his hands, Chase quickly rolled to the side, taking Norah with him. He was on top of her now as he planted his hands against the mattress on either side of her head and pressed his body weight against hers.

"God I missed you," Chase breathed.

"I missed you too," Norah said and traced the outline of his face with her fingertip.

"And I missed this." A sexy moan escaped from Norah's lips as Chase moved his pelvis against hers. Grinding against each other with their clothes on made this feel somewhat like an adolescent make-out session, but he'd be damned if it wasn't hot as hell. Norah seemed to feel the same as her fingers dug into his shoulders and she alternated between moaning and saying his name. Just the sound of that alone could send him over the edge.

Chase moved then, working his way down her body and hooking his fingers into the sides of her panties. The corner of his mouth lifted into a sly grin as he looked to her and gave them a tug. When she returned his smile he took that as a silent okay and slid the sheer fabric down her smooth thighs and legs. He dropped them to the floor as he stood at the edge of the bed and reached for her hands. Pulling her to a sitting position, Chase reached down and took the delicate pink fabric of Norah's lingerie and slid it up and over her head, letting it drop to the floor as well.

His eyes roamed over her naked body, over the curve of her hip, her waist, and the swell of her breasts. Everything about her was unbelievably perfect and unbelievably all his.

Reaching for the fly of his pants, Chase unbuttoned and unzipped them before pushing them and his boxers down his legs. He stepped out of them and opened the top drawer of his nightstand, pulling out a square foil packet. As he covered himself he felt a pair of hands slide around his waist from behind him. Cool lips touched his shoulder and he slowly turned to see Norah looking up at him with lust filled eyes.

"You're taking too long." Her lips twitched as she shoved gently at his chest.

Chase fell to the bed, his back hitting the mattress as Norah crawled on top of him. His hands slid up and down her thighs as she looked at him, her bottom lip tucked beneath her teeth as she slowly lowered herself onto him.

Chase let out a long, deep groan and let his head fall back against the mattress. Goddamn, it felt so unbelievably good to be inside of her again. With her hands firmly planted on his chest, Norah began to move her hips, rocking back and forth against him with gentle rhythmic movements. His head was spinning. His vision started to blur. The combination of her warmth and the way she moved felt so ridiculously good that he was going to lose it any minute. Hell, he was surprised he'd lasted even this long. Moving his hands to her hips, Chase gripped them firmly and sat up.

"Oh my God." Norah's tone was somewhere between a gasp and a moan as Chase pulled her to him, harder.

He moved one of his hands to her breast, teasing the hardened tip as he trailed open-mouthed kisses along her collarbone and to her other breast. When he took her into his mouth he heard her moaning his name and felt her body quiver as she started to move her hips faster.

Chase could tell she was close to coming. He was too. He moved his hands underneath her arms and to her shoulders, pulling her to him as he met her every move. When he knew he couldn't hold out much longer, Chase pressed his mouth to that tender spot on her neck and sucked.

"*Oh!*" Norah exclaimed.

The moment her body began to pulse around him he

lost it, groaning against her skin as he came so hard that stars clouded his vision. He held onto her, pressing his forehead against her chest as he tried to gain control of his breathing.

"Wow," Norah said, her voice wobbling as she too tried to catch her breath. "That was some hello kiss."

Chase laughed, letting out a short burst of air against her skin before looking up to her and meeting her eyes. With one hand pressed firmly to her back, Chase moved the other to her hip and twisted his body so Norah was lying on the mattress beneath him.

"If you thought that was something…" He pressed his lips to hers and then her cheek, her chin, and her neck.

"Chase," Norah said softly as she ran her fingers through his hair.

"Hmm?" he asked, his mouth between her breasts as he continued down her body.

"We have all weekend to make up for lost time," she said. "We don't have to make it all up right now."

He dipped his tongue out as he hit her stomach and traced a line down to her belly button.

Norah trembled.

He grinned as he went below her belly button. "Do you want me to stop?" Sliding off the edge of the bed to his knees, Chase pressed his mouth to the inner part of her thigh.

She let out a soft gasp and he felt her body tense.

"Norah?" Chase said, pressing his lips to her skin once more, inching closer and closer. "Do you want me to stop?" His mouth found the heart of her femininity and he felt her body tense again as his tongue glided against her.

"No," Norah breathed and moaned. "I don't want you to stop."

"Good," Chase said in a husky tone, running his

hands up and down her smooth thighs as he glanced up to her. "Because I've missed the hell out of you and I am nowhere near to being done."

CHAPTER THIRTY-ONE

Dallas at night was absolutely breathtaking. In the distance, lights outlined the buildings and skyscrapers shone bright against the darkened sky as Norah stared out the passenger window of Chase's SUV. Keeping her eyes on the skyline, Norah attempted to focus on the beauty of it but couldn't keep her mind from wandering. At least a dozen thoughts swirled around in her head, increasing her nervousness and turning her stomach into one huge knot.

This was such a big night for Chase—so big that Norah was beginning to regret telling him that she'd accompany him to the dinner meeting. She'd never been to anything like this before and had no idea what her role was in the grand scheme of things. Was she supposed to just sit there and look pretty while the men talked business?

She laughed to herself as that thought ran through her brain. If Chase had wanted someone like that, he would've been better off asking someone besides her to go to this thing with him. Keeping her mouth shut and her opinions to herself wasn't one of her strong points. Be that as it may, Norah knew nothing of architecture, so she probably would be silent for that conversation. Or maybe she wouldn't even be around when the guys were discussing their business venture. It could be one of those scenarios where they leave the table to talk things over drinks, leaving their spouses—or dates—behind at the table. What the heck was she going to do if that happened? She tried not to worry over something as silly as that and took comfort in the fact that at least Chase's mother would be one of those women.

"What's on your mind?"

Chase's smooth voice drug her out of her thoughts, and she turned slowly to look at him. Her eyes gazed over him from head to toe, and she noted how incredibly charming he looked in his charcoal gray suit, crisp white button down shirt, and navy blue tie.

"I was just taking all of this in," Norah said, gesturing to the scenery passing by. "The traffic here may suck, but this view is really something."

Chase smiled as he stared out the windshield to the road in front of him; his left hand gripped the steering wheel while his other arm draped lazily over the center console.

"Any of these buildings your design?" she asked, thankful for the distraction.

"Nah," Chase said with a slight shake of his head before glancing over to her. "But if you really want to see some of my work, I can take you tomorrow."

"I'd like that."

A few streets later, Chase pulled his SUV off the road and stopped at a brick front building. Twinkling lights peeked through greenery growing up and around the iron fence surrounding a small outdoor dining area, giving the restaurant a soft, welcoming glow. A young man with gel spiked hair and a red vest covering his white button down walked around to the driver's side, holding the door open for Chase to step out. After Chase accepted the ticket from the valet, he walked around the front of the vehicle and reached for Norah's door. He held his hand out to her, which she graciously accepted, as he helped her from her seat. Clutching her wristlet in her hand, Norah used her other to smooth out her simple, sleeveless, little black dress as she walked with Chase to the entrance of the building.

"Stop fidgeting," Chase whispered in her ear with a teasing tone.

His voice sent a thrill down her neck, making her skin prickle with goose bumps.

"I'm just making sure my dress isn't wrinkled," Norah explained. She felt Chase's fingers gently take hold of her elbow, pulling her to a stop beneath an archway of twinkling lights and greenery.

"I can tell you're nervous," Chase said, moving both of his hands to her upper arms and stroking his thumbs softly against her skin. "There's nothing to be nervous about."

Norah let out a soft sigh as she stared up into Chase's green eyes. "I just don't know what I'm supposed to do."

The corner of his mouth lifted as his expression softened. "Just be with me," Chase said as he brought one of his hands to cup her jaw.

Resting her own hand over his, Norah nuzzled into his palm as she nodded. Chase shifted then, moving to stand next to her, and held his arm out for her to take. She rested her hand in the crook of his elbow as they made their way into the restaurant.

"Good evening, sir," the host greeted Chase, giving him a warm and welcoming smile from behind his podium before briefly turning to Norah. "Madam. May I have the name of your reservation please?"

As Chase spoke with the thin, well-dressed host, Norah took the opportunity to glance about the space. To the right was what appeared to be the main dining area which was beautifully done. The cream colored walls were set aglow by the modern fireplace mounted on the wall. Small tables covered in white linen were surrounded by mahogany chairs with soft tan leather stretched across the back and the seat. When Chase had mentioned they would be dining at a steakhouse, she surely hadn't envisioned this.

"Ah yes," the host said. "We've reserved one of our private dining rooms for your meal. If you'd like to be seated, I'll be happy to show you to the dining room. However, the members of your party who have arrived are enjoying cocktails in our lounge."

"Thank you," Chase told the young man. "I think we'll join our party in the bar for now."

The bronze haired host smiled again as he gestured to the room behind him. A small bar made of rich, deep mahogany wood lined the entire back wall. Dim lighting and the darker walls gave the space an intimate feel. Oddly enough, it somewhat reminded her of the Rusty Spur, only a way fancier version. This little reminder of home comforted her and some of the nervousness she'd been holding onto started to fade away.

"Chase, m'boy!"

Norah turned at the mention of Chase's name being called from across the room and saw an older man waving them over. He had the same dark hair as Chase, only his was adorned with streaks of silver, the same bone structure and almost the same build. This had to be Chase's father. Three other people stood nearby, and Norah instantly recognized one of them as Susan O'Donnell.

"Son," Chase's father said as he reached his hand out and touched Chase's shoulder before gesturing to the other man. "You remember Jerry Michaels."

"I do," Chase said and outstretched his hand towards the silver haired man. "How've you been?"

"Gettin' old but I sure can't complain," Jerry said to Chase with a grin that crinkled the tanned skin around his eyes. "This is my wife, Lisa."

"Pleasure to meet you, ma'am," Chase as he and shook the woman's hand.

"And who's this jewel you're keeping tucked away?" Jerry asked Chase with a teasing tone as he gestured to Norah.

Chase turned with a smile and wrapped an arm around Norah, gently resting his palm on her lower back as he brought her closer to the group. "This would be Norah."

"What a pretty name," Jerry said and shook Norah's hand.

"Thank you, sir," Norah replied.

"Norah," Chase said, gaining her attention and directing her to his father. "This is my father, Darren."

"It's very nice to meet you, sir," Norah greeted Darren with a warm smile and a handshake.

Darren O'Donnell returned her smile, giving Norah the impression that he was pleased to meet her. His eyes on the other hand told a different story, momentarily confusing her. They were colder than his smile—an effect from the alcohol, maybe? She wasn't sure how long the others had been here before they'd arrived and how many drinks they'd had already. It was the only logical explanation she could come up with for his expression.

"And, of course," Chase said, pulling Norah out of her thoughts. "You remember my mother."

Susan O'Donnell's welcoming smile was genuine as she stepped forward and gently pulled Norah in for a hug. "It is so good to see you again, Norah."

"You too, ma'am," Norah replied, stepping out of the hug and allowing Chase's mother to hold her at arm's length.

"That dress is absolutely stunning on you," Susan said to Norah before turning to Chase with a grin. "My son is one lucky guy." Susan sent Chase a wink, and Norah started to feel the heat of a blush in her cheeks. "Come, Norah," Susan said, looping her arm with Norah's and gesturing for Lisa to follow them a ways down the bar. "Let's get away from the men before they get talking about golf. Darren was just out there this morning, so I know he'll want to brag about how well he did."

Lisa let out a tiny laugh as she ordered a merlot from the bartender. "Jerry too. I think you got us away just in time."

Susan laughed softly and ordered a glass of chardonnay.

"Anything for you, miss?" the bartender asked Norah.

"Chardonnay, please," Norah said and accepted the delicate stemware from the man across the bar.

"So Norah," Lisa said after taking a sip of her wine. "How long have you and Chase been together?"

"A few weeks," Norah told Lisa and then took a sip of her wine.

"New love," Lisa said with a sigh. "How I miss those days. Don't you, Susan?"

"Things were a lot different back then," Susan replied with a nod. "We were young, reckless, and didn't have a care in the world."

"True. Very true," Lisa said, gracefully brushing her obviously dyed auburn hair from her face. "I was only eighteen when I met Jerry. We met at a party thrown by a mutual friend and I knew within the first twenty minutes of talking to him that I was going to marry him. What about you, Susan?"

"Darren and I met when I was twenty-two," Susan said. "I was working at a women's clothing store, and he came in one day looking for a gift for his girlfriend for their date that night. He asked me for my help, and we spent a ridiculous amount of time walking around that store. He'd finally found this pretty lavender dress and asked me if I could wrap it up for him. I did, of course, and when I handed it to him after he paid for it, he turned right around and handed it back to me. He told me that I was going to need that for our date that night."

"So there really wasn't a girlfriend after all?" Lisa asked in awe with her hand resting over her heart. "That is so sweet and charming." She took another sip of her wine and turned to Norah. "And what about you, Norah. How did you and Chase meet?"

"Well," Norah said and briefly looked down to her glass. "Chase and I actually met in the bar I work at back home."

"Oh," Lisa said, seeming to be taken aback by her statement. "You work in a bar?"

The tone of Lisa's voice as she asked the question made Norah's skin crawl. Was it a problem that she worked in a bar?

"Yes, ma'am," Norah answered, squaring her shoulders and standing a little straighter.

"Hmm," Lisa said. "And is this what you 'do' for a living?"

Norah narrowed her eyes slightly at Lisa's air quotes. She didn't understand what this lady's problem was with her working at a bar. It was honest work, and she'd be damned if anybody was going to make her feel ashamed for that.

"Her family also owns a horse ranch," Susan said to Lisa. "They breed and sell some of the finest Quarter horses around."

With a bewildered expression, Norah looked to Susan. She knew that Chase's mother was just trying to smooth over the conversation and pull it in another direction—or at least she hoped that's what Susan was doing. But she didn't need Chase's mother to protect her from this hoity-toity snob. She wasn't embarrassed by who she was and where she came from, and she was just about to make that clear when Lisa's voice broke through her thoughts.

"I've always wanted to visit a real working ranch," Lisa said to Norah. "Tell me. Do you allow guests to stay?"

So now this lady was inviting herself to stay at Norah's family's ranch? Seriously? This night was not getting off to a great start. Norah looked down at her glass of chardonnay and wished she were holding something a lot stronger. She had a feeling that she was going to need it to get through the rest of this funfest.

"Well, look who finally decided to show up." It was Jerry's voice that Norah heard from behind her. She let out a silent sigh of relief for the much-needed distraction and took a sip of her wine.

"You know me," another man said. "Fashionably late as usual."

"Don't go taking the blame, sweetheart," a woman said in a sugary sweet voice. "Jerry and Lisa know that I'm never on time for anything."

"Now that the rest of us have arrived," Lisa said with an annoyed tone under her breath to Susan and Norah, "we can finally be seated." She picked up her clutch from the bar top and gestured with a slight nod of her head for Susan and Norah to follow.

Norah allowed the two older women to walk past her before she turned and looked up. Suddenly, it felt as though the walls of the room were closing in on her. She froze and just stared with a blank expression at the man standing across from Darren O'Donnell.

This had to be a dream—or a horrible nightmare.

Her heart began to thump rapidly against her ribcage as she looked upon a face she'd never met yet instantly recognized.

Finding it difficult to breathe, Norah set her glass of wine on the bar and decided to make a run for the ladies' room to get her bearings straight. But just before she turned to go, the man looked over in her direction, and she locked eyes with none other than her father.

CHAPTER THIRTY-TWO

Ice clinked against his glass as Chase lifted it to his lips and took a sip, the alcohol leaving a satisfying burn as it traveled down his throat. He half listened in on his father and Jerry's conversation about how they did on the golf course that morning. The topic didn't interest him in the slightest, but he smiled and commented when it was necessary to keep up a good appearance.

Glancing over to his left, Chase looked to see how Norah was holding up. If she was still nervous she sure wasn't showing it. She looked completely confident standing there talking to the two older women, with her back straight and chin held high. He smiled slightly to himself as he watched her, and a feeling of pride washed over him. For her to come with him tonight was a big deal. He'd asked a lot of her to do this, seeing as they'd only been together for a few weeks, and for her to just jump in without hesitation, well, that meant a lot to Chase. More than she probably even realized.

"Well, look who finally decided to show up," Jerry said rather boisterously, and Chase turned his attention back to the men next to him.

"You know me," the man walking up to them said. He appeared to be around Chase's father's age, with his sandy brown hair perfectly coifed and brushed away from his clean-shaven face. A gold Rolex adorned the man's wrist from beneath the sleeve of his tailor made suit as he shook hands with Jerry. "Fashionably late as usual."

"Don't go taking the blame, sweetheart," the woman on his arm said, resting a perfectly manicured hand over her significant other's chest. "Jerry and Lisa know that I'm never on time for anything." Her raven hair was worn loose in soft curls cascading down her back and around her shoulders. She was an attractive woman, and clearly years younger than the man she was with, but the heavy make-up she wore made her appear older.

Chase hadn't noticed at first that his mother and Jerry's wife had rejoined them. Confused, Chase turned slightly, expecting to see Norah, but he didn't.

"Let me introduce you to our guests," Jerry said, slapping the other man on the shoulder. "This is Darren O'Donnell and his lovely wife Susan."

Chase watched as his mother and father stepped forward to shake hands with the man and woman.

Where the heck was Norah?

"And this young lad is Darren's son, Chase," Jerry said.

Chase reached out and gave the man a firm handshake. "Pleasure to meet you, sir."

"A father and son team," the man said. "I like that."

Jerry placed his hand back on the man's shoulder and looked to the rest of the group once more. "Folks, this is my business partner, Michael McKade, and his wife, Pamela."

Chase had turned his head looking for Norah but snapped back around at Jerry's introduction.

McKade?

That was quite the coincidence. Chase had only ever met four McKades, and only just recently. He looked the man over inquisitively. In some respects the man did resemble Norah's older brothers. But it couldn't be, could it?

"You don't suppose he's a relative of Norah's, do you?" Susan leaned in and jokingly whispered to Chase.

He let out a soft laugh and turned again, looking for Norah.

"Speaking of Norah," Chase said quietly to his mother. "You don't by any chance know where she is, do you?"

Susan looked behind her and frowned slightly. "I don't. Maybe she went to the ladies' room. You want me to go check?"

"No, that's okay," Chase said and rested his hand on his mothers arm. "I'll take a walk that way and see if I run into her. Go on to the dining room and we'll meet you all there."

Making his way away from the group, Chase walked down the length of the bar and exited the room. His mind was everywhere, wondering if the man in the other room could indeed be Norah's father. He was going purely off of a notion, seeing as Norah had never really shared any information about her absent father, but it was just too much of a coincidence for the man in the other room to be anything else. Thinking of absences, Norah's disappearance right as Michael and his wife entered the lounge concerned Chase and further attested that he was right. Would she be upset with him for bringing her here tonight? Oh God. Would she think that he knew all along about this Michael McKade character and kept it a secret from her? He was going crazy with wonder, but right now he just needed to stop and focus on finding her.

Standing at the sink in the ladies' room, Norah ran cold water over her hand and then pressed her palm to the back of her neck. She took in slow deep breaths and let the sound of the running water sooth her nerves. It worked to an extent, and she grabbed a paper towel, wiped her hands, and then used it to turn off the faucet. Discarding the used towel in the trash, Norah opened the door and made her way out into the hallway.

Chase was walking towards her but stopped when he locked eyes with her. She'd held strong so far, refusing to let her emotions get the best of her. But seeing Chase and the worry stricken look on his all too handsome face made her want to break down and run straight into his arms.

"There you are," Chase said, his face softening with a smile as he stepped towards her. "I thought I'd lost you."

"Sorry about that," Norah said and ran her fingertips across her forehead, brushing a strand of her blond hair away from her eye. "I was just in the ladies' room." An obvious fact but she gestured to the door anyway.

"So," Chase said with the slightest bit of hesitation in his voice. "Jerry's partner and his wife are here now."

Norah nodded. "Yeah, I saw them walk in."

"You did?"

She nodded again and looked to the floor briefly before letting out a sigh and returning her eyes to Chase's. "There's something I need to tell you." She took in a deep, settling breath and let it out forcefully. "That man out there, Jerry's business partner? That's my dad."

"I wondered. He just introduced himself and then I gave him a second look and...oh, Norah," Chase said and shook his head slightly before reaching his arms out and pulling her to him in one of the most comforting embraces she'd ever experienced. "Would you believe me if I told you that I had no idea this was going to happen?

His breath brushed against her hair, sending a shiver down her spine as she settled into him.

"If I had known, I wouldn't have asked..." He pulled away from her slightly with pinched eyes and shook his head before opening his eyes to look at her. "I am so sorry."

"Chase," she said softly and lifted her hand to cup his jaw. "Don't apologize. Let's just get this thing over with. Everyone's probably wondering where we are."

His eyes widened with unspoken questions as he looked to her. "You want to stay?" Chase asked incredulously. "Norah, I can't ask you to—"

"You're not asking," she said, cutting him off. "I'm offering." She gave him a gentle smile. "Besides, it's not like that man has any idea who I am. We're complete strangers, and we can stay that way. I made you a promise, and I intend to keep it."

"But, Norah—"

"No 'buts,'" Norah said and took in a deep breath. "I'm not going to let my personal affairs mess with your career opportunities. Go ahead to the dining room and I'll meet you there in a few minutes. I won't be long." When she saw Chase's hesitation she added, "Please."

With a heavy sigh, Chase nodded his head then leaned forward and pressed his lips against her forehead. She watched him walk away before taking the opposite direction and heading back out to the bar. It was empty as Norah took a seat in one of the leather, padded barstools.

"What can I get for you, miss?" the bartender asked.

"Jameson," Norah said. "Neat, please."

The bartender poured the amber colored liquid into a glass and then placed it on a coaster in front of Norah. She lifted the glass and took a generous sip before setting it back down to the bar.

"Excuse me, miss."

Norah hadn't heard anyone walk up behind her and was a bit startled at the sound of the man's voice. She was just about to turn to answer him when he slid onto the barstool next to her.

It was him. Her father.

Her heart felt as though it had come to a complete stop before it sped off within her chest.

"You wouldn't happen to be the young lady accompanying a Mr. Chase O'Donnell this evening, would you?"

Oh God. Did he know? And if he did know, *how* did he know? Maybe she was just jumping to conclusions.

"Yes," she answered. "I am."

"Norah," he said. "Am I right?"

She gave him a soft nod. "You are."

"And are you from Dallas, Norah?" he asked.

Norah took in a deep breath and let it out slowly. "I think you know that I'm not."

He gave her a curious grin as he rested his elbow on the bar. "Why would you think that?"

"Because I know who you are, Michael McKade," she told him. "I've seen enough photos stashed away in dusty albums of you to know that you're my father."

Michael McKade just stared at her with an awestruck expression. "I can't believe it's you," he said. "That you're here, sitting right in front of me. You look so much like your mother."

Norah looked away from her father and swirled the amber liquid in her glass before taking another sip.

"How old are you now? Twenty-two? Twenty-three?"

"Twenty-five," she answered him flatly, staring down to her glass and running her fingers along the edge of the coaster.

"Wow," he said in a somewhat astonished tone and motioned for the bartender to bring him a drink. "So how are you? How are your brothers?"

Small talk. Her father was actually trying to have

small talk with her as if it were only weeks that had gone by instead of years. She took in a breath and tried to keep her cool.

"Fine," she told him. "We're all doing just fine."

"Good," Michael said, nodding his head as he accepted his drink from the bartender. "That's really good to hear."

An awkward silence filled the space between them as the seconds ticked by.

"So," Michael said, dragging the word out. "You're here with Chase. Does that mean the two of you are an item?"

She nodded.

He stared at her and pursed his lips, as if he were asking himself whether to continue or not.

"Have you two been together long?"

"What are you doing?" Norah asked Michael, her tone even as she looked over to him.

"What am I...?" he said with a confused expression. "I'm just trying to talk to you and find out about your life. I apologize if I've offended you somehow, but I honestly just wanted to know how you were."

She let out a disgusted huff and downed another sip. "You want to know how I'm doing?" she asked with a half laugh, her expression a mixture of anger and confusion. "Now?"

And there went her cool composure.

He appeared to be caught off guard by her question, so she continued.

"Why now?" she asked. "How about when I was growing up? Would you like to know how I was *then*? Because, as you very well know, I grew up without a father."

"Norah—"

"It sucked," she said, completely cutting him off and not allowing him a chance to speak. "I was the only girl in school who didn't get to go to the father-daughter dances. And when it came time for me to go to prom? I would hear all of my friends complaining about how their dads threatened their dates and how embarrassing it all was. As silly as it may sound," she poked her finger into her chest, "I wanted that." Norah looked into Michael's hazel eyes questioningly and tried to control her emotions.

Don't cry. Do not cry.

"You just left," she said softly. "And you never even bothered to try to contact us. How could you just abandon your kids like that?"

Looking away from Norah, Michael gently drummed his fingers on the bar top before placing his hand palm down against it. "Things may not have worked out with your mother and me," he said, looking back to Norah. "But there wasn't a day that went by that I didn't think of the three of you."

"If that's true," Norah said, "then why didn't you even attempt to stay in our lives somehow?"

He released a weighted sigh. "I wasn't cut out for the life your mother wanted us to have," Michael told Norah. "The ranch, the horses—all of that was her dream. Not mine." He paused. "She was the one who also wanted a big family."

Norah gave her father a puzzled looked and raised an eyebrow. "What are you saying?"

"Zane was a surprise," Michael said. "I loved your mother, but if Zane hadn't come along I'm not sure we would've stayed together for as long as we did. Having you and Luke seemed like the natural thing to do after that, and for a while I was content. But then I realized that I just wasn't made for that kind of lifestyle. Or fatherhood.

I just wasn't good at any of it. So I left to find something that I was good at and I did. I've become a very successful man."

Air escaped from her lungs and Norah found it hard to breathe. "So, let me get this straight? You never wanted to have children with my mother, but you did anyway and your life turned out better without us in the picture?"

"I didn't say that."

"Yeah," Norah said. "You did." She scoffed and rolled her eyes. "You know, all my life I've wondered who my father was and what he was like. I'd often imagine that you were off somewhere saving the world from hunger or doing something good for humanity. Somewhere far away in an underdeveloped country and the only reason you never called was because there was no means of communication. But now?" She expelled a heavy sigh. "Now I realize that you're just a giant dick in an expensive suit who only cares about himself."

"Now Norah," Michael said, his growing irritation evident in his voice. "Just hold on a second."

Downing the last of her whiskey, Norah stood up from her barstool and slapped a few bills on the counter. "I'd say it was a pleasure meeting you, Michael, but I'd be lying."

Holding tight to her wristlet, Norah turned and walked away, keeping Michael McKade exactly where he belonged—in the past.

CHAPTER THIRTY-THREE

Norah's body was buzzing when she entered the private dining room, partly from the alcohol traveling through her system and partly from adrenaline. All those years full of questions and bottled up emotions finally got the sweet release they deserved. The only thing that would have made giving her dear old dad a piece of her mind better would be if Zane and Luke had been with her so they could speak their piece as well.

Man, that felt unbelievable.

But then she caught sight of Chase sitting with his back to her, and she started to feel as though telling Michael McKade off on this particular evening wasn't the greatest idea after all. She was there for Chase, and Chase was there to impress Jerry and Michael. She hadn't thought about how her actions would reflect upon Chase, or his father for that matter. How could she have been so careless?

She pulled out the chair next to Chase and sat down.

"Hey," Chase said softly, turning to her with a smile and then changing his expression to concern. "What's wrong?"

Was she that readable?

With a slight shake of her head, Norah looked down to her hands in her lap before glancing up to Chase. "I think I may have done something really stupid," she told him quietly.

"I doubt that," Chase said. "But you want to tell me anyway?"

Just then Michael entered the room and walked over

to sit next to his wife.

"Later," Norah said to Chase.

Her heart was pounding again. There was a time and a place for everything, and here and now wasn't it. Why'd she have to act so foolishly? How was she supposed to get through the rest of this night now? Taking in calming breaths, Norah glanced up to Michael. Apparently the man was either a really good actor or Norah's words hadn't affected him in the slightest. He was laughing and joining in on a joke Jerry had told to Darren, and not at all looking in Norah's direction. It bothered her—it shouldn't have, but it did. For a man who seemed almost happy to see her a short while ago, he now had the nerve to sit there and completely ignore her? She wouldn't let it get to her, and she didn't for the entire rest of the meal. Instead, she chatted with the ladies at the table while the men held their own conversations.

"Well, gentlemen," Jerry said, slapping his napkin on the table and leaning his back against the chair. "I don't know about you, but I could go for another drink."

"I'll take you up on that offer," Michael chimed in. "Darren, how about you and your son join us and we'll talk further about how our businesses can benefit from working together?"

"Of course," Darren said and stood from the table.

"I'll be back shortly," Chase said to Norah and gently squeezed her hand before he, too, stood and exited the room.

As soon as the men were out of ear shot Pamela stood and grabbed her clutch from the table. "I'm going to make a trip to the ladies' room," she announced. "Would anyone like to join me?" She looked to Susan and Lisa, but not Norah.

That was rude and little odd.

"I will," Lisa answered. "We'll be right back, ladies."

The room fell silent for a few moments after Pamela and Lisa left as the server cleared away the plates and silverware from the table.

"I must say," Susan said to Norah as the server exited the room with his hands full of dirty dishes. "You're either the strongest person I know or you just really know how to hide your emotions well."

"Pardon?" Norah said, turning to Chase's mother with a raised eyebrow.

"How you were able to sit here all night long with your estranged father sitting right across the table from you and not even bat an eye at how awkward it was is beyond me." Susan shook her head slightly and took a sip of her wine.

"How did you know about that?" Norah asked softly.

Susan gave Norah a soft smile. "Chase told me. He knew he'd eventually get pulled away and he wanted you to have someone to confide in, in case you needed to."

Well that was sweet. Even when he couldn't be with her, Chase was making sure she was taken care of. "Thank you for that, Mrs. O'Donnell," Norah said.

"Call me Susan," Chase's mother said and gently pat Norah's knee. "You held your own tonight, Norah, and you should be very proud of that."

She thanked Susan once more and took comfort knowing she had someone to talk to. But she didn't know Susan O'Donnell well enough to go spilling her family drama, even though the older woman technically knew of it already. What Norah wanted was Chase. Thinking of burrowing herself into his embrace calmed her, and she'd get to do that at some point. But she needed someone to talk to right now.

"I think I'm going to head to the ladies' room as

well," Norah said to Susan. "Would you excuse me for a moment, please?"

Susan nodded and Norah exited the room, pulling her cell phone from her wristlet as she walked down the corridor. She dialed Andi's number and waited, leaning against the wall and tapping her toe on the floor as she listened to ring, after ring, after ring. Finally Andi's voicemail came on and Norah pressed the end button on her phone. With a sigh, she slowly pushed open the bathroom door and stepped inside. The trilling sound of laughter came from the other side of the short wall, hiding the rest of the room from the door.

"You can't be serious," Norah heard a woman say. Could that be Lisa Michaels' voice?

"I wish I were kidding," another woman said. Pamela McKade maybe? "What the hell does she think she's doing here anyway? Michael left that life behind him a long time ago, so what right does she have to show up now?"

Whoa. Were they talking about *her*?

"Maybe she tagged along with that Chase O'Donnell because she knew that Michael would be here tonight," Lisa said. "The girl works in a bar for Christ's sake. Who knows? Maybe she's hard up for cash and is out to get some kind of compensation."

Were they serious? She didn't want anything from that asshole.

"Well if she thinks that she's getting a dime from us, then she's absolutely crazy," Pamela said. "I don't owe her anything, or those brothers of hers. And if she's here on behalf her mother, well than she can just kiss my perfect little ass and go back to Bumfuck, Texas, where she belongs."

Norah's jaw dropped. It took every bit of restraint she

had to keep her mouth shut, even though she really wanted to tell Pamela where she could take that perfect little ass of hers and what she could do with that attitude. She couldn't do that to Chase, though. Not when there was so much riding on how well this dinner meeting went.

"What was Darren's son thinking anyway," Pamela continued, "bringing her here? This is a fine dining establishment, not a hoedown. Did you see that dress she was wearing?"

Instinctively, Norah looked down and ran a hand over the simple black fabric.

"I've seen prostitutes with better taste," Pamela said. "And don't even get me started on those shoes or her hair. It's almost as if she's never been to a formal event before." A devious laugh echoed off the walls. "Formal where she's from probably just means showing up in camo that doesn't have any mud or horse shit on it."

Lisa laughed. "Pamela, you are so bad."

"I shouldn't make fun of the poor girl," Pamela said, her tone softening. "This is probably a big night for her, being the first real guy she's been on a date with that wasn't her cousin."

"Oh my God," Lisa said, laughing even more.

Norah's stomach started to turn. She didn't want to admit it, but the personal jabs hurt like hell.

"She doesn't fit in here," Pamela said with Lisa agreeing. "Chase could do a hell of a lot better than some trashy bartender."

A lump rose in her throat and she swallowed hard. Tears formed in her eyes, and Norah knew that all of her strength had disappeared. There was only so much one person could take, and she had had about enough for one night. She quietly left the bathroom and snuck through the dining room to escape outside. The cool night air grazed over her skin, leaving a trail of goose bumps in its path. Norah closed her eyes and took in deep breaths.

"Miss?"

She opened her eyes to find the young valet from earlier that night.

"I'd be happy to pull your car around for you, if you'd like," he said in a pleasant tone. "May I have your ticket?"

Norah shook her head slightly and cleared her throat before answering the young man. "My date has the ticket," she said, and gestured to the restaurant with her thumb. "I was just…"

She looked around, taking in the appearance of the restaurant and the street. Everything was so close together—too close. Even though she was outside in the open, she started to feel a little claustrophobic. The lights, the cars, the noise, the people…it was all too much. Pamela may have been right about one thing; Norah didn't fit in here.

"I was just getting some air," Norah told the valet.

He smiled and gave her a nod as he walked back to his station.

A wrought iron bench sat off to the side, and Norah strolled over to it and took a seat, crossing one leg over the other at the knee. With a soft sigh, she leaned her head back and looked up to the night sky. She sat like that for a while, just letting the events of the night replay over and over again in her mind—her father admitting he hadn't wanted her, and his new wife taking cheap shots at her behind her back. Her breath hitched and she swallowed hard.

Be strong. Don't give them the satisfaction of seeing your pain.

Blinking away the tears, Norah lifted her head and

uncrossed her legs as she stood from the bench. She'd get through this. One way or another she would make it through this night. After giving herself a silent pep talk, Norah started to walk back to the restaurant but paused when her cell phone rang.

Pulling it from her wristlet, she glanced at the caller id and then answered. "Hey, Andi."

"Norah," Andi said with worry in her voice. "You okay?"

Letting out a heavy sigh, Norah dipped her head and covered her eyes with her free hand. "No," she said. "No, I'm really not okay."

"Oh no," Andi said. "What's going on? What happened?"

Norah walked along the sidewalk as she told Andi everything, stopping a few feet past the wrought iron fence of the outside dining area.

"You want me to come up there?" Andi said. "'Cause I'll do it. I'm sure between the two of us we can set your deadbeat father and Mommy Dearest straight."

A small laugh escaped from Norah. "And I'm sure everyone would wait patiently for your five hour drive."

"Hey, at least I got you to laugh," Andi said. "I'm really sorry Norah, and I really do wish I were there with you right now to console you."

"It's fine," Norah said. "I'll be coming home tomorrow night and then I'll put all of this mess in the past and be done with it."

"Now that's the attitude to have," Andi said. "Well, call me when you leave for home. When you get back I'll come over. We can watch old movies and stuff our faces with ice cream and gummy bears."

Norah laughed once more. "That sounds awesome. Thanks for talking, Andi. G'night."

Placing her cell phone back in her wristlet, Norah turned and started back towards the restaurant. As she approached she saw Chase walking through the archway, appearing to be searching for something—most likely her.

"Hey," he said when he noticed her and walked over. "I really do keep losing you tonight. You okay?"

"Yeah," Norah told him. "I was just getting some fresh air."

He reached out for her and rested his hands on her hips. "No, seriously," Chase said as he looked down to meet her eyes. "Are you okay?"

"I'm fine," she lied. "I'm just," she paused and sighed, "tired." Lifting her hand, Norah ran her fingers along the lapel of his suit jacket. "Shouldn't you be in there rubbing elbows with Jerry and Michael?"

He gave her a half smile, and she knew that he knew that she wasn't being truthful about being okay.

"We're all done for tonight," Chase told her as he stroked his thumbs back and forth against the fabric of her dress. "I went back to the dining room to let you know, but you'd disappeared again." He smiled and rested his forehead against hers.

She returned his smile and brought her other hand up, taking hold of the other lapel and running both of her hands up and down the fabric simultaneously. "So am I allowed to know how your meeting went?"

"I think it went well," Chase said. "They liked what my father had to say and we've set up another meeting for the first of the week to go over some designs so that I can get an idea of what they're looking for."

"That's great news, Chase," Norah told him and leaned her head back just slightly so she could look at him. "I'm really happy things worked out well for you tonight."

He looked to her with mixed expressions: wonder,

worry, confusion. "A lot happened tonight, Norah," Chase said softly. "Are you sure you don't want to talk—"

"There they are."

Chase turned and Norah looked around his shoulder to find everyone from their party walking towards them as they exited the restaurant.

"We were wondering where you two had run off to," Jerry said and outstretched his hand towards Chase. "It was good seeing you again, son."

"You too, sir," Chase said to Jerry and shook his hand.

Norah pasted on a smile as she went from person to person, shaking hands and saying goodbyes for the night. Not so surprising, no words were exchanged between her and Michael. He just graced her with a tight-lipped smile and a sharp nod before taking hold of Pamela's hand and walking to his sleek, black BMW sedan.

"You ready to go home?" Chase asked when everyone had gone their separate ways and then held out his hand for hers.

Home.

The simple word had never held much value for her until this very moment. And as Norah gave Chase a soft nod and wrapped her hand around his, she knew that his definition of home was entirely different from hers.

CHAPTER THIRTY-FOUR

For the entire drive back to his apartment, Norah was quiet. Every once in a while Chase would steal a glance at her, and every time she'd be staring out the passenger window in a daze. At one point he reached over to her lap and rested his hand over top of hers, giving it a gentle squeeze in a silent show of his support. Only then did she look away from the outside world to look at him, gifting him a brief, soft smile before turning away again.

This was killing him. They'd had no opportunities to talk about what had happened and now, when they were alone and clearly had the time to talk, Norah wouldn't even look at him for more than a couple of seconds.

It was the same story when they arrived in the parking garage, walking side by side in silence to the elevator. And the same went for the ride up to his floor and the walk down the hallway. When he opened his door for her and she walked in ahead of him, Chase finally couldn't take it anymore. Closing the door behind him and dropping his keys on the counter, Chase reached out for Norah and pulled her to a stop.

"Talk to me," he said after turning her to face him. "Don't shut me out, Norah. Please."

She sighed and leaned into him, pressing her cheek against his chest and wrapping her arms around his waist. "I don't want to shut you out," Norah said softly. "But I've just got so much running through my mind right now."

"Like what?" Chase rested his chin on her head and stroked the back of her hair with his hand as he held her.

"I keep thinking about everything that happened tonight." She let out another sigh and lifted her head to look at him. "I talked to my dad."

Chase's eyes widened slightly. "You did?"

Norah nodded. "I went back to the bar right after you and I talked in the hall. The place was empty when I sat down and then a few seconds later he was sitting right next to me."

"Did he know who you were?" Chase asked.

Norah gave him another nod. "He told me I looked just like my mother." She took in a shaky breath and looked back to the buttons on his shirt. "I don't know what happened," Norah said in a barely audible voice. "He asked about me and my brothers, and I just…snapped. I told him that I couldn't believe how'd he just left us and didn't even bother to stay in our lives."

She sniffed and Chase realized that she was crying. A tear slipped from her eye and rolled down her cheek. Chase brought his hand to her face, cupping her jaw as he swiped away her tear with the pad of his thumb.

"Did he say anything?" he asked her, his voice low and full of concern.

"He said a lot of things." Norah scoffed. "But I think the thing that sticks with me most is that his life turned out better because he left us." Covering her hand over his, Norah gently pulled him away from her face and backed out of his arms. She walked over to the counter and grabbed a paper towel, folding it and dabbing it beneath her eyes.

"I'm so sorry," Chase said as he turned towards her.

"Oh no, wait," she said with a small, sarcastic laugh. "It gets better." Gripping the paper towel in her hand, Norah's expression hardened. "Later, after you guys left to talk business over drinks, I happened to overhear Pamela and Lisa completely trashing me in the bathroom."

That comment surprised him.

"They did what?" he asked, completely in shock and infuriated by what she'd just told him.

"God, Chase," Norah said, her voice breaking. "Do you know how completely mortified and humiliated I am? The things they said…" She pinched her eyes shut and shook her head before looking back to him.

Chase could feel his body tense as rage pulsed through him. At the same time, his heart was breaking over Norah's pain.

"What did you say to them?" he asked.

She gave him a puzzled expression. "What was I supposed to say, Chase? Everything I wanted to say or do would've ended up reflecting poorly on you."

"So you just—what?—stood there in the shadows and listened to them talk about you behind your back?" Chase asked with an incredulous tone.

"You say that like it's a bad thing," she countered. "I did what I thought was best for you and kept my mouth shut." Then she quietly added, "I'd already crossed a line with my father and I wasn't about to do the same with his wife."

Scraping a hand through his hair, Chase let out a heavy sigh. "That's the thing, Norah. You don't keep your mouth shut, and you don't back down that easily—I've seen it firsthand. That's not who you are." He closed the distance between them, lifting his hand to brush her hair behind her shoulder before resting his palm against her neck. "I don't want you to ever feel like you can't stand up for yourself. But that's beside the point because none of that should've happened tonight."

He gazed into her blue eyes and the hurt burning within them cut him deep.

"I can't make this night go away," Chase told her. "But I will make it up to you. I don't know how, but I will find a way to make all of this right."

"Chase—"

He stopped her with a kiss—soft, delicate movements of his lips against hers.

"I promise," he whispered, his breath brushed against her mouth as he leaned his forehead against hers.

"I don't want to talk about it anymore," Norah said, using the same quiet tone as Chase. "I'm so worn out, physically and mentally. I just want to go to sleep and forget about it all for awhile. Can we just go to bed?"

With a nod, Chase moved his hand from her neck, gliding his fingertips down her arm and interlacing his fingers with hers. "Let's go."

The next afternoon Chase and Norah headed off to his parents' house for a barbeque that his mother had decided to have at the last minute.

"So this is your childhood neighborhood?" Norah asked as she stared out the window, the light peaking through the trees cast a glow on her golden hair. "It's lovely."

"Thanks," Chase said as he glanced back and forth between her and the road in front of him. "Are you sure this is okay? Because we don't have to go."

She turned to him and gave him an understanding smile. "It's fine, really."

"You say that," Chase said, "but you only have a few hours left before you leave. Are you sure you don't want to do something else?"

"Like what?" she asked him.

"I don't know," Chase said and added a shrug. "But I'm sure we could come up with something to pass the time." He looked to her and gave her a sexy grin.

"You need to stop," Norah said with a short laugh and shoved at his shoulder. "I think it was nice of your mom to invite us for dinner. I really like her."

"She likes you too," Chase said and reached for Norah's hand, lacing his fingers with hers over the center console.

Norah brought her other hand over and ran her fingers tips along his arm as she stared out the windshield with him. "Which one is it?" She nodded to the houses passing by.

"We're coming up on it," Chase said. "Three houses down on the left. The white one with dark green shutters."

A few moments later Chase pulled his SUV into his parents' driveway and parked behind his mother's sedan.

"This is beautiful, Chase," Norah said. "Which one of these windows is your old bedroom?"

He stepped out of the vehicle and walked around to her side, holding the door open for her as she stepped out onto the pavement.

"My room was in the back of the house," he told her.

"Oh," she said and tucked her bottom lip between her teeth. "Am I gonna get to see it?"

He grinned at her curiously and raised an eyebrow.

"Don't even go there, O'Donnell." She laughed and slapped at his chest as they walked up the pathway to the front door. "I wanted to see what you liked as a child, all of your old toys and how your room was decorated. You probably had superhero bed sheets, didn't you?"

His grin widened. "I did," he said. "Superman to be exact. But my old room has been redecorated for quite some time and is now used for guests." Stopping at the front door, Chase turned to Norah and reached for her, placing his palms on the small of her back and pulling her to his body. "But if you really want to see *Man of Steel,* I'm sure we could make arrangements."

"Oh gross, stop." She laughed and playfully shoved at his chest.

"You know you like it," he teased and leaned towards her.

"You're a mess," she said, and he could feel her breathing kick up a notch as he pressed his lips to hers.

The front door opened a second later, and Chase had to firmly plant his feet as to not be knocked over by Maddie.

"Uncle Chase!" the little girl squealed and flung her arms around his waist. "You came!"

"Hey, Mad," Chase said, wrapping an arm around his niece in an awkward side hug.

"And you brought your girlfriend," Maddie said, keeping her arms around Chase and smiling at Norah.

He laughed and patted her back as he too smiled at Norah. "Yes, I brought my girlfriend."

"I'll go tell everyone you're here," Maddie said and removed her hold of Chase before running back into the house. "Hey, everybody! Uncle Chase and Norah are here!"

Norah let out a soft laugh and Chase joined her.

"She's excited," Norah said.

"She's always excited," Chase said and took Norah's hand as they walked through the front door.

"Oh my," Norah breathed.

Chase followed her gaze as she took in her surroundings and tried to see things from her point of view: the warm, golden hue of the walls, the dark stained hardwood floors that carried into the staircase leading up to the second story, and the balcony that overlooked the foyer.

"This is so nice," Norah said in awe.

"Come on," Chase said and flashed her a smile. He led her through the kitchen and dinette before walking out the sliding glass door to the backyard patio.

"Hey, guys," Susan said, her face brightening with a smile as she waved to Chase and Norah. "Come on over. Your father's manning the grill and everything should be done shortly."

Darren didn't bother turning away from his station. Instead, he lifted the tongs in his hand and waved, simply acknowledging that they were there.

Such a polite man, his father was.

But Chase didn't let his father's poor manners get to him. He wanted the last few hours of Norah's visit to be drama free, and that's exactly what he was going to give her. They hadn't spoken anymore on the topic of her father or the other events that had happened the previous night. Norah hadn't brought it up, and even though he desperately wanted to make sure she was okay, he hadn't broached the subject either. She'd already been through enough this weekend and he'd made a promise to make it up to her somehow. The only way he could think of making it up to her at the moment was to keep her busy and her mind free.

"You wanna go play horseshoes with Sarah and Keith?" Chase asked Norah and nodded over to his sister and brother-in-law.

"Sure," she said.

Over the next couple of hours they ate, played games, laughed, and talked. It was one of the nicest days Chase could remember having with his family, solely because Norah was by his side. It felt so natural for her to be there with him, and the way she interacted with his parents, sister, brother-in-law, and nieces made her seem like she was already part of the family. She fit so perfectly into his life that he wanted to beg her to stay here with him. Maybe he would do just that. He was only going to be here for another week before returning to Buford to finalize things with the ranch. Maybe he could convince her to stay with him and feel things out—see if she liked living in a big city.

"Who wants dessert?" His mother's voice cut through his thoughts.

"Me!" Maddie shouted.

"Me too!" Chelsea chimed in.

"Okay, okay," Susan said and stood from the patio table. "Norah, would you be a dear and help me?"

"Sure," Norah said, standing from the table and giving Chase a soft smile as she headed off into the house with his mother.

"Chase," Darren's gruff voice called from beside him. "A word."

Darren stood and walked into the house. Chase let out an exasperated sigh and gave his sister a look before going with his father. He followed Darren to his office and stepped inside the room after him.

"Door," Darren said, his back turned to Chase.

With a puzzled expression, Chase closed the door behind him, leaving a two-inch gap between the door and the frame.

"Everything okay, Dad?"

Darren turned and gave Chase a hard stare. "What the hell do you think you're doing?"

Chase deepened his puzzled expression, thoroughly confused by what his father was asking him.

"Don't look at me like that," Darren spat out. "What

are you doing with that girl out there?"

Jesus. This was about Norah? Chase let out a sigh and lifted the corner of his mouth into an amused smirk.

"Okay, Dad," Chase said. "Let's have it. What's wrong with her?"

"You know damn well, Chase," Darren said. "She's a distraction, and you need to cut her loose."

Chase let out a short burst of air and darted his eyes briefly around the room.

"Do not laugh at me, boy. I need all of your focus on this project for Michael and Michaels," Darren said. "And I don't think you can do your job properly while you're busy rolling around in the hay with *her*." He pointed absently in the direction of the kitchen.

Rolling around in the hay? He'd let that comment slide for now even though it pissed him off to no end.

"Not do my job properly?" Chase asked, the disbelief in his voice front and center. "When have I not completed anything you've asked me to do since I've been away?"

Darren fell silent but just stared at Chase with an expression that said he wasn't in the mood for back talk.

"You can't say that I haven't because," Chase poked his finger into the center of his own chest, "I've done my job."

"And barely got me the designs I needed for The Channing Group before they were due," Darren added snidely.

"Because you jumped up the due date on them—"

"Look! The bottom line is I gave you permission to leave work to fix up that stupid ranch you inherited on the terms that you'd spend the rest of your time working on your projects, not getting your rocks off with some bartender who managed to stick her claws in you. I won't have you screw things up because you're worried about keeping a cheap piece of ass."

Chase could feel his blood starting to boil. "A cheap piece of ass?" He narrowed his eyes and gritted his teeth, flexing his jaw as he tried to compose himself. "Norah's just some bartender I like to keep around because she's a good lay. Other than that I have no use for her and she means absolutely nothing to me." He heaved a heavy breath and then another as he tried to calm himself. "Is that what you want me to say? Because if that's what you're expecting to hear then you can go fuck yourself because that's not at all how I feel about her."

"You watch your mouth, boy," Darren said, anger deepening his voice as he crossed the room to Chase.

"I am not a boy," Chase retorted and stood his ground. "I'm a grown man, so stop treating me like I'm a goddamn child. I've never given you a reason to doubt me, so you can stop with the bullshit." He turned, clenching and unclenching his fists by his side as he walked to the door.

"This is an important client, Chase. A *very* important one. I need your head in the game," Darren called after him, "and you back in Dallas full time."

Chase turned and opened his mouth to retort but Darren cut him off sharply.

"This discussion is over. You're either back here full time starting tomorrow or…"

"Or what?"

"Be at the office no later than eight." Darren gave him a hard look.

Biting the inside of his cheek, Chase returned his father's glare as he flung open the door and exited the room.

CHAPTER THIRTY-FIVE

She felt as though she were walking on phantom limbs. Norah's whole body went numb as she made her way back to the kitchen, clutching the large serving plate Susan had asked her to grab from the hall closet to her chest as if it were a protective shield. A lot of good that did her though. Chase's deep, rough voice echoed in her mind haunting her and slicing through to her very core.

Norah's just some bartender I like to keep around because she's a good lay. Other than that I have no use for her, and she means absolutely nothing to me.

She hadn't meant to eavesdrop. The closet had been two doors away from Darren O'Donnell's office, and she hadn't paid any attention to the deep, rough voices behind the door until she heard her name. It was as if her senses kicked into overdrive, allowing her to hear everything loud and clear without having to take another step towards the door. How did she not see this coming? That Chase was...using her for his own personal pleasure while he was stuck in Buford.

Because he's fed you nothing but sweet lines and acted like he truly cared for you as a ploy to get in your pants.

God. It didn't make any sense whatsoever. They'd spent so much time together over the past month. And she knew that Chase wanted her, hell she'd wanted him too, but she honestly thought that there was more between them than just lust. She'd felt a connection with him and—*damn it!*—actually gone and fallen in love with the guy.

Wade's deception creeped into her thoughts, swirling together with Chase's harsh words, and Norah felt like she was going to be sick.

Fool me once, shame on you. But fool me twice, shame on me.

She was an idiot to trust Chase.

And then she heard her brother's voice, *I think you're going to want more than he's willing to offer.*

Why on earth hadn't she just listened to Luke's advice? If she had, then she wouldn't be in this mess. She'd be back home in Buford, working behind the bar at the Rusty Spur and doing chores around the ranch, where she belonged.

"That's the one."

Norah tore herself away from her inner thoughts and looked to see Susan O'Donnell standing on the other side of the counter wearing a warm smile.

"You can set it down on the counter, sweetie," Susan said to Norah. "Thank you for grabbing it for me."

"You're welcome," Norah said and forced a smile and a nod to Chase's mother.

Footsteps sounded on the hardwood floor behind her a few moments later, and Norah stiffened when she felt Chase's hand rest lightly on the small of her back.

Get off me. Don't touch me. I never want to feel your hands on me ever again.

Chase must've noticed the change in her body because he leaned in towards her and asked, "Are you okay?"

His breath brushed across her ear, and normally the small action would send shivers down her spine and make her skin break out in goose bumps. But now all it did was make her stomach turn and knot into a tight little ball.

Keeping her eyes focused on the items spread across

the counter, Norah gave Chase a slight nod. She couldn't look at him. Even now as the image of his face sprang into her mind it angered her more by the second. That handsome face she'd kissed hundreds of times now sickened her instead of making her knees go weak.

They stayed at Chase's parents' house long enough to eat the dessert his mother had plated and then they were saying their goodbyes.

Maddie and Chelsea, the sweetest, most rambunctious little girls Norah had ever known, wrapped their little bodies around Norah's legs so tight that she couldn't move.

"Can we see your horses the next time we come to visit Uncle Chase?" Maddie asked, looking up to Norah with pleading eyes.

God, she couldn't do this. How was Norah supposed to explain to this wonderful child that she wouldn't be in the picture by the time they visited again with their Uncle Chase?

"Maybe," Norah told Maddie and brushed the girl's hair away from her forehead with a motherly touch.

The simple answer seemed to be good enough for the young girl. Her face lit up and she squeezed Norah once more before letting her go and running to Chase.

"Norah," Susan said and gently pulled her in for a hug. "Thank you for coming over today. I know you and Chase probably had better things to do than spend the rest of your trip with his boring old family." Susan turned her head slightly and grinned at Chase.

"Thank you for having me, Susan," Norah said, pulling away from Susan's embrace. "And I don't think I could've imagined a better way to spend my last few hours in Dallas." She pasted on her best smile and glanced over to Chase before looking back to Susan. "It's been nice getting to know who Chase really is."

"Aw," Susan said and cradled the side of Norah's face with her hand before resting it on her shoulder. "You are the sweetest thing."

After saying goodbye to Sarah and Keith, Norah turned and headed for Chase's SUV. Darren O'Donnell hadn't bothered to step outside during their departure. Figures. The man seemed like a real jerk, and Norah thought to herself that the apple didn't fall far from the tree.

During the drive back to Chase's apartment, Norah plastered herself against the passenger side door attempting to put as much space between her and Chase as possible.

"You're awfully quiet," Chase said.

She didn't reply. She just kept her focus on the buildings and never-ending concrete as Chase's SUV sped down the road. When they'd hit the door of his apartment, Chase finally must've had enough of the silence between them. After he unlocked and opened the door he placed his arm across the frame, completely blocking her path.

"What's going on?"

"Move your arm, Chase."

"Not until you tell me what's wrong."

Norah ducked under his arm and entered the apartment. She heard the door close behind her as she hurried to Chase's bedroom to grab her things.

"Why are you whipping through here like an angry tornado?" Chase asked, standing in the doorway as she threw the rest of her things in her overnight bag.

And then he was right beside her, reaching out for her and curling his hands around her upper arms.

"Norah—"

Shrugging out of his hands, Norah turned and slapped

his arms away from her. "Don't. Touch. Me." She pointed a finger directly at him before shoving at the items in her bag so she could zip it up.

"What the hell, Norah?" Chase asked, his expression perplexed. "Seriously. What's the matter?"

Grabbing the zipper of her bag, Norah pulled it quickly but, in her haste, it snagged on a piece of her clothing and she had to yank at it to get it unstuck.

"I shouldn't have gotten involved with you," Norah said, cursing under her breath at that damn zipper that just wouldn't budge.

"Wha—" Chase started but stopped, seeming to collect his thoughts. "I don't understand."

"Coming here, being with you," Norah said. "It was all a big mistake. Son of a—!" She punched at the bag and decided to leave the zipper alone. Grabbing the strap, Norah shouldered the bag and pushed past Chase to the other room.

"Because of what happened last night?" Chase asked as he followed her. "Norah, I had no idea that your father—"

"This is not about my father," Norah said as she looked around the room for her truck keys. "Or his wife for that matter."

Damn it, where'd she put them?

"Then for the love of God, Norah, please just tell me what's going on because I'm absolutely clueless over here."

Her eyes roamed the room once more before she shot Chase a hard glare. "You wanna know what this is all about? You're an asshole. The end."

Found them. She walked over to the end table and snatched her keys from behind the lamp.

"Well that explains everything," Chase shot off in a

sarcastic tone. "You care to elaborate?"

She walked past him, clutching her keys in her left hand as she went for her cell phone charger back in Chase's room. Why hadn't she just packed all her shit up earlier?

Because earlier today you really didn't want to leave.

"Goddamn it, Norah, talk to me."

Ripping her charger from the wall, Norah spun and found herself face to face with Chase. His breathing matched her own, his chest dramatically rising with every intake of air. And then she snapped.

"I'm just some bartender you like to keep around because I'm a 'good lay,'" Norah said, tears stinging her eyes. "And other than that you have no use for me and I mean absolutely nothing to you."

She watched as Chase's facial expression changed to one of recognition and his mouth fell slack.

"You can't even deny saying it because I heard it with my own ears, Chase." She swallowed hard around the lump rising in her throat and took in a ragged breath before walking around him.

"Hold up a second," Chase said, running after her and grabbing her arm.

"Get off of me." Norah looked down to his hand curled around her wrist and tightened her jaw.

"I need you to listen to me for a second," he said.

Norah shook her head and attempted to free herself from his grip. "I think I've heard enough from your mouth. Now let go."

"Please. Just listen."

She tugged again.

"Norah, I didn't mean—"

Balling her other hand into a fist, Norah swung her arm around and delivered a solid right hook to Chase's jaw. He let go of her wrist and stumbled backwards slightly, looking to her with a dumbfounded expression.

She lifted her chin as she stared at him, daring him to do or say anything else. But he didn't. So she adjusted the strap on her shoulder, gave him one more hard look, and stormed through the door. Her hands were shaking, almost violently, as she shuffled through her purse in search of her cell phone, pulled it free and dialed a familiar number. They were still shaking when brought her phone to her ear, and she took in deep breaths to try and calm her nerves as she stepped into the elevator.

"Andi," Norah said, her voice breaking slightly. "I'm on my way home."

CHAPTER THIRTY-SIX

For the next half hour, Chase paced his apartment as he let what had just happened with Norah sink in. How could he have been so dumb to let his father get to him like that? And even worse, Norah had heard him being a smartass but didn't know that's what he was doing. His poor decision had bit him in the butt, royally. Now Norah was on her way back to Buford and there was nothing he could do about it.

Sure he could go after her, but as that thought popped in his brain he brought his hand up to his face and rubbed at his jaw where she'd rocked him with that killer right hook of hers. That was enough of a statement for him that Norah didn't want him chasing after her.

Letting out an exasperated sigh, Chase's pacing took him to his bedroom. He plopped down on the edge of the bed and scrubbed his hands over his face before pushing them through his hair.

This is a fine mess you've gotten yourself in, O'Donnell. You had the girl of your dreams and now you've lost her.

Chase fell back against the bed and as he did he caught the faint scent of Norah's perfume still lingering on the comforter. He inhaled deeply and closed his eyes. Visions of her danced in his mind, visions so real that he almost felt like he could reach for her and she'd be right there. But she was gone. Really and truly gone. And it was all his fault.

Way to go, Chase. Way to go.

Knock knock knock knock.

Norah opened her red-rimmed eyes and looked to the clock on her nightstand.

7:02 a.m.

That couldn't be Andi. When they'd spoken last night, after her hasty departure from Chase's apartment, Andi had told Norah that she'd be waiting for her at Norah's house when she got home so they could talk. But Norah insisted Andi wait and come over the next morning. The only thing she had wanted to do when she arrived back at her house was curl up in a ball in the center of her bed and have a good cry.

The knocking sounded again, and Norah sat up from her bed, rubbed her hands over her face and through her hair, and flung the covers back to get up. She almost reached for her robe but then realized that she was still wearing her navy blue sleeveless shirt with the little pink rose pattern and her jeans. Making her way down the hall and through her tiny living room, Norah reached for the front door and opened it.

"Jesus, Norah," Luke said, the shocked look on his face replacing the irritated one that had been there for a split second before. "You look like shit."

"Thanks," she said sarcastically. She stepped away from the door, leaving it wide-open, and made her way to the kitchen.

She heard the door close and then Luke's boots stepping on the hardwood floor as he followed her. Opening the cabinet next to her fridge, Norah grabbed a can of coffee grounds and a filter before closing the door and proceeding to make a pot of coffee.

"What are you doing here?" Norah asked.

"Haven't talked to you in awhile," Luke said with a shrug. "Just figured I'd stop by and see how things were going."

She scoffed. "In other words, you're checking up on me."

The corner of his mouth lifted. "Guess I am."

Norah shook her head and smiled half-heartedly. "Want some?" she asked Luke as she ran water into the coffee pot before pouring it into the back of the machine and closing the lid. She replaced the pot on the warmer and pressed a few buttons before stepping away to put the coffee grounds back.

"Sure. I'll take a cup," Luke said, occupying the doorway and leaning against the frame with his arms crossed over his chest. "So what's up with you? Why do you look like that?" He uncrossed one of his arms and gestured to all of her.

"Like I just woke up?" Norah asked.

"Like you slept in your clothes and you've been cryin'," Luke elaborated.

He had her there. There was no use lying to him about anything. Not anymore. The strong urge to blurt out everything that had transpired over the weekend overpowered her. But not as much as the urge to completely break down in tears in front of her older brother as all of those horrible memories came flooding back. Her bottom lip quivered and her eyes quickly filled with tears as she looked away from Luke and to the floor, covering her face with both of her hands.

"Whoa," Luke said in a surprised tone and then she felt his arms circling around her shoulders, pulling her to his chest. "Nor, what's goin' on?"

Her sobs consumed her. She removed her hands from her face and wrapped her arms tightly around Luke's waist, gripping onto the back of his shirt as she buried her face into his shoulder.

"You're killin' me here, sis," Luke said, his voice soft and gentle as he leaned his chin on top of her head. "Tell me what's goin' on so I can fix it. I can't stand to see you cryin' like this."

She pulled away from him slightly and rubbed at her eyes before touching his shirt where her tears had left a wet spot. "Oh, your shirt," she said and sniffed.

"It's fine," Luke said and bent his knees so he was almost eye to eye with her. "Talk to me."

Norah took in a ragged breath and then another before she told Luke everything; her secretly seeing Chase behind everyone's back, sneaking off to Dallas to be with him, meeting their father, the things his witch of a wife said about her, and—the icing on the cake—the things she overheard Chase say about her.

Luke blew out a long breath of air and shook his head.

"Luke?" Norah said.

"I'm sorry," he said and shook his head again before he looked to her. "That's just a lot of information to process in a short amount of time."

"I know," she told him. "I'm sorry."

"Why didn't you just tell us you were seeing Chase?" Luke asked.

Norah raised an eyebrow and gave him an incredulous glare.

"Okay," Luke said. "I know Zane and I are a bit protective, but we do it out of love."

"I know," Norah said, her voice barely above a whisper.

"Does *anyone* know what's been going on?" Luke asked.

Norah nodded her head. "Andi does but she was sworn to secrecy. I called her after everything happened."

"So Mom and Zane don't know about your run-in with Dad?"

She shook her head.

"When you plannin' on tell them?"

"Sooner rather than later," Norah said and wiped away a tear from her cheek with her fingertip. "I'd like get my thoughts and myself together so I'm not blubbering like this when I tell them though."

"Good plan," Luke said and gave her a meaningful smile. "I'll head out so you can do what you've gotta do." He tugged her close, pecked a kiss on top of her hair and gave her a brotherly hug before he stepped away from her. He almost made it from the kitchen when he stopped and turned back to her. "Hey, Nor?"

"Yeah?"

"About Chase…"

Oh God.

"I don't want to say 'I told you so,' so I'm not," Luke said. "But I will say this…"

And here comes the lecture.

"He's an idiot for messin' things up with you. I know this hurts right now, but it'll get better in time."

Norah just stared dumbfounded at her brother. That was it? No you-should've-known-better-than-to-get-mixed-up-with-that-guy talk?

"I'll see you later, sis." He tipped the brim of his hat and then he was gone.

Norah stared off after him for a few moments, lost in her own thoughts, before she snapped herself out of it and poured herself a cup of coffee. Taking a sip of the hot, steaming brew, Norah glanced around for her cell phone and remembered she'd turned the ringtone off last night after she'd climbed in bed. She walked to her room, opened the nightstand drawer, and grabbed her phone. The screen lit up and the phone made a happy little tune as she turned the ringtone back on. She took another sip of her coffee and her eyes widened when she looked down to the screen and noticed she had sixteen missed phone calls and one voicemail. Her heart fell to her stomach as she pressed her screen to see whom the missed calls were from.

Chase.

Chase.

Chase.

Chase…

She kept scrolling and scrolling to see if any of the missed calls were from anyone *but* him, but they weren't.

Taking in a deep breath, Norah pressed her phone against her ear to listen to the voicemail.

"Norah," A sigh. "I—"

She pulled the phone away from her ear and promptly deleted the message. Just the sound of his voice had set her on edge. Her hands were beginning to shake so badly that she had to set her coffee mug on her nightstand.

If she were ever going to get over Chase O'Donnell, then she needed to distance herself as much as she could from him. Picking the phone back up, Norah blew out a breath of air as she looked up the number for her service provider and dialed them. After pressing a few buttons to get her to the department she needed to speak to, Norah waited patiently until she was connected to a real life person before stating, "I need to block a number, please."

On Tuesday afternoon, Chase sat across from Michael McKade and Jerry Michaels as he presented his ideas for their up and coming office building.

"I like what you've come up with," Jerry stated.

"Thank you, sir," Chase replied.

"I'd change a few things here and there but all minor stuff." Jerry leaned back in his black leather executive chair and looked to his partner. "What do you think, Michael?"

Michael McKade looked over the designs for what seemed like a very long time before answering Jerry. "I like it," he said with a nod. "But I will agree that a few changes will need to be made." And then Michael rattled off his list of things to move, take away, and add, which basically meant scrapping Chase's design all together and coming up with a new design of his own.

Chase pressed his tongue to his cheek and suppressed an annoyed sigh.

"Not a problem," Chase said. "I can have all of those changes made and a new design drawn up for you in a few days."

"Sounds like a plan, son," Jerry said and stood from the conference table.

Chase stood as well and walked around the table, meeting Jerry and Michael and shaking both of their hands.

"I'll be in touch with you in a few days then," Jerry said. "I have a conference call to prepare myself for if you'll excuse me."

Chase nodded to Jerry and walked back to his side of the table as the older man left the room. He began to gather his things and place them in his portfolio when he noticed that Michael was still in the room with him.

"Got a minute?" Michael asked, tapping his fingers on the lacquered mahogany tabletop as he looked to Chase with a devilish smile.

Chase was a bit thrown by this but nodded his head. "Of course."

Placing his hands in the front pockets of his dress pants, Michael walked around the table to the wall of windows that looked out upon the city and stared. "I feel as though I need to be honest with you, Chase, and let you know that your father's firm isn't the only firm we're looking at to design our new office building." He turned to look at Chase. "You're actually one of three." Looking down to the floor, Michael began to walk the length of the room. "Our company is highly desirable, but I'm sure you knew that already." He glanced briefly at Chase. "So it doesn't surprise me when people attempt to—how do I put this politely?—buy my affection."

Chase hid his confusion. Where was this guy going with this?"

"Usually people choose an expensive dinner or, my personal favorite," Michael placed his hand on his chest, "a box of Cuban cigars. But I have to say that no one has ever attempted to earn my business by reuniting me with my daughter."

What the hell? Chase's head snapped to Michael and he gave the man a shocked yet perplexed look. He opened his mouth to speak but Michael silenced him by holding his hand up.

"I'm not sure who's brilliant idea it was or how you even managed to get her to agree to it," Michael said, "but you fellas have got some big cojones for even attempting to pull it off."

"I think there's been a misunderstanding," Chase said but apparently Michael hadn't heard him because he just continued to talk.

"Sadly our little reunion didn't go that well," Michael said. "I'm sure you knew that though, but I will applaud your efforts." He grinned. "She's an outspoken little thing. Reminds me a lot of her mother."

Chase was about to lose it if Michael started talking poorly about Norah and her family. But he didn't, so Chase took his chance during the silence and attempted to clear up the situation.

"Mr. McKade, I honestly can say that my father and I weren't trying to make ourselves appear any better than the other firms who are trying to gain your business by reuniting you with your daughter," Chase explained. "We pride ourselves in our work, and I would hope that you'd choose the best architect for your project based on their level of skill and what they can bring to the table. I've designed many buildings here in Dallas and not once have I had to use bribery to gain those clients. I let my work speak for itself, and I hope you keep that in mind when choosing a firm."

Michael looked Chase up and down as he chewed on the inside corner of his lip. "Thank you for that, Chase. I'll make sure I do keep that in mind."

CHAPTER THIRTY-SEVEN

One week later...

"Chase!" Darren O'Donnell stormed into Chase's office, slamming the door against the wall before crossing the small space to Chase's desk.

"Dad?" Chase said, startled from the abrupt intrusion. "What the hell's the matter with you?"

"What the hell's the matter with *me*?" Darren asked, steam practically blowing from his ears and nostrils. "What the hell's the matter with *you*? What did you say last week when you went to Michael and Michaels?"

"Nothing," Chase said, bewildered by how infuriated his father was. "I just went over the designs and took notes on some changes they wanted. It should've taken me a couple of days to fix it all, but I busted my ass and had everything done and back to them the next afternoon. Why? What's going on?"

Darren's face was so red that Chase started to worry about the man's health.

"I just got a call from Michael McKade letting me know that they've decided to go with another firm," Darren said. "And he told me to personally thank you for giving him something to think on."

Shit. Chase closed his eyes and blew out a breath of air as he slumped back in his office chair.

"What did you say to him?"

"Okay, first," Chase said and gestured to the chair next to his father. "Why don't you sit down, Dad? You look like you're about to have an aneurism."

"I want to know what you said, Chase," Darren said between gritted teeth. "Now."

"Fine," Chase said and slapped his hands down on his desk. "After I went over the designs Michael started going on about how we were one of three firms competing for this job and that he'd never had anyone go so far to bribe him as we did."

"Bribe him?" Darren asked. "What was he talking about?"

Chase let out a sigh. "He thinks we, or I, brought Norah with me to our dinner meeting to make us look better than the other firms."

Darren snorted. "Since when does bringing a *ridin', ropin' cowgirl bartender*," he said, emphasizing his words with an exaggerated hick accent, "make us look good?"

"Since that 'ridin', ropin' cowgirl bartender' is his daughter."

Darren's eyes widened.

"Anyway," Chase said. "I told him that it wasn't true and that our firm has never had to use bribery—that our work speaks for itself. I also told him that he should choose the best architect for his project based on their level of skill and what they can bring to the table."

"Jesus Christ, Chase," Darren said, holding is face in his hand. "You just told the owner of a multi-million dollar company how to run his business. You don't think that sounded a bit cocky? That you belittled him at all?"

"No," Chase answered honestly. "No, I don't think that at all. I think I saved face for *your* business by standing firm on the fact that we don't have to suck up to win bids on projects."

Darren muttered something unintelligible under his breath and Chase questioned him.

"I said I shouldn't have sent you," Darren spat out.

"Thanks to you *my* business failed in winning the bid for the Michael and Michaels project."

"You're mad because I stood up for the right thing?" Chase asked. "That I stood up for *you* and tried to make *you* look like an honorable business man?" He scoffed. "Jesus, Dad, I don't know what you want from me."

"I wanted you to do your job," Darren said. "*'Don't screw this up'* were my exact words, and that's what you did."

"Well, if I'm such a fuck up," Chase said, standing to meet his father eye to eye, "then why don't you just fire me already and get it over with?"

"Maybe I will," Darren sneered.

Chase had to work hard to calm his nerves. He wanted to hit something, and bad. And right now his father's face was looking to be the perfect target.

"I'll do you one better," Chase said, his voice low but to the point. "I quit."

"Fine," Darren said and motioned washing his hands. "I'm done with you."

Chase grabbed his suit jacket from the back of his chair and grabbed his keys before heading for the door.

"Why don't you go on and run back to your little whore while you're at it?"

That was the last straw. Chase dropped his jacket and keys and spun around, throwing his arm up and under his father's chin as he slammed him against the wall and pinned him there. "Don't you ever—*ever!*—call her that again. You hear me?"

"Get. Out," Darren choked, his face turning blood red from lack of air. "Now."

Chase dropped his arm and stepped back, watching his father bend over and gasp for air before picking up his jacket and keys. He straightened his tie and ran a hand through his hair as he looked around the small office area. All eyes were focused on him. With a nod to his clearly confused and startled audience, Chase made his way to the elevator. Once he was inside, he couldn't help but feel as though a great weight had just been lifted from his shoulders.

Chase's cell phone rang. Why he still thought it could be Norah on the other end, he wasn't sure.

Because you're hoping she'll forgive your sorry ass and take you back, that's why.

True. He was still hoping that someway and somehow Norah would forgive him. Taking him back would be the ultimate bonus, but he'd settle for being on speaking terms with her. It had felt as though someone had stabbed him in the chest when he'd called her the morning after she'd left Dallas and he'd received the prerecorded message saying that his number had been blocked. That had stung like hell knowing that she'd gone that far as to never have to hear from him ever again.

After the fourth ring, Chase answered his phone.

"Chase?" His mother's voice sounded pained before he heard her start to cry.

"Oh, Mom," Chase said gently. "Come on, now. Don't cry."

"I'm sorry, it's just…" She paused to take in a few breaths. "I know you and your father have never had the best relationship but I honestly never saw it coming to this extreme."

Of course Darren had called and told his mother what had happened. But, knowing his father, he probably embellished the story by saying Chase had also taken a swing at him.

"Look, Mom," Chase said. "I'm sorry too. I know this kind of stuff worries you but try not to let it. Okay? Dad and I...we just can't get along, and I don't know why. He's got some sort of chip on his shoulder when it comes to me, and I think it's best for now if I place some distance between us."

"What are you saying?"

"I'm gonna go back to the ranch," Chase told his mother. "I've got more things to do around there and then when that's all done I'll figure out my next move."

"Okay," Susan said and sniffed. "I love you, son. Please call me as often as you can."

"I will, Mom," Chase said. "I love you too."

This was a bad idea.

Chase sat in his SUV drumming his fingers on the steering wheel as he stared at the door of the Rusty Spur. He just sat there watching as people came and went, in the building and out the building, the music growing louder each time the door opened and then fading as the door closed. This had gone on for a good twenty minutes now as he contemplated on whether or not he should go in or if he should just head straight to the ranch. If he were a smart man, he would choose the latter.

Chase chewed on the corner of his lip as he thought it over for a few more minutes before deciding, *Screw it*, and removed his keys from the ignition before stepping out of his SUV. Crossing the parking lot, Chase grabbed the door handle as a man and a woman came stumbling out of the building, laughing with their hands all over one another. He shook his head as he let them pass and then entered the smoky air of the bar. It wasn't as packed as he'd expected it to be. Quite a few tables were vacant, as were bar stools, so it didn't take him long to single out Norah from the crowd.

She was standing next to one of the tables, smiling and talking to a group of men with her tray tucked beneath her arm. But then she must've felt as if someone were staring at her because she looked up and around before settling her gaze directly on him.

Norah hated that feeling she got when she knew someone was staring at her. Usually it meant that some creep was checking her out, so she turned her attention slightly away from the old high school friends she was talking to and glanced around the room. Her heart came to a dead stop when she saw him.

What was he doing here?

She just stood there and stared at him with a dumbfounded expression. Maybe it wasn't him. Maybe it was just her subconscious playing a nasty trick on her. She'd had that happen more than once since everything went down over a week ago. But then he started to walk in her direction and Norah knew that this wasn't a figment of her imagination. Excusing herself from her friends, Norah quickly turned and started for the bar.

"Norah," Chase called after her. "Wait a second. Please."

"What are you doing here, Chase?" Norah asked, rounding the corner of the bar and setting her tray on the back counter. This was not happening.

Chase rested his arm on the lacquered wood top and watched her for a moment. "I wanted to see you, to talk to you."

She didn't look in Chase's direction as she took an order from a customer, reached into the cooler and handed the man a longneck beer.

"What happened that last day we were together…" Chase started, looking down to his arm on the bar top and blowing out a breath of air before looking up again. "Norah, can you please just talk to me for a second? I need you to hear me out."

Anger flooded her veins. "You need me to hear you out?" she asked. "I think I've heard enough from you to last me a lifetime, so right now I'm going to ask that *you* hear *me* out and leave. Now."

"Norah," Chase pleaded.

"I'm not doing this, Chase." She stared him down, hoping to drive her point home. But as she looked into Chase's green eyes she was reminded of all the good memories she had of him, and her heart shattered. "Just go."

"Please don't do this," Chase said, his voice so soft and pained that she almost gave in.

She felt her throat tighten and swallowed hard against the action.

"I can't even look at you," she told him, barely able to get the words around the lump in her throat. "Please, just leave me alone."

"Is everything okay, Norah?" Trace, the bouncer, asked as he walked up and stood next to Chase.

Breathing hard and fighting back her impending tears, Norah held onto Chase's gaze and told Trace, "No."

She watched as Chase's shoulders slumped just slightly. "Norah—"

"Come on, guy," Trace said, placing a hand on Chase's shoulder and directing him away from the bar.

"Time for you to call it a night."

Her hands were trembling as she watched Chase being escorted from the bar. A mix of emotions ran through her in that moment: shock, disbelief, wonder, sorrow, anger. And all of them swirled together creating one dreaded sensation that left her feeling like a hollow shell. She hated him, hated him for what he did, for what he said, and for showing up here tonight. But the thing that she hated most was the fact that she didn't want to hate him at all.

CHAPTER THIRTY-EIGHT

The night sky was pitch black when Chase pulled up to the ranch and parked his SUV next to the house. He sat there for a long moment, replaying Norah's words to him over and over again in his mind.

I can't even look at you.

The pained expression on her face as she spoke those words ripped his heart into pieces. He shouldn't have gone there, at least not tonight. His spur of the moment decision had backfired severely.

Stepping out of his vehicle, he closed the door shut behind him and looked to the barn when he heard one of the horses whinny. The pole light by the barn guided him as he made his way across the yard and slid open the large door. Two heads popped over the stall doors and Chase smiled.

"Hey, guys," he said and walked over to the first stall. "Remember me?"

Chase reached a hand out and rubbed at the white blaze that decorated the gelding's face. He looked over into the stall and gave the horse a few gentle pats on his neck before moving to the next one.

"It looks like you guys have been taken care of well while I've been gone." He ran his hand up and down the gray mare's neck and she nudged him with her muzzle. "Sorry," Chase said with a soft laugh. "Guys and *lady*."

Moving over to the third stall, Chase looked over and saw the pony standing in the corner. "Hey, Buckshot," Chase said, then frowned. "You didn't eat your oats."

He opened the stall door and took a handful of oats

before slowly walking up to the pony.

"Here you go, old fella." He held his hand out flat beneath the pony's mouth, but all it did was sniff and turn its head slightly. "Not hungry?" Chase said and used his other hand to pet the pony's shaggy mane.

The gray mare craned her neck over the stall and let out a soft whinny. "Jealous?" Chase asked and outstretched his hand with the oats to her. "Here you go." She nibbled at the oats and Chase gently pet the side of her face when she'd finished eating.

"All right, guys," Chase said as he made his way from the stall, "and lady." He shut the stall door, locked it, and then headed down the dirt packed aisle to exit the barn. "You all have a good night, and I'll see you in the morning."

Chase awoke to the sound of someone knocking on the back door. Sunlight spilled through the curtains as he crawled out of bed and made his way from the room.

"Coming," Chase called from the hall as he slipped his t-shirt over his head.

Excitement and anticipation moved through him. Every bit of him hoped that when he opened that door he'd see Norah. Maybe she'd changed her mind about hearing him out? But when he reached for the door and pulled it open, Norah was not the person standing across from him.

"Son of a bitch," Luke muttered.

And before Chase had time to do anything, Luke hauled off and punched him square in the jaw.

Stumbling backwards, Chase hit the table and awkwardly caught his balance. "What the hell, man?"

"You've got a lot of nerve showing up here, O'Donnell," Luke said, fists balled by his sides as he hovered in the open doorway.

"On my own property? Chase rubbed his jaw and glared at Luke. "How rude of me."

"No, what's rude was how you treated my baby sister," Luke said. "I warned you not to hurt her and said if you did I'd have to break your jaw."

"Well, thanks for sticking to your word," Chase mocked. "It may not be broken but you got your point across. Feel free to leave now that you've got what you came for."

"Don't flatter yourself." Luke snorted sarcastically. "I came by to take care of the horses. Just because you're an asshole doesn't mean they should suffer."

"Yeah, well don't bother," Chase said. "I can do it myself."

The corner of Luke's mouth turned up as he let out a huff and started to walk backwards across the porch. "Stay away from my sister," Luke warned, pointing his index finger at Chase. "Or the next time, I swear to God, I *will* break your jaw."

Chase crossed his arms over his chest as he walked out onto the porch, staring Luke down as he made his way over to his truck. A cloud of dust and dirt kicked up beneath Luke's tires as he sped out of the driveway and down the road. Shaking his head, Chase slipped into his work boots and ran his hand through his hair before placing his baseball cap on his head and making his way out to the barn. The door screeched as he slid it to the side and stepped into the weather-beaten building.

"Hey, Doc," Chase said, nodding to the gelding before heading towards the tack room to grab the horse's halter. But Chase stopped in his tracks when he noticed

Missy pacing around in a circle in her stall. Wondering what she was up to, Chase furrowed his eyebrows and crossed the small space.

"Hey there, girl," he said and reached his hand over the stall door. "What's going on?"

The mare kept pacing and dipped her head over into the adjacent stall.

Chase looked to Missy with a puzzled expression and backed away from her stall door. Taking a few steps to the left, Chase rested his hand on the wooden ledge and looked over into Buckshot's stall. His chest tightened.

"Oh no."

"Norah?"

Jumping slightly at the sound of her name, Norah turned her attention away from the window and looked to her mother. "I'm sorry, Mom," she said, shaking her head. "Did you need me?"

"Can you hand me the butter from the fridge, please?" Linda asked, standing in front of the stove and stirring the contents of a cast iron pan.

With a soft nod, Norah walked over to the fridge, grabbed the glass butter dish, and handed it over to her mother.

"Thank you, sweetie," Linda said, then looked briefly to Norah. "Are you okay? You seem distant."

"Hmm?" Norah asked. "Oh, yeah, I'm okay."

Linda dipped her head and shot Norah a disbelieving look.

"What? I'm fine."

"I think I've gotten pretty good at telling when one of my children is lying to me," Linda said with a half smile.

"I'd also say I'm pretty good at guessing when something's wrong." She looked away from Norah and down to the pan as she stirred a wooden spoon around the edges.

"You're right," Norah admitted and let out a sigh. "I've just got so much on my mind right now. With everything that happened with Dad, his wife, and…"

"And Chase," her mother finished for her when she let her sentence trail off.

Norah nodded solemnly.

"You miss him, don't you?" Grabbing a large bowl from the counter, Linda turned off the stove and emptied the contents of the pan into the dish.

Norah hesitated for a long moment before replying with a soft, "Yes." She crossed her arms over her chest, hugging herself tightly as she shook her head and let out a small laugh. "It doesn't make any sense though, does it?"

"Of course it makes sense, sweetie," Linda said, setting the food off to the side and wiping her hands on a dish towel before turning to face Norah. "What the two of you had was special."

A sarcastic huff escaped from Norah's lips. "What we had was a lie."

"Norah…" Linda said, her voice and expression woeful as she looked to her daughter.

"It's okay, Mom." She forced a gentle smile. "I honestly thought at one point that Chase and I would…" Tucking her bottom lip between her teeth, Norah shook her head and looked to the floor as a wave of emotion ran through her.

Her mother's arms enveloped her and pulled her close. "I hate to see you like this," Linda spoke softly. "But these hard times that life brings us only make us stronger in the end. You'll get through this." She pulled back and lifted Norah's chin between her forefinger and thumb. "I know you will."

Holding back the tears that filled her eyes, Norah nodded and let her mother's words sink in. "Thanks, Mom."

"Come on. Come on." Chase gritted his teeth as he turned the key in the ignition for the umpteenth time, praying and cursing that the tractor would start this time. The engine sputtered and produced a bit of black smoke before it made a horrible choking sound and completely shut down. Slamming his hand against the steering wheel, Chase let out a long string of curse words and let his head fall forward as he blew out a breath of air.

What a shitty morning and Luke's little surprise visit wasn't even the worst of it. Walking out to the barn and finding that the pony had passed away overnight had nearly sent Chase over the edge. He'd never considered himself a crier, but he sure came damn close to it as he entered the stall and knelt down next to the animal, another part of his life gone forever.

The sound of a vehicle approaching caught his attention, and he lifted his head to see a pick-up truck pulling up the driveway. Sunlight glared off the hood, making it impossible for him to see who the driver was. Squinting against the brightness, Chase watched as the truck came to a stop in the middle of the yard and the driver stepped out.

Well, this was just great. Two McKades in one day. What were the odds?

Zane looked around before seeing Chase in the shed and then strolled across the yard towards him, the brim of his cowboy hat hiding his face as he approached.

"Chase," Zane said, his expression unreadable as he looked up to Chase sitting on the tractor.

Chase didn't bother moving from his seat as Zane entered the building. "Zane," he acknowledged with a nod.

A thick silence filled the space between them as the two men stared at each other.

"I take it my brother's already been by." Zane nodded and pointed to the bruise decorating Chase's jaw.

"Yep," Chase answered coolly. "You here to deliver a message as well?" Blood pumping fiercely through his veins, Chase hopped down from the tractor and glared at Zane. "What's it gonna be? Black eye? Bloody nose? Or are you gonna to stick with the McKade tradition and break my jaw? Your sister and your brother already tried so—what the hell?—let's see if the third time's the charm."

"Whoa, take it easy, Chase." Zane held his hands up to show that he wasn't a threat. "I didn't come here for that."

Crossing his arms over his chest, Chase stared at Zane, unconvinced. "Then why are you here?"

"To talk," Zane said and relaxed his hands.

"About what?"

Zane gave Chase a knowing look.

"There's nothing to talk about."

"You broke my sister's heart," Zane said. "I think we have a lot to talk about."

"Look," Chase said, uncrossing his arms and calming down a bit. "I get that you and your brother are doing the whole looking-out-for-your-sister thing, but what happened is between me and Norah. And, no offense, I'd just rather not discuss it with you."

"None taken," Zane said. "But I'm not leaving here

until you tell me why you did what you did."

Chase expelled a heavy sigh and stood silent for a long moment as he stared across the space to Zane. "Okay," he said. "You wanna know why I did what I did? I'm an idiot, plain and simple. I did something stupid, said some things that were even more stupid, and I ended up hurting someone I care very much about." He paused and collected his thoughts. "I never meant for any of this to happen. And I sure as hell didn't mean to put her through the shit she's been through. If I had a way to un-do it all, I would in a heartbeat. I wouldn't even do it just to win her back. I'd do it so she'd never feel the heartache and painful regret that she's feeling now."

Zane studied Chase for what seemed like a very long time. "You really do care about her, don't you?"

Chase nodded. "I do."

"I believe you," Zane said but quickly added, "but don't go thinking that I'm gonna help you get her back. You're on your own with that one. If Norah decides she wants to be with you…" He paused. "Well, I won't stand in your way."

"Thanks, Zane."

"But if you screw up again you know I'm gonna have to—"

"Break my jaw," Chase said for him. "Yeah, I know."

The corner of Zane's lips curled up into a grin. "So, what's wrong with your tractor?"

CHAPTER THIRTY-NINE

Norah jogged up the steps of Merle's store and shoved her list in her back pocket as she pushed open the door. The string of jingle bells attached to the handle signaled her entrance and an elderly woman peered out from around the corner behind the counter.

"Hey, hon," she called out to Norah.

"Hi, Miss Ida," Norah said. "How are you doin' today?"

Ida emerged from behind the wall and adjusted her reading glasses on the tip of her nose. "My arthritis is actin' up a bit, but other than that I'm good," she said. "What brings you in?"

"Just picking up a few things for the ranch," Norah said. "I'm gonna need some oats but I have other things to pick up as well."

"No problem, sweetie," Ida said. "You go on and get your other items and then I'll have one of the boys load your truck for you."

Norah thanked the older woman and began making her way around the store. She'd just rounded the corner of the aisle that held horse supplies when she saw him.

Chase stood in front of a selection of halters, one looped over his shoulder as he held two more in each hand. He seemed to be pondering his purchase when he glanced up and over to her.

Her chest tightened the instant his eyes met hers.

She couldn't move. She just stood there staring at him with her mouth gaping open. What was he still doing in town? Chase's body language screamed of hesitation, but then he slowly started to walk towards her. Her breathing quickened with her escalated heartbeat, and for a second Norah felt like turning and running away.

Don't be ridiculous and cause a scene right in the middle of gossip central.

Taking in a deep breath to calm herself, Norah firmly planted her feet and waited as Chase approached her.

"Hey," he said, stopping just short of two feet away from her.

At least the man was smart enough to give her some distance.

"Chase," Norah replied and did her best to avoid looking him in the eye. "I didn't expect to see you here."

The corner of his mouth lifted slightly as he briefly dipped his gaze before looking back to her. "I was just picking up a few things for the horses." He lifted his hands to show her the halters. "Can't decide which one to get for Missy."

This felt extremely odd. Standing here talking to Chase should have been uncomfortable, given their recent history. But she found herself falling back into a familiar place and decided, w*hat the hell?*

Norah looked to Chase's hands and pointed to the one off to the right. "The purple one would look really nice on her."

Chase nodded and stuck the other halter back on the wall. "Purple it is then."

"I don't know if you saw them or not," Norah said, "but the pony halters are right on the end. A red one would look nice on Buckshot."

Chase nodded again and looked down to the halter in his hands, running the nylon through his fingers. "It would've looked real nice on him," he said "But he, uh, actually died a couple of days ago."

"Oh," Norah said, her voice barely above a whisper. "Oh my gosh, Chase, I'm so sorry."

"It's fine," he said. "He was old, and it was his time. I don't know what I would've done though if your brother hadn't dropped by and helped me."

"My brother?" Norah questioned.

"Yeah," Chase told her. "Zane had stopped by that morning to, uh…talk."

As Norah stared at Chase in disbelief, surprised by what he'd just told her, she noticed the bruise hidden beneath the stubble on his jaw and gasped.

"Oh my God," Norah said, not realizing she'd stepped forward and was now inches away from Chase. "Did he do that?" She gestured to his jaw.

"This?" Chase asked and angled his face for her to see the mark better. "No." He grinned. "This was courtesy of Luke." He let out a small laugh and turned to face her head on, still grinning. "Now I know where you learned that killer right hook of yours."

Unable to help herself, Norah smiled.

"Norah, hon?"

Norah turned her head and found Ida standing at the end of the aisle.

"Oh, I'm sorry," Ida quickly apologized. "I was just gonna tell you that the boys have to step out for a delivery. So if you want to pull your truck around to the back real quick I'll have them load your order before they leave."

"I'll be right there," Norah said to Ida before looking back to Chase. "Well I better get going."

"Yeah," Chase said quietly and locked his eyes with hers. "It was good seeing you."

She nodded, keeping her eyes on his. "You too." She lingered there for another short moment before looking away from him and turning around. Walking down the aisle, Norah had only made it a few feet away before hearing Chase call after her. She turned back around and found him closing the distance between them.

"I know this probably isn't the right time to do this," Chase said, almost rushing through the words. "But I just want to tell you that I'm sorry, for everything."

She didn't know what to say. Her mind was everywhere as she absorbed the situation. This short encounter had been a nice reminder that she and Chase used to be friends and made it easy to forget the things he'd said when he didn't know she was listening. But his apology brought those not so fond memories to the forefront of her mind and filled her with regret. Now Norah knew exactly what she wanted to say to him but couldn't get the words past the tightness of her throat. So she turned away from him, not wanting him to see how his words affected her, and left.

Norah stood behind the bar, leaning down with her elbow on the wooden top and her head in her hand as she looked out upon the crowd of people that filled the Rusty Spur.

"Are you bored or something?"

Glancing to her left, Norah found Andi standing next to her placing dirty glasses into the sink of sudsy water.

"No," Norah said. "I was just thinking about stuff." She looked around the room once more before pushing herself up from the counter and spinning around to rest her back against it. "Can I ask you something?" Norah said to Andi as she crossed her arms over her chest.

"Sure," Andi said. "What's up?"

"Do you think I'm being childish with this whole Chase thing?"

"Childish?" Andi questioned Norah, furrowing her eyebrows in confusion. "I'm not following you."

"I blocked his number so he couldn't call me, and the two times I've seen him since then I wouldn't let him talk to me about what happened."

"That's not childish," Andi said. "You're just doing what you have to do in order to help yourself get over him."

"You think so?"

Andi nodded and stared at Norah inquisitively for a long moment. "It's not working though, is it?"

Norah pinched her lips tight and shook her head. "Part of me wants to just be able to forget about everything and put it in the past." She sighed heavily. "But the other part of me wants an explanation and to hear what he has to say."

"So why don't you do that?" Andi asked.

"Do what?"

"Hear what he has to say." Andi then reached into the cooler, pulled out a longneck beer and passed it across the counter to a waiting customer. "It's going to eat you alive, arguing with yourself like that. He's still in town, right? So just go talk to him, get an explanation from him and then take things from there. You might just end up getting the closure you need."

Norah nodded her head as she thought about Andi's advice.

"Well?" Andi said.

"Well what?"

"Why are you still standing here?"

Norah shot Andi a confused look. "What? You want me to go talk to him now?"

"Sure," Andi said. "You're not going to be able to concentrate on anything else until you do. So go."

"But what about—"

"Don't worry about Red," Andi told Norah. "If he asks where you are I'll tell him you went home with a headache."

A smile spread across Norah's face as she reached for her truck keys by the register. "Thanks, Andi."

"You're welcome," Andi said and returned Norah's smile. "Now go on. Get out of here."

Chase was driving to the Rusty Spur, trying to talk himself out of going and convince himself that it was just a bad idea all around, when he caught sight of headlights coming towards him in the distance. He rarely ever passed anyone this late at night on these back roads, so when the vehicle approached Chase took a good look at it as his headlights brought it into full view.

That couldn't be…?

He looked up to his rearview mirror and saw the red glow of brake lights. Pressing his foot against his own brakes, Chase shifted his SUV into park and watched as the vehicle behind him pulled a u-turn. He squinted against the bright lights as the vehicle parked behind him and then watched as the driver's side door opened.

He stepped out of his SUV and into the night air, leaving his door open as he made his way towards his back tire. Standing in the headlights, Chase waited as Norah walked up to him with a determined look on her face. Her pace slowed and she came to a stop, leaving a good six feet of space between them and a whole lot of silence.

Chase chewed on the inside of his cheek, waiting to see if she was going to yell at him, or cuss him out, or punch him again. But she did none of those. She just stood there across from him and stared.

"I was actually just headed up your way," Chase said when the silence had become too much for him to handle. "I didn't know if you'd be working or not but—"

"Why did you say those things about me?"

Not really surprised by her hostility towards him, Chase opened his mouth to speak but she cut him off.

"It just doesn't make any sense to me, Chase," Norah said. "And, trust me, I've tried to piece it all together, but I can't make any of it fit. The time we spent together? How we were?" She let out an exasperated sigh. "I felt something for you that I've never felt with another man. And I honestly thought you felt the same about me. So please, just tell me. Did I really mean nothing to you?"

Chase had to work hard to calm his breathing. Hearing her say it like that ripped him in two.

"No," he said.

The pained look on her face almost did him in. "Then why did you say it?" Her voice broke and her eyes glistened with tears.

"My dad and I were arguing," Chase explained. "He was being a real jerk and said some things about you, and I got mad." He took in a deep breath and let it out very slowly. "God, Norah, when you overheard me I was completely being sarcastic, just telling my dad what he wanted to hear. None of those horrible things I said were true. And right after I said it I told him that he was an idiot if he thought that was the way I felt about you." He took a step in her direction but stopped himself from going any further when she took a step back. "Now I wish I'd handled things differently and not let him get to me. If I could take it all back, Norah, I would. I never meant for you to get hurt, especially by me."

Her bottom lip was between her teeth as she took in a shaky breath. "Why'd you come back?"

That question threw him. How'd they get to this topic? He was just about to answer her with, *to beg for your forgiveness and win you back*, when she continued.

"This was easier to deal with when you weren't around," she told him, then glanced down to the gravel road before looking back to him. "The first thing I think of when I see you are all the hurtful things you said about me." She swallowed hard. "But then I remember all the good times we had and I find it hard to stay mad at you." Her lip quivered and she took in another shaky breath. "How am I supposed to get over you?"

He was no longer whole. His heart, his mind, his entire being felt torn to shreds. "I don't want you to get over me."

Tears flowed freely down Norah's cheeks.

"Norah, I've lost so much in such a short amount of time, and I don't want to add you to that list." He slowly made his way over to her, one guarded step at a time. "You mean the world to me. Coming here and meeting you has been the best thing that's ever happened to me. And falling in love with you?" He shrugged slightly. "That was just a bonus."

She stared at him, awestruck. "Professing your love for me doesn't mean I'm going to instantly forgive you."

"I don't expect you to." He grinned, just slightly, as he looked into her blue eyes. "I don't care how long it takes for you to forgive me." He let out a soft chuckle. "Hell, I'm just glad you're talking to me."

He watched her as she took in deep breaths through her nose and blew them out through her mouth. "I don't know if I can do this, Chase. I'm so confused."

"About what?"

"What to do," Norah answered in a soft-spoken tone. "I hate you for what you said, whether you meant it or not, because it still hurt." Her breath hitched. "But at the same time, I don't want to hate you."

"Then don't." He reached out for her hands, relief washing over him when she didn't shy away. "Give me another chance, Norah. Please."

Taking in a ragged breath, Norah closed her eyes and a tear slipped down her cheek. "I don't know, Chase. I need some time to think."

"Okay," Chase said as Norah slowly pulled her hands away from his. "Take all the time you need."

Tucking her bottom lip between her teeth, Norah nodded and turned away from him. He watched her walk back to her truck, climb into the driver's seat and slowly drive past him down the long, dark road. Standing there in the middle of the road, Chase stared off after her hoping she'd slow down or that he'd see the glow of her brake lights. When she disappeared completely from his view, Chase let out a heavy sigh and walked back to his SUV. He ditched his plans of going to the bar, turned his vehicle around in the road, and headed back to the ranch.

Tears blurred her vision to the point where she was unable to see the road clearly. Not wanting to add an accident to her growing list of horrible events, Norah pulled her truck to a sliding stop on the side of the road. After shifting the vehicle into park, she crossed her arms over the steering wheel then rested her forehead against them. Her shoulders shook as she let herself cry.

Her head hurt and her heart ached as she thought about everything Chase had just told her. She wanted to believe him and believe that he truly did care for her. But she just couldn't bring herself to forgive him right then and there, no matter how much she wanted to. It had taken every bit of restraint she had not to throw herself into his arms and forget about all the bad things that had happened.

Lifting her head from the steering wheel, Norah brought her hands to her face and wiped the tears from beneath her eyes and cheeks with her fingertips. She needed to get away, to escape from reality, if only for just a little while, to clear her mind so she could think straight. Taking in a few deep and calming breaths, Norah shifted her truck into drive and headed for her family's ranch.

When she neared her mother's house, she flipped off her headlights and then turned onto the driveway shutting the ignition off to her truck and letting it coast to the barn. After exiting the truck and quietly closing the door behind her, Norah entered the barn and saddled her horse. A few minutes later she was riding out of the yard, the cool night air brushed over her exposed skin and through her hair as she urged Cheyenne into a gentle lope. They rode like that for a while, and once they were surrounded by nothing but wide-open space and a blanket of stars, Norah slowed Cheyenne's pace to a slow walk and gave the horse a few gentle pats against her neck.

"Good girl, Cheyenne," Norah praised softly and ran her fingers through the mare's pale mane. "I'm sorry I haven't spent much time with you lately. I wish I had a good excuse, but I don't." She let out a soft sigh. "Spending all of my time with Chase seems pretty dumb now, considering the predicament I'm in." A tiny laugh escaped from her lips. "You are so lucky you don't have to deal with men."

She brought Cheyenne to a stop and let her eyes roam

over the land. Moonlight grazed the tips of the tall grass, giving it the effect of calm water. It was a beautiful sight and filled her with the peace and serenity she so desperately needed. A soft breeze blew through the air, and Norah closed her eyes, taking in a deep breath before leaning over and resting her cheek against Cheyenne's mane.

"I don't know what I should do, girl," Norah said, running the palm of her hand up and down the mare's neck. "He's never lied to be before, so I don't know why I'm so hesitant to believe him now." She sighed. "I guess I'm just scared. What if I forgive him and then something like this happens again? I don't think I could deal with another Chase O'Donnell heartache. I love his stupid ass so much, and this is killing me."

She took in a ragged breath and then blew it out slowly. Sitting back up and positioning herself back in the saddle, Norah sniffed and wiped at her cheek with the back of her hand. She gripped the reins and gently laid them against her horse's neck, turning her back in the direction of her mother's house. It'd been a long night, and Norah had a lot to think about. But deep down she already knew what she wanted. She just needed to find the courage to admit it.

CHAPTER FORTY

The pungent aroma of horse manure filled his nostrils as he dumped the contents of the shovel into the wheelbarrow. With a heavy sigh, Chase rested the blade of the shovel onto the hard, packed dirt floor and folded his arms over the handle. Sweat dripped down his temples, down the side of his neck, and then trickled lazily down his torso leaving his gray t-shirt and the waistline of his jeans damp. He removed his worn navy baseball cap from his head, feeling slightly cooler as the air hit his sweat-matted hair, and wiped the back of his arm across his forehead. His intentions were to remove the beads of moisture that gathered there, but all he managed to do was add more and smear it all together.

Every muscle in his back and arms ached, which surprised the hell out of him since he thought he'd be used to this ranch stuff by now. He stretched in an effort to ease some of his discomfort and then went to replace his baseball hat back on his head, but stopped. The bright yellow streak of dried paint caught his eye, and his chest tightened.

He was thankful that Norah had finally given him a chance to explain himself, and he'd been sincere with her when he told her to take all the time she needed to think things over. But if he were going to be completely honest with himself, he'd hoped she wouldn't take this long. Part of him—the extremely optimistic part—had envisioned her changing her mind and coming back to him right after she drove off. At the most he figured she'd sleep on it and call him as soon as she woke up. And yet here it was, late morning of the very next day, and he still hadn't heard from her.

He laid awake in his bed for hours after he'd arrived home last night as the memory of their conversation playing over and over again in his mind. And it was the first thing he thought of when he'd woken up that morning. Wondering when or if she'd call him was driving him crazy. So in an effort to save at least some of his sanity, Chase had dressed and gone outside to start on his morning chores.

He'd started with turning the horses out and then made his way up to the loft to grab a hay bale. After deciding that the place was a complete mess, Chase had taken the initiative to restack all of the bales. Once that was done he tossed one bale out of the loft door, made his way down the ladder and fed portions of it to each horse. He'd then headed back for the barn and to the tack room to grab a shovel and start cleaning out the stalls. When he walked into the room, he decided it was a complete mess as well and began reorganizing all of the tack. Sweat quickly beaded on his skin from the stuffy close quarters, and he impatiently wiped the back of his hand beneath his nose to remove one of the droplets. After he'd finished the unnecessary task, Chase had finally gone to work cleaning out the stalls.

He heaved a heavy sigh as he stared down at his hat for a long moment before gripping the brim and adjusting it into place on his head. He then took hold of the bottom hem of his shirt and brought it to his face to wipe the sweat away. Lifting the handles of the wheelbarrow, Chase pushed the filled cart through the barn doors and to the manure pile. He was on his way back to the barn when his cell phone rang. Dropping his hold on the handles of the wheelbarrow, Chase reached for his phone then froze when he saw Norah's name appear on the screen. Excitement and anticipation filled him as he quickly pressed the button to answer the call.

"Hello?" he said, softly clearing his throat and calming his voice.

"Hi, Chase," Norah said. "I'm not calling you at a bad time, am I?"

"No," Chase told her. "Not at all. What's up?"

He heard a soft sigh come from her end of the phone followed by silence.

"Norah?"

"I'm here," she said. "I, uh…I was wondering if you had plans for later. I thought if you weren't busy that maybe I could stop by and we could talk."

His mouth curved into a smile. "Yeah. We can talk. What time were you thinking of stopping by?"

"Sixish?" she said.

"Okay," Chase replied. "I'll see you then."

When Norah ended the call a few seconds later, Chase didn't waste any time and quickly made another phone call.

"Chase," his mother answered in a sweet tone. "How are you doing?"

"I'm okay," Chase told her. "You got a second?"

"Sure," Susan said. "What's going on?"

"Norah's coming over later to talk, and I need your help with something."

"What do you need?"

Chase rubbed his hand against the back of his neck. "I need a recipe."

Norah pulled up to Chase's house at quarter to six. Her

heart beat frantically in her chest as she parked her truck next to his SUV. Turning off the ignition, she stared out the windshield to the house for a long moment gathering her nerve. She took in a calming breath and stepped out of her vehicle before making her way over to the porch. As she walked up the steps she caught the faint smell of something burning. Eyebrows furrowed in confusion, Norah lifted her hand and cautiously knocked on the door.

Chase opened the door with a surprised yet puzzled expression. "Hey," he said, then turned to look at something in the house before turning back to her. "You're early."

She gave him a bemused smirk. "I said I'd be here around six, and it's quarter till now."

"Shit," he murmured and glanced back into the house.

"Is everything all right?" Norah asked.

"Yeah," Chase said, looking back to her. "Yeah, everything's okay. I was just hoping to be done by the time you got here." He flashed her a smile and stepped aside, gesturing for her to walk past him. "Come on in."

A soft halo of smoke circled the ceiling of the kitchen as she moved past him and further into the room. She coughed and waved her hand in front of her face.

"What are you doing?" Norah asked, turning to look at Chase.

"Besides trying to burn my house down?" he teased as he opened and closed the door in an attempt to fan some of the smoke from the room. "I was trying to cook you dinner. Can you open that window over there for me?"

"Sure," Norah said, then crossed the room and slid the window up. As she turned back around, she glanced over the countertops. They were a complete mess. Flour covered the surface and the bag it came in sat there with a large rip running down the center. A popping, spitting sound caught her attention, and she looked to the stove. Chase was trying to make her fried chicken. She smiled softly before looking at him and noticing that his faded blue t-shirt was speckled with grease spots. "I thought you didn't cook?"

Chase turned to look at her as he stopped swinging the door and left it wide-open. "I don't," he said, then added with a small laugh, "Obviously." He gestured to the plate of burnt food as he walked over to the stove. The oil in the pan popped as Chase removed another piece of blackened chicken, and he flinched.

Norah attempted to suppress an amused smile but Chase caught her and asked, "What's so funny?"

"Nothing," she said with a slight shake of her head. "Do you want some help?"

"That kind of defeats the purpose of me cooking for you but..." He let out an exasperated sigh and stepped back from the stove. "Yeah, I do want your help. If I keep this up I really will burn my house down."

Norah let out a small laugh and walked over to the stove, taking the tongs from Chase's outstretched hand and adjusting the heat setting on the burner. "So what made you decide to cook dinner for me?" she asked, keeping her eyes focused on the cast iron pan in front of her.

Chase had walked over to the fridge and was now on his way back to her with a beer in each hand. "Just wanted to do something nice for you." He shrugged, popped the top off one of the beers and handed it over to her. "I'd planned on having everything made and on the table by the time you got here and was gonna light some candles and have all this mess cleaned up." He popped the top off of his beer and took a sip.

"So in other words, you were trying to suck up to

me," Norah said with a smirk as she pulled the last few pieces of chicken from the pan and turned off the flame. They weren't black like the other pieces, but they were definitely browner than they should've been. At least they were still edible.

"I guess I was." Chase brought his bottle to his lips and took a long drink. "I failed pretty miserably though, huh?" He chuckled softly. "I can design entire buildings but I can't follow a simple recipe. There's something not right about that."

"I wouldn't say you failed completely," Norah told him, then took a sip of her own beer. "The gesture was nice, but it wasn't necessary. I just wanted to talk to you."

"I know," he said, then nodded his head in the direction of the back door. "Since dinner's ruined, you wanna go out to the porch?"

"Sure," she said and followed him out of the house. She walked to the corner of the porch and rested against the corner rail.

Chase had paused by the steps, leaning his tall frame against the post as he looked across to her. "So what did you want to talk to me about?"

This was it. Now or never. Her heart hammered inside her chest but Norah gathered up her courage and began.

"I've done a lot of thinking since everything went down, and even more since last night," Norah told him, looking down to the bottle in her hands. "And I don't think I'll ever be able to forget what happened while we were in Dallas." She looked up and locked eyes with him. "But I really want to try to put it in the past and be done with it. All of it. If you say that you didn't mean those things you said to your father, well, then I believe you. You've always been upfront and honest with me, so I really shouldn't start to doubt you now." She paused, took in a breath then let it out forcefully. "The bottom line is...I don't want to be mad at you anymore. I don't want to go on not seeing you or talking to you every day." She searched his face and gave a tiny shrug of her shoulders. "I just want to be with you."

Chase perched his beer on the railing and walked over to her at a leisurely pace. "I *have* always been honest with you, about *everything.* And I would never lie to you or do anything to intentionally hurt you. My life is better because you're in it." He grinned. "At the risk of sounding completely sappy, you're my entire world and without you I have nothing."

Tears began to form in her eyes, and she blinked against the warmth.

"I love you so damn much, Norah," Chase said, stepping to her and resting his hands on her hips.

Her heart turned over with love as she took in a shaky breath and looked to Chase's beautiful green eyes.

"The past two weeks have been the worst—not seeing you, not talking to you." He paused. "Call me crazy," he said softly, "but I think I missed you."

She laughed through her tears and took in another shaky breath. "I missed you too, you jerk."

"Don't forget I'm also an idiot," Chase said in a low voice.

"And stupid," Norah added with another tiny laugh.

The corner of his mouth lifted into a sideways grin as he slowly circled his arms around her waist and pulled her to him.

"I really do love you, Norah," Chase said, resting his forehead against hers. "More than anything."

"I love you too, Chase," Norah said. "With all my heart. Being with you just feels right."

"So is it safe to say that we've worked things out?"
Norah nodded. "I think it is."

"Then stay with me. Please."

"Tonight?"

He pulled back to look at her and Norah met his eyes.
The tips of his fingers trailed lightly down her cheek as he
nodded softly. "And tomorrow. And every day after that."
He brought his hand up and rested his palm against her
neck just below her ear, his thumb stroked back and forth
against her jaw.

"What about when you move back to Dallas?" Norah
asked, placing her hand over his and looking up at him
with tear filled eyes. "What do we do then?"

"I'm not going back to Dallas," Chase answered her
with a slight shake of his head.

That information surprised her and she was sure the
look on her face showed it. "You're not?"

"Nope," Chase said, then added, "It's kind of a long
story, but I'll tell you all about it if you promise to stay
with me. Say yes."

"Bossy much?" Norah teased.

He grinned. "You know you like it. So, what do you
say?"

Norah's eyes darted to his mouth then back to his
eyes again, feeling every bit of love and renewed hope that
shone within them. She took her bottom lip between her
teeth and nodded. "Okay."

A slow smile tipped the corners of his mouth as
Chase moved in to kiss her—long, hard, and passionately.

"Thank you," Chase whispered against her lips.

"For what?" Norah asked.

"Coming back to me," Chase told her, pressing his
forehead to hers and twisting his fingers in her hair. "I've
felt so lost without you."

"Me too," Norah answered him in a whisper.

"Yeah?"

"Yeah." Norah nodded. "So no more messin' this up. Okay? From either of us." She leaned her head back to look at him. "Deal?"

He gave her an amused grin. "Deal."

"Good," she said, then pulled him down for one sweet, slow kiss. "Because I'm going to hold you to that."

Chase smiled. "I hope you do."

EPILOGUE

Four months later…

"Come on," Chase said, taking Norah's hand in his as they walked up the porch steps. "I've got something I want to show you."

Her curiosity peaked. "What are you up to, O'Donnell?"

He turned to her and grinned. "Just come on."

She let Chase lead her inside and over to the kitchen table where he took a seat in one of the chairs, pulling her down to his lap in the process. She sat with her legs across his thighs as he reached his arms around her and pulled his laptop towards him. The screen came to life when Chase ran his finger over the mouse pad.

"Well," Chase said, tugging her close to his body. "What do you think?"

Norah stared at the screen, narrowing her eyes and leaning a bit closer to get a better look. "I don't know what I'm looking at."

Chase let out a soft chuckle. "It's the new barn I'm going to have built."

"New barn?" Norah questioned with an incredulous tone and turned to look at him. "What's wrong with the one you have now?"

"It's not big enough," Chase said casually and did something on his laptop that made the image appear bigger.

"Big enough for what?" Norah asked. "You only have two horses."

"Yeah, well I plan on having more than that once I start bringing in rescues."

She'd turned back to the laptop to view his drawing again, but now she snapped back around to look at him, wide-eyed and in shock. "What did you say?"

"I wanted to tell you a while ago," Chase told her. "But I wanted to wait to see if I could afford the new barn first. Can't offer shelter if I don't have it."

"So," Norah said, still trying to process what he was saying. "You're turning your ranch into a horse rescue?"

"Yeah," Chase said. "You said it'd always been a dream of yours and, well, I kind of hoped this could be something we'd do together."

"You want me to be your partner?"

Chase's mouth turned into a one-sided grin. "Something like that." He leaned forward then, reached around the laptop and came back with a tiny black box in his hand.

Norah's heart slammed against her chest. "Oh my," she breathed.

"I didn't get your father's blessing," Chase teased, taking her hand in his. "But I did get the rest of your family's."

She was breathing so hard that it was almost embarrassing. "And they all said yes? Even Luke?"

He grinned again. "Even Luke." Chase looked down to her hand in his and stroked her fingers before returning his gaze to her eyes. "Will you marry me?"

Taking her bottom lip between her teeth, Norah smiled as tears glistened in her eyes. "Yes." She nodded and let out a tiny laugh. "Yes, of course I will."

Chase's grin widened as he let go of her hand long enough to open the box, revealing three shimmering princess-cut diamonds set on a polished platinum band.

"Oh my God, Chase," Norah said, her tone and facial expression showing her surprise.

"Do you like it?" He took the ring from the box and slipped it onto her left hand's ring finger.

"It's beautiful," she said, staring down at her hand and wiggling her fingers so the diamonds sparkled in the light. "You did a really good job picking it out."

Chase let out a small laugh. "I'd love to take credit for the whole thing, but I actually had my mom and Sarah help."

"They know?" Norah asked, turning to look at him.

He nodded. "And they couldn't be happier. They're so excited to welcome you into the family."

Norah couldn't help but notice that he hadn't mentioned his father in that statement. But it made perfect sense since the two men still weren't on speaking terms with one another.

"I should probably warn you though," Chase said with a teasing smile, bringing Norah out of her thoughts. "Now that we're engaged, don't be surprised if my mom starts bugging us about grandkids."

"Grandkids?" Norah asked, then let out a soft laugh.

"The woman is itchin' for more," Chase said. "I don't know about you, but I'm in no rush."

"I'm in no rush either," Norah said, giving Chase a sexy come-hither look as she stood up from his lap and straddled him. "But that doesn't mean we can't practice."

"Practice, huh?" Chase said, running his hands up and down her back before resting his palms against her rear.

"Mmm-hmm," Norah said, placing her arms over his shoulders and leaning towards him until her nose touched his. "Lots and *lots* of practice."

Chase's mouth was on hers then as he stood from the chair and carried her to the bedroom where he made long, sweet love to her. Afterwards, Norah rested her head against Chase's chest and listened to his heartbeat. A soft smile curled up the corners of her lips. She could stay like this forever, and she would because being in Chase's arms was exactly where she belonged.

The End

ABOUT THE AUTHOR

In November 2011 author Kimberly Lewis stepped into the writing world with her first contemporary Western romance, *When the Heart Falls*.

Born and raised on the Eastern Shore of Maryland, this country girl caught the creative bug at an early age, doing everything from drawing to writing short stories.

After rediscovering her love of romance novels, Kimberly found the inspiration to pick up a pen—or in this case a laptop—and began writing her first novel. Since then she has continued to write and credits her husband and her wonderfully crazy family and friends, who with their love and joking demeanor provide her with the ideas that inspire her novels.

In her spare time she enjoys reading, horseback riding, and spending time with her amazing family.

To learn more about Kimberly and her books, please visit her at kimberlylewisnovels.com

For more from Kimberly Lewis, read on for a preview of

Zane

THE MCKADES OF TEXAS, BOOK 1

ZANE
(THE MCKADES OF TEXAS, BOOK 1)
Copyright © 2012 by Kimberly Lewis

She's looking for safety...

Kellan Anderson is in hillbilly hell—or at least that's what it feels like. After enduring endless counts of abuse from her now ex-boyfriend, Kellan makes a run for her life and finds herself in cowboy country. Leaving her fancy clothes and expensive lifestyle behind her, she trades in her high heels for cowboy boots and changes her name to Andi Ford. With her painful past threatening to catch up with her, hiding out in this small town seems easy enough—until one blond hair, blue eyed cowboy steps in the picture.

...Will she find it in the arms of a cowboy?

Zane McKade has sworn off women, determining that they are all liars and cheats—including the new waitress at the local bar. After a rather unpleasant first encounter with the beautiful brunette, Zane's radar is set to high as he believes this woman is not who she claims to be. When his intimidation methods fail to break through Andi's barrier he decides to turn on the charm to get her to tell the truth. But Zane's plan begins to backfire as the more time he spends charming Andi, the more he finds himself breaking his own rules and falling for her.

Enjoy the following excerpt from *Zane*

Kellan saw the man coming her way and a nervous feeling began to grow in the pit of her stomach. She hadn't noticed it when he rode up, but he was *incredibly* good looking. The man had to be a least six two, with long muscular legs leading up to narrow hips that angled into a *very* masculine upper body. He looked like an athlete. He looked…solid. And although his pale blue shirt was soaked with sweat, it somehow added to his overall appeal. He stopped at her table and glared at her. Only then did she realize that this man was not coming over for friendly chit-chat and her mood shifted.

"Is that your red sports car out there?" Zane asked, tilting his head and jerking his thumb towards the parking lot.

"Yes," Kellan told him. *What's it to you?* She stared up at him, waiting for him to continue. But when he just stared back, his deep blue eyes shooting daggers at her, she decided enough was enough. "Is there something I can help you with?"

Zane's jaw flexed. "You could have four miles ago."

"What?" She was utterly confused as to what mileage had to do with his apparent anger towards her.

"I don't look familiar to you?" He stared at her, his eyebrows coming together in frustration.

She looked the man over from head to toe. "No, I'm sorry you don't."

Zane let out an exasperated sigh. "How about now?" He raised his arms above his head and waved them just like he had done when he was trying to flag her down.

He looked completely ridiculous and she fought back the urge to laugh at him. But the more she looked at him she realized that he did look strangely familiar. *Oh my…* He was the man on the side of the road next to the pickup truck just outside of town.

"Oh," Kellan said. "Yes, I do remember you now. I'm sorry I didn't recognize you with your shirt on." She loaded her voice with sarcasm and crossed her arms over her chest. If he was going to have an attitude with her, then she was going to give it right back.

Zane's eyes narrowed. "Well, would you care to explain why you just blew past me like that?"

Kellan laughed, quietly as to not draw attention. "Why did I blow past you? Hmm, let me think. Um, maybe it has to do with the fact that you were partially naked and in the middle of nowhere."

Well damn. He hadn't thought about that. He'd been all riled up thinking that some *guy* just ignored him. Now, thinking about it from her perspective, he could see why she didn't pull over to help him. As it was though, his built up anger from everything that had transpired today got the best of him and he continued with his rant.

"I was *not* half naked," he said, his voice low as he briefly glanced around the room to see if anyone could hear them speaking.

"Look, *cowboy*." She said the word as though it were an insult and not an affirmation of what he obviously was. "I'm sorry you're having a bad day, but don't come over here and take it out on me. I had a good reason for not stopping earlier and I'm not going to apologize for looking after my own safety. You could've been a murderer for all I knew."

Zane knew that he should just man up and walk away, but he just couldn't do that now after her snarky "cowboy" remark. Why'd she have to go and say it like that anyway?

"Look, *princess*," he said with the same tone she had used. "This ain't Hollywood. Take your sunglasses off. You're inside and you look like a damn fool."

Kellan's jaw fell in disbelief.

Zane smiled, feeling triumphant that he got in the last word. He turned and started to walk away from her.

"Screw you, *cowboy*!" she yelled after him, saying the word exactly as she had before. "And that horse you rode in on."

And—*Whoops!*—now everyone in the diner had turned to look at them.

Zane turned around to her with amusement on his

face. "Very original, *princess*."

Available Now

Coming Soon:

Luke (The McKades of Texas, Book 3)

34572706R00198

Made in the USA
Middletown, DE
26 August 2016